TAINTED VISIONS

A Novel by T. J. Tanksley

Dedicated to Kathy

With appreciation for assistance from
Barb, Karen, Terri, Rosie, Naomi and others.

Cover Artwork by Nichole Ray, Las Vegas.

DISCLAIMERS:

This entire work is intended and presented as a work of fiction, resulting from the author's imagination. Thus, the characters, places and events are imaginary characters and events. If there is any significant resemblance to any real persons or to any real businesses, it would be intended as fictional or would merely be a coincidence.

Additionally, although this fictional work deals with legal issues that could possibly occur to people in real life, nothing stated by any character in this novel or by the narrator should be regarded as any type of legal advice whatsoever, and no statement in this novel whatsoever is intended to be relied upon, or should be relied upon, as any type of interpretation of any statutory law or case law of any jurisdiction whatsoever; consult a licensed attorney in your jurisdiction for any needed legal advice or guidance. Similarly, nothing pertaining to any physical or medical conditions is to be relied upon as any type of medical information; consult a licensed physician for any physiological or medical concerns.

*****

Tainted Visions

COPYRIGHT © 2017

Las Vegas, Nevada, Circa 1990—Off Strip

ONE

Louis Tennyson Lynch already felt awkward enough being in his employee's home on a Sunday afternoon, sitting in the den with an infant's toy on the floor and the faint smell of family breakfast still in the air, but he also risked being late to meet his wife at a charity event. And, though he was managing to be patient, he still didn't understand why Abel Santoro had requested this "special private meeting".

"Santo," Lynch finally said as amiably as he could, "just tell me what's bothering you. It can't have anything to do with the great work you've been doing for me ever since I enticed you up here from Tucson."

"Thanks, sir," said Abel, "but I'm going crazy right now. I forgot to even have the darn papers ready. Be right back…"

Lynch rolled his eyes as Abel rushed out of the room. *These artistic types…*

Alone, Lynch immediately fixated upon a wooden sculpture he'd previously noticed at Abel's housewarming. The nude female piece glistened in the natural desert light coming in through an uncovered window. Even with its small breasts—in a city of swollen ones—its graceful beauty revealed that Abel's talent went far beyond the magic he could do with the cabinetry and paneling he installed in the customs homes that Lynch built and sold.

In Lynch's mind, however, even the finest wood carving could not have replicated some of the best features of the suspected model: her creamy olive complexion, shoulder-length auburn hair and electric-green eyes. Although she was out of the house at the moment, just as Abel had said she'd be, Lynch couldn't help but recall how appealing Abel's wife Dawn was in person. But, on this day, dreading that he would soon have to meet and socialize with his own wife of thirty years plus, the sculpture started to annoy him.

How in hell does he get her?

"Here they are," Abel said as he re-entered the room holding some papers.

But, no sooner had Abel set them on the desk than he resumed pacing, his large-boned body, far more powerful than his craft-work required, shifting back and forth while Lynch still waited.

Finally, Abel stopped. "I asked you here today, sir, because you are very wise and my family owes everything to you, even being able to buy this house."

"Oh, come on, Abel", Lynch blurted back with a smirk, "that's bullshit. You're talented and you earned it."

"Thanks for the kind words, sir, but my skills are quickly leaving me," Abel replied, his eyes widening. "I have to work longer now on my jobs, even if nobody else notices, because I get horrible headaches that mess up my concentration."

"Really, Abel? I sure hadn't noticed that you were having any problems."

"I'm afraid so," said Abel, as he stood rigidly, a look of defeat in his eyes.

"Listen, Santo, things like that can come up. You should see a top-notch doctor, maybe a specialist. I can put you in touch with the best. It might even be a damn allergy or something else you have no clue about."

Abel's head dropped. "Already been diagnosed, sir." His eyes then shifted toward the window. "The docs say it's inoperable brain cancer—stage four of what they call 'astrocytoma', which I had to learn to pronounce. Ever heard of it?"

Lynch made no response.

"They say I'm kinda young to have it so bad, but no matter. I still only have about four months to live, maybe a little longer. But pretty soon I won't be good for anything. I might even start having seizures."

"Oh my," Lynch grimaced.

Abel reached into his pocket and pulled out a prescription bottle, which he held up for view. "Already on pain killers."

Poor bastard.

"Yeah, 'shit happens' all right, just like they say."

"I'm very sorry for you, Abel. You're so young and with a family."

Sorry for me, too.

"Mr. Lynch, I fear big time for my family. Our baby's not even two. Dawn will be way over her head with the mortgage, the furniture that we're still paying off, two car payments, all the bills. And my dying slowly will cost lots more than we can afford."

Yeah...

"But please understand, sir," Abel held up his hand, "I didn't ask you over just to hear me whine. I'm getting to something else."

While Abel then took a measured breath, Lynch sat tight for whatever was coming.

"One thing I did right, sir, was to get life insurance, two hundred fifty thousand worth. It also pays double for accidental death. I liked that because I figured, if it happened to me while my kid was still little, that would be how."

"Well, that was very smart of you, Santo."

"Maybe sir, but how was I supposed to know I'd get this damn thing," he said, pointing to his head then quickly wiping his eyes. "and if I tried to buy more, maybe they would have done more tests first. At least with the two-fifty," Abel said in a quivering voice, "Dawn could pay off the house and have some left over."

"How is Dawn taking all this?" Lynch asked, figuring that would be a worthy question at the moment.

"Oh, no sir. You're the only one who knows, other than the docs," replied Abel.

"Really, Abel?"

"Seriously, yes...At first, I was afraid to tell her. But now, I'm trying to keep it all from her for another reason and you'll soon hear why."

"Okay, if you say so, Santo..."

Abel picked up the papers and held them up with an eerie calmness. "Here's the reason I asked you over today, sir. They call this a 'Plain English' life insurance policy. It pays double for accidental death, but it looks like it pays zero if the guy dies during the first two years by, uh...shall we say, his own hand. And I've still got about eight months to go before two years is up."

Lynch gave a non-committal nod.

"So, I'm asking your opinion in complete trust. What if the insurance company could somehow prove that an accidental death during that first two years wasn't really an accident...if doctors said that the guy was terminal anyway, wouldn't the insurance still have to pay the normal amount?"

"But you're only talking about 'what ifs'..."

Abel handed over the papers. "Could you possibly take a look, sir, and tell me what you think?"

Lynch began ostensibly flipping through the pages, while noticing out of the corner of his eye that Abel was pacing again.

Abel then abruptly stopped pacing and, despite the minimal time that had elapsed, resumed his plea. "I know this is Las Vegas, sir, but I've never gambled here, even for small amounts. And I don't want to play double or nothing on this, if you know what I mean. I'd stick it out somehow if I had to, just to make sure Dawn got the two-fifty. But..."

Lynch, with the policy still in hand, looked at Abel. "Santo, as a close friend, which I hope I can call myself, I first want to repeat how very sad I am that such a thing is happening to you, and I'd very much like to help. But this is really a legal question, and you know I'm not a lawyer."

Abel shook his head. "But I don't know any lawyers, sir, and I'm afraid to just pick one out of the phone book for this. Would you know one who could maybe find out the answer...without saying who it's for? I know I'm asking a lot, Mr. Lynch, but I'm getting desperate."

Lynch glanced again at the page Abel had marked, then put it down. "Listen, Abel, speaking strictly as a non-lawyer, what you're hypothetically talking about makes sense to me. But we're moving awfully fast here. Maybe something can still be..."

"Don't I wish, sir, but I already did all the testing." With that, Abel's eyes shifted toward the window. "I guess I'll just have to handle this myself as best I can, sir. It wasn't right to try and involve you..."

Lynch stayed silent.

"...But when I'm gone, sir, no matter how or when it happens, could you possibly keep an eye on my wife, Dawn, and help her remember that I bought life insurance so she puts in her claim? It would give me such peace to know that someone like you was going to keep an eye on her."

While Lynch thought about Dawn, this time as a soon-to-be widow, Abel waited, his eyes wide and imploring.

"Santo, as long as you put the question to me, I have some views of my own about your wife's future..."

"What's that, sir?"

"Well, for starters, even with the insurance money, she could still use income and a career. Think about it, and you'll see I'm right."

Abel unhesitatingly nodded.

"Fine then," Lynch continued. "She should start working at my office, part-time for now and it can expand later. I'll be able to look after her, just like you want, and we'll train her at her own pace. Eventually, she could get her real estate license. Would that be any comfort to you?"

"Oh, I'd absolutely love that, sir, and we've got a good nanny for Cora...But, could she start out part-time?"

"Sure, Santo."

"Mr. Lynch," said Abel with some apparent new concern, "I'll give her a reason for doing this, like maybe it's just a precaution in case my work ever dries up. But she can't be told the real reason..."

"Of course not, Abel. Just have her get in touch with my staff. I'll alert them."

"I will, sir. Thank you so much," said Abel, as he collapsed in a chair and gave a long sigh.

"Are you okay for at least awhile, Santo?"

"Yeah, I can still do more work, but pretty soon you'll need another guy."

"What I meant is that I'd like you to take your family to my place in Laguna Beach for a few days of fun. It's beautiful there. Meanwhile, I'll have my attorneys look into your question on a confidential basis."

"Oh my God, sir, that would be so incredible of you! I knew I could count on you."

TWO

Weeks later, Abel Santoro trudged along through the early morning shadows in his neighborhood, his legs and lungs burning in pain, almost enough to numb out the dull ache in his head. All the while, he made the best of any musical inspiration that might emanate from his portable Walkman radio, a prior birthday present from his wife.

Facing fatigue, with little sleep the night before, he could see the chosen spot ahead. There, his route would take him along a shaded street on which large trucks frequently drove—especially this time of the morning—hauling dirt or gravel for nearby residential construction sites.

Within a few more steps, a familiar song about love and heartbreak started to play. As he listened, Abel willed back tears with all his resolve, not wanting to back out again.

As if by divine arrangement, a large truck had just finished its turn and was now headed downhill in his direction.

Realizing he'd have to speed up to make the spot and still allow for last second adjustments, Abel forced himself to run even harder, converting his inner turmoil into base energy.

"No excuses now," he muttered to himself. "You're fucking worthless alive."

As the truck approached, Abel ran on the sidewalk parallel to the street, knowing that he was virtually secluded by the roadside trees and their shadows.

"Dawn and Cora, I love you so much."

After more heart-pounding seconds, with his energy all but spent, he left the sidewalk and ran between the trees into the path of the oncoming truck.

He turned his head and tried to brace himself for whatever might be felt before being crushed into oblivion. But his resolve immediately dissipated, as it had before. Some inner consciousness mustered all his remaining strength to try to reverse his body back from the truck's path.

His last-second effort, however, was not enough. Neither was the violent swerve of the truck, as its brakes screeched obscenely into the early morning air. The truck's massive bumper threw Abel's body into a limp rotation, whipping his head into the asphalt.

*****

Dawn tried not to worry about how long Abel had been gone, but it was now starting to bother her. She got out of bed, where she had been leisurely reading, and went into the bathroom to wash up.

More minutes passed.

She decided to start getting ready to go look for him, but hoped he'd be back before she got out the door.

Eventually, after putting on some jeans and a light sweater, she tried to transfer her daughter Cora from her crib into her car seat without waking her, but no luck.

"No go to Nanny G's," Dawn whispered to her child, "Just a little ride this time."

Within a half mile, she approached an accident scene. A construction truck had jumped the curb and plowed into the landscaping. Though it all looked quite bizarre, a noxious fear seized her.

With the traffic minimal, she stopped her car near the police officer filling out paperwork and rolled down her window. "Excuse me sir, I'm looking for my husband. He went jogging..."

Before he could say a word, the look on his face terrified her.

"If your husband was this jogger, he's in an ambulance that just left here for Desert Meadows Memorial. I'm very sorry but that's all I know."

*****

The morning became a horrific blur.

With Cora safe at Nanny Gin's, Dawn endured long hours at the hospital without any hopeful news.

Finally, a weary surgeon emerged from the operating room. "He's temporarily stabilized," said the surgeon, "but he has not regained consciousness. I don't want you to build up any unrealistic expectations, Mrs. Santoro. It doesn't look good."

*****

Three hours later, while her head pounded from not eating, word came to her.

"I'm sorry, Mrs. Santoro," another somber-faced doctor announced with a look of concern as to her ability to handle it. "We tried, but the injuries were just too extensive."

Dawn's knees buckled as her hands covered her face. She shook her head repeatedly. "Oh my God, he's gone! Abel's gone!"

"Mrs. Santoro, you're under incredible stress right now. I urge you to try to gather yourself before going anywhere. We have a chapel here that would give you some quiet and privacy, or perhaps you have someone who can come and pick you up?"

*****

Heavy minutes passed in the chapel's surreal quiet.

She repeatedly closed her eyes and reopened them, hoping that she was really somewhere else, and this day was not what she had been led to believe. She even stepped over to the entrance door and peeked out into the hallway. Yes, she still was in a hospital. She shook her head and sobbed, over and over again.

Finally realizing that things had to be done, as painful as they might be, she made her way back to the hospital lobby area and phoned Abel's work. At her request, she was immediately transferred to Lynch.

"Mr. Lynch, I can hardly believe this myself, but you need to know. Abel was killed this morning...hit by a truck. I'm still at the hospital."

There was a long silence.

"Oh my God, Dawn...what a terrible shock! I am so sorry for you...and for Abel. He was so young."

"I know, Mr. Lynch. That's what makes it even harder for me to accept...Why Abel?"

"Dawn...are you okay? I mean, under the circumstances. Is there anything I can do?"

"Mr. Lynch...uh, I don't know. Right now, I...someone here suggested I see a grief counselor, but..."

"Dawn, I'll tell my staff to be on call for any help you need, so don't hesitate at all. And we'll get going on the arrangements for Abel. Just tell the hospital people to call us. You've got enough to deal with right now."

"Oh, that would be a big relief, Mr. Lynch. Thank you so much."

"Dawn, seriously, will you be able to manage?"

"I'll make it somehow, sir...I have to with a little daughter." She sobbed, "I'm all she has now, and I should probably be getting back to her..."

"Dawn, let me know of anything at all I can do to help. I mean it."

THREE

Ever since Dawn had started working part-time, the home of retired school teacher Gwen Rogers—"Nanny G", as she was often called—had been a familiar and fun place for Cora. But, on the fateful day that Abel was hit, it had been a Godsend. Handling the unfolding tragedy at the hospital herself was overwhelming enough, without having to also try to watch and shield a young child in such a setting.

As Dawn walked up to the front door, she thought about the fact that Gwen was a widow herself. She took a deep breath before knocking and tried to shake herself loose, seeking an appearance that approximated normal for fear that Cora might otherwise sense the catastrophe.

The music that Dawn could barely hear immediately stopped and soon Nanny G opened the door. Though Gwen was well into middle age, she was still a handsome-looking woman with kind eyes that instantly showed how lucky school children would have been to have her as their teacher.

But on this day, having been tipped off by Dawn before her drive over, Gwen's eyes probed into Dawn's soul as both women stood in the doorway, while both understood that there would be no mention of Abel in Cora's presence.

"Mommeee," Cora said excitedly in delivering her hug.

"How would you like to come in and sit awhile?" Gwen asked. "We could keep each other company."

"Oh, that sounds nice, Gwen," said Dawn with an eager shake of her head. "I'm in no hurry right now to go anywhere else."

"Good, then, let's order in some pizza and you can stay as late as you wish."

Dawn tried to let herself be absorbed by the cheery inside of Gwen's child-friendly house. With kiddie books all around, building blocks on the floor, Play Dough on the kitchen table next to remnants of a peanut butter sandwich, and Cora's drawings taped to the refrigerator, she felt an infusion of life that temporarily neutralized her crippling sorrow.

While the pizza was on order, and Cora's attention was diverted, Gwen looked into Dawn's eyes and gently shook her head. "I know this doesn't sound like me, but I've got a bottle of wine that's been waiting to be opened. You're more than welcome to have some and to even spend the night if you want."

"Oh, thank you so much, Gwen. I am definitely tempted to just sit down with that bottle and a big straw. But I'm afraid it would bypass my empty stomach and go straight to my head, which is already pounding. Maybe one glass when the pizza arrives...if that's okay."

*****

Despite the temporary refuge that Gwen had provided, as Cora's bed-time approached, Dawn determined that it would be best to get her daughter home and at least try to stay close to a normal routine.

Once Cora was buckled in her car seat, Gwen gave Dawn a long sisterly embrace. "Try to take things as slow and easy as you can," she whispered. "And don't even think about trying to explain anything to Cora until the time is right, which, at her age, won't be anytime soon. For now, just say 'Daddy went bye-bye'."

Though Dawn felt fully drained upon arriving home, she would force herself to carry out her typical routine for Cora's bed-time. Grateful that she had not binged on wine, she would try her best to act as if it was just another night. She would then give into her exhaustion, and seek a temporary reprieve from her numbing sadness, in sleep.

The two played with Cora's little doll-house, then read children's stories until the child was ready for bed. Thankfully, there were no questions about Daddy, *this time*.

When Dawn was finally able to lay herself down, however, all she could do was linger in agony. That she so badly needed sleep somehow made it all the more elusive.

Eventually, biological needs forced her to get up for the bathroom, but she determined not to look at herself in the mirror. She feared seeing a person who looked far beyond the breaking point, or worse—seeing a horrifying zombie, instead of a young mother.

She maneuvered back to her bed and, just before midnight, she was able to surrender her decimated self into sleep.

FOUR

The next morning, Dawn lay rigidly on her back, awake but not daring to peek at the other side of the bed, clinging to the barest hope that it had all been a nightmare.

More seconds dragged by.

No other breathing could be heard in the room.

Finally, admitting to herself that Abel was anything but a quiet sleeper, the gambit ended. Upon venturing a look, she knew that her widowhood was as real as the rest of the bed was empty and undisturbed. She cried in agony.

"Why am I being punished?" she said in a choking whisper. "Forget me, what about Cora?"

As she continued lying there, random bursts of sadness would overwhelm her. Each time, more sobbing would follow until she started to wonder if she physically had any more tears to give at this moment.

Eventually, during a pause, she for some reason began to think about how similar tears had been emitted by so many women before her over countless millennia. Even if most were probably older, she now knew exactly how they felt, having joined their sisterhood of misery.

But her personal loss again vied for her attention. She realized that there were still ghostly traces of him all around. His pillow was within her reach. His work clothes, with even more of his smell, were in the closet along with his shoes. And his hamper, she suspected, was probably half full, at least.

As haunting as all this was, something worse haunted her. Eventually, all his traces would dissipate until his only remnants for her to cherish would be their beautiful daughter and his elegant handiwork around her house.

The urge to greedily breathe in his remaining scent compelled her to lay there doing so, until she finally told herself that it would linger on for at least another day, if not longer.

But what to do with his clothes, she wondered. Just throw everything away? Could she even do that?

Wash them, and give them all to charity?

She stared at the ceiling, overwhelmed by the moment. "There's no need to decide right now," she whispered. "When I'm up to it, I'll move his things in the spare room. Charity can wait."

She took his pillow into her arms, letting her tears flow onto it until she could cry no more and the new reality seized her. She could not make time wait until she was ready for life without him. With a young daughter to care for, it was going to be all about coping, minute-by-minute, hour-by-hour, and simply pressing on for who knows how long in an empty version of herself.

FIVE

Gorgeous bouquets decorated the mortuary chapel: from Abel's main supplier, from Lynch, and even from the trucking company.

People who knew Abel on the job praised him openly and one-on-one to her.

And, having gotten so much help from Lynch's office on the arrangements, Dawn was pleased at how dignified and flawless everything went.

But there was little comfort in the words of the arranged minister. He spoke as if Abel's death was merely an episode in a story already known to all—as if Dawn somehow knew what lay ahead for herself, when nothing could have been further from the truth. She felt completely unprepared.

*****

During the slow walk back from the grave-site, she sensed that people were keeping just enough distance away so as not to crowd her, but to be available if she wanted to talk to them.

A personal friend, however, did stay close. Dawn had known Julie Navert, whom Dawn often called "Jewels", since child-birthing classes. The perky and rambunctious brunette, who worked as a real estate agent and never hid her materialistic aspirations, hadn't been the slightest bit embarrassed to be the only single woman to enroll in the class. Then, weeks into the program, Julie handled her tragic miscarriage incredibly well in Dawn's eyes. As the two walked together on this day, Julie held her arm around Dawn, as if, by virtue of her own experience, she could help Dawn absorb the grief.

Despite Julie's support, however, Dawn couldn't help but resume crying. She eased herself onto a nearby bench to try to compose herself, with Julie quietly taking a seat next to her.

Eventually, Dawn looked up to see Lou Lynch patiently standing a few feet away. He looked like he was prepared to say something, but that he would keep whatever it was to himself for as long as necessary until he knew she was ready to listen.

Dawn wiped her eyes. "I'm sorry, Mr. Lynch...It's just so hard right now."

He slowly nodded, then stepped cautiously forward and took a seat on the opposite side of the bench from Julie.

Julie excused herself, but remained nearby.

"Don't apologize, Dawn," said Lynch. "You have every right to sit here and cry as long as you want."

"I'm trying to stop, Mr. Lynch. Crying's not what it's cracked up to be, anyway."

"Dawn, I have something to tell you, but only when you're ready..."

"Oh...You can go ahead, sir. It's okay."

"It's just that, when people here spoke so highly of Abel, which is all true, I wanted you to know that he spoke just as highly of you. As much as he liked his work, he told me that it was you who made him happiest—you and your daughter, of course. He said he considered himself the luckiest man in the world to have such a family."

"Really, sir? I didn't know Abel talked openly like that."

"He certainly did to me."

Dawn felt more tears about to come. "Oh my...Thank you for that, sir."

"As I see it, Dawn, although Abel died young, he had more happiness than some men ever have no matter how long they live."

Overcoming the tears, she looked at Lynch. Was he trying to say something?

He looked down, seemingly with a touch of embarrassment.

"Mr. Lynch, I don't know about other men, but I sure thought Abel was happy."

"Well I do know about other men, Dawn, and I'm speaking the truth."

Okay...but where this is going?

"Dawn."

"Yes?"

"Are you're going to be able to manage, under the circumstances?"

"Yes sir. I'll make it."

"That's the spirit."

She gave a weak nod.

"So, then, Dawn, when you do feel up to working again—after more time off of course—you can be full-time if you want. Keeping busy could be good for you."

"Honestly, sir, I hadn't even thought about that yet."

"Understood...Nobody's expecting you to."

"But I'll definitely be needing the money."

SIX

Lying in bed the next morning, she thought about Lynch's advice to "keep busy" by working full-time. She shook her head. "This isn't like breaking up in high school or something..."

She wondered how he could have even brought that up, while still at the site of Abel's funeral.

"Anyway," she whispered, "I'm not ready to go back to work. And it's not going to be tomorrow or the next day either...I know you'll manage without me."

She thought further. "But there is something that will keep me busy for a little while. No offense, Abel, but it's now time to move your clothes into the spare room. I just hope I can handle that much."

Having had no appetite for breakfast, the initial two hours she spent converting the spare room from chaotic storage to something more dignified left her feeling drained and numb. But maybe it was just as well, she figured. If her senses were keen, it would only inflame her grief with each item of his that she removed from what once was *their* bedroom.

Still, as she laid out his clothes on the bed, her hands had enough energy to tremble with an awkward guilt, as if Abel might walk in on her at any moment and rightfully ask what she was doing with his things. She wondered if she was becoming delirious.

At one point, she even *tried* to envision Abel, as if he were standing right before her. If she was going to have to endure the pain, she at least wanted to see him in the process. But, when that brought no relief, she simply surrendered, letting grief have its way with her.

After finally managing to finish with his clothes, she got out a shoe-box full of family photos that had been intended for an album and picked out three for the time being: one of Abel alone, one with her, and one of their family. She then set them where they could be gazed at any time she felt the need, including right now.

Yes, I was married to that man.

Yes, we were happy—while it lasted.

*****

Later that day, on her return home with Cora from a fast food restaurant, the sight of a neighbor sorting the mail on their front porch made Dawn realize that she had not been checking her own since that hellish day. At least she could not recall doing so.

She ventured to her mailbox with Cora in tow. It was stuffed. Junk fliers. A sympathy card. And there were bills from the mortgage company and on an auto loan.

As she carried it all into the house, her stomach churned from the combination of the cheap hamburger and the painful reminders of debts. Unlike Lynch, who had not bothered her at all since the day of the funeral, the rest of the world was not going to stop just so that she could continue to grieve.

She tossed the two bills onto the kitchen table and stared at them. There'd be more to come: the other car payment, the furniture loan, the credit card, utilities, and anything else.

She glanced around the house. Every item, not yet fully paid for, was a threat.

Grieving had found a new partner in her life: Fear. It had been patiently waiting for her full attention. And, like her grieving, it was not going away anytime soon. It was just settling in.

She looked at Cora, already resuming play with her doll-house set, happily unaware of the new reality. But how far into the future would Cora still feel safe and secure? How many years, or even months?

Though there was no answer, Dawn saw one message in her child's play. If it was the last thing Dawn did, she had to hold onto the house, with all the memories and Abel's work embodied in it.

It was also unavoidably clear that she needed to go back to work while the invitation to be a full-time employee was still open. She vowed that she would be working by this time next week.

New life, here I come, ready or not.

Not.

SEVEN

Seeing no compelling reason to keep Abel's pickup truck, with another year and a half of monthly payments and the extra insurance costs—not to mention having to look at it every day—Dawn sat at the kitchen table staring at the keys and trying to gather her courage.

It has to be now...

As she headed toward the dealership, with Cora dropped off at Nanny G's, her tears began to flow along with the memories. All the trips in the truck with Abel. The art shows. The picnics. The other outings.

It had also been Abel's transportation since she first met him at an art fair in Tucson, where he'd had a booth displaying his wood-crafting talents. She had stopped in, after her junior college drama and dance classes, just to wander and browse. But she had been instantly captivated by his exquisite wood sculptures and his soft-spoken masculinity. Today, however, the residual smells of his work-life, and of Abel himself, haunted her as she made the loneliest of drives.

She knew that she was in no frame of mind to try to bargain with a car salesman, not that she would ever be good at that. But, as she got closer to the dealership, that dreaded encounter took a momentary backseat to a haunting thought. Did Abel, or his spirit, somehow know what was about to happen?

"I'm sorry Abel," she said openly, "but we—I mean I—cannot afford it. If I don't take drastic steps, the bank

25

account will soon be empty, and then all I'll have is a credit card to max out."

*****

The bare cubicle she had been directed to at the dealership had started to feel like solitary confinement until a short balding man, wearing a functional grey suit, appeared and greeted her. Although he seemed to have other things on his mind, he flashed a quick smile and invited her to walk a few steps to his personal office, which turned out to be only a slight improvement over the cubicle.

"Unfortunately, Mrs. Santoro, because payments are still due on your truck and it's not a popular model, twelve hundred is the best we can do."

She made no effort to conceal her disappointment.

"You know, ma'am," he resumed speaking before she could have even tried to say something, "you might get a little more by selling it yourself. That is," he said, while shaking his head with obvious distaste, "if you want to subject yourself to all that hassle. But then again, if you fail to sell it and then come back to us, I couldn't guarantee we'd make you the same offer."

Dawn cringed. The idea of trying to sell Abel's truck herself was more repugnant than the salesman could even know. "Oh my. Then I'm not quite sure what to do."

Except that I need this done Now!

"We just can't go any higher, ma'am...unless you might be looking to trade in on a new model?"

26

"Trading in is not what I need, sir. I'm only here because my husband just died and I now have two cars, with extra payments I can't afford."

"Oh, sorry for your loss, ma'am...So, have you considered maybe trading both your older cars in toward something new or close to new?"

"Not at all. No."

"Well, now that you're single again, might I at least show you some of the newer and sportier models? We could throw some numbers around and..."

"No thank you."

You crude asshole.

"Well, in that case," said the salesman, "how about this? In addition to what I quoted you for your husband's pickup, you can bring your other car in any time and have a free oil change and safety check-up. And, whenever you feel ready to buy again, I'm sure we'll have the right car for you."

"Fine."

"So then, did you bring in all the papers today for this pickup? On a used vehicle like this, we do like to get any maintenance records if you might happen to have them."

"No. I mean it didn't occur to me. I'd have to look to see what there is."

"Don't worry about it, Mrs. Santoro. After we do the deal here, we're going to drive you back to your house anyway. Our driver can then wait while you take a quick look for us in your husband's papers or drawer—wherever he might have kept things like that."

Having to search for where Abel might have kept maintenance records was enough of a downer, let alone trying to do so while a guy waited on her front porch...until an unexpected find grabbed her full attention: Aceworth Insurance Company—Life Policy.

"Oh my God, that's right," she voiced, as she picked up the policy and started to browse its contents. "Abel bought this after Cora was born...Holy...two hundred fifty thousand!"

Grasping the policy, she took a couple steps then turned and collapsed backward onto her bed. She stared upward. "I can now mourn in peace. Oh thank you so much, Abel...from me and from Cora."

EIGHT

"How tragic for you," said local Aceworth insurance agent George Knight, whom Dawn had called right after sending the car dealer's driver on his way with a tip but no papers to take back. "Your husband was so young. But, then again, how fortunate that he had a policy."

"Oh, I realize that, sir. Believe me."

After Knight then elicited her age, employment, and child's age, all with inexplicable enthusiasm, he promised to call right back.

In a short while, her phone rang. "Mrs. Santoro, George Knight again. Thank you for your patience and let me again express my condolences."

"Thank you."

"Now, Mrs. Santoro, this is obviously a very trying time for you..."

"Yes."

"For that very reason, I view it as part of my professional obligation to try to assist you in making prudent decisions with your money. Far too often, people in situations like you now find yourself in fail to plan properly, and they go on to regret it for the rest of their life."

"Uh, excuse me, Mr. Knight, but, did you find out when I'll receive the life insurance money?"

"Oh, certainly. Once we submit the claim, it gets processed at Aceworth, but I don't see why an adjuster would have any issues. And, with Mr. Santoro having been hit by a truck, as you informed me, I assume you are aware that the coverage doubles to five hundred thousand..."

It what?

"...which happens to be enough for some comprehensive financial planning."

"Oh, my..."

"But it's not such a large amount, Mrs. Santoro, that it can just be spent loosely. If I may say so, you have the opportunity with this money to prudently plan for your lifetime, including help with your retirement, your child's education, and perhaps some modest income as well."

"For sure, sir. I understand..."

"That's good, Mrs. Santoro, and I therefore see it as my duty to sit down with you, as soon as you feel up to it, of course."

"Okay, but..."

"I have already evaluated your personal information with our company resources, which are tops in the industry. And, as soon as we can meet, I'll be able to present an ideal plan for you that is part annuity and part mutual funds, all designed to maximize the life and usage of your funds."

"I see."

"Mrs. Santoro, when do you think you could come in to discuss everything and to also sign your claim form? Or, if you prefer, I could come to your home."

"Oh, I'm not sure."

"Does later today work for you perhaps? I can work past five if needed."

"You did say five hundred thousand?"

"Yes, Mrs. Santoro. A sizable sum, to be sure, but I want to help you maximize it for your future security. If today doesn't work, perhaps tomorrow?"

Instead of answering, she hastily scanned the policy.

"Mrs. Santoro?"

"Yes," she finally replied, "I'll come to your office in the next few days, sir. How about if I call you when I'm about to head there?"

"Uh...okay, Mrs. Santoro, if that works best for you."

Even before she hung up, however, Dawn had in mind a different plan. She would listen politely. But, no matter what Knight said, the house and her car were going to be paid off in full. *Maybe* she'd consider a proposal from Knight for a part of the remainder.

*****

Later that same day, her home telephone unexpectedly rang. "Hello, Mrs. Santoro, my name is Donald Wimbley. I'm a local investment counselor, and I believe that you really need my services right now..."

"Uh, how did you..."

"Mrs. Santoro, I'm sorry for your loss, but it's frankly my duty to know those who are in need and keep them from making avoidable mistakes with their life insurance payout. Whatever amount you are expecting, I'm concerned that your insurance agent will try to sell you proprietary products that are not the best available. By being independent, I can offer you the best financial products that make the most sense for you. You do have children, don't you?"

"Yes, one, but..."

"Well then, you'll want to plan for their college. At least let me meet with you before you go with anyone else's program. Can we schedule it?"

"Uh, I need some time to catch my breath first, if that's okay, sir. Can I get back to you?"

"Okay, Mrs. Santoro, but take this opportunity seriously because it could save you thousands in the long run. If I don't hear back in a few days, I'll touch base again."

After Dawn took Wimbley's number—*as if* she would actually call him back—she resigned herself to more of the same in the days to come.

NINE

"I know you're still grieving," said Lynch in his call to her the next morning, "but I just want you to know that we all miss you. The whole office looks forward to your return when you are ready."

Really?

"That's sweet, Mr. Lynch. But it's still so hard for me to accept that Abel is gone. So, yes, I am still grieving."

"Understood, certainly."

"And, actually, sir, I've had so little energy and sometimes get woozy. I'd be mortified if I got sick in front of everybody there."

"No, no. Don't force yourself. There's no pressure."

"But sir, as long as we are talking, I'm actually not a hundred percent sure that I will be coming back."

"Oh really, Dawn?"

"It's not that I don't appreciate the opportunity, Mr. Lynch..."

"But you haven't actually made up your mind on that yet, have you Dawn?"

"No sir. I wouldn't even trust myself right now to decide something like that."

"But, if you don't come back to work, how are you going to manage financially, if I might ask?"

"I appreciate your concern, sir, but, it turns out that Abel had life insurance. I found the policy, and I'm going to make a claim."

"I see...But are you sure it will be enough for you, not to come back to work at all?"

"It looks like it's enough to take away all my money pressures for a while. And then later, when I start feeling more positive, I should be able to decide and plan things. I might even open up my own little business..."

"Your own business...in real estate?"

"Oh, no. Maybe a children's dance and acting studio. They don't seem to have many here..."

"I just hope you realize how tough that is, Dawn. Most new businesses fail. By working for me, you won't be putting your nest-egg at risk and I'd do whatever I could to help you succeed. Didn't you like your work here?"

"It's not so much that, sir. It's just been kind of a dream of mine and Abel used to say that he'd support me on it when the time was right."

"I see."

"I do appreciate you concern, Mr. Lynch, but I'm not about to do anything foolish."

"Okay...then how about this, Dawn. I have a very good accountant who also does financial counseling and management. At least get some quality professional advice first...whether you ultimately follow it or not."

*****

"Mrs. Santoro," said the caller, "I'm Karen Dunlap, CPA. A client of mine, Lou Lynch, told me a little about

34

your situation and asked me to see what assistance I could provide with your financial planning."

"Oh yes, hello...I guess I could do a first meeting. I'm just surprised at how quickly you're calling after Mr. Lynch mentioned you..."

"Dawn, if we can use first names, by now you're probably getting various solicitations triggered by the public record of your husband's most unfortunate passing, for which I am very sorry for you...Don't let those people bother you."

"Okay...Thanks for the tip, Karen."

"So then, you're wondering about me..."

"Well, I do trust Mr. Lynch..."

"Dawn, I'm offering to help you manage your insurance proceeds at absolutely no cost to you, courtesy of Mr. Lynch. And, rest assured that I have nothing to sell you myself. No commissions."

"But are you aware, Karen, that I don't have the money yet? I actually just found the life insurance policy."

"That's fine. We'll help you put in a formal claim when you come in. Just bring in a copy along with the death certificate."

"Oh, okay."

A death "certificate"...Isn't the death itself crappy enough?

*****

Two days later, while sitting in the reception room of Karen Dunlap's office, and clutching copies of the requested papers, Dawn felt an unexpected guilt. She was about to turn her husband's death into money.

But, then again—she reminded herself— she'd gladly give up the money if she could have Abel back. And she also had to think about little Cora.

When Karen soon emerged from her office, she smiled warmly, with compassion in her eyes, so as to put Dawn at ease.

Sitting in Karen's plush office, Dawn tried to relax while Karen looked over the policy. Having already had a dry run with Knight, she was not overly worried about what Karen might suggest.

"So," said Karen, "it appears that we will be working with five hundred, given your husband's unfortunate accidental death, as Mr. Lynch informed me...which was so sad to hear about."

"That's what the agent said...and thank you, Karen."

"Okay. So, do you have any initial thoughts, Dawn, either short-term or for the future? We can talk about anything you want."

"Absolutely, Karen. I really want to pay off my house. It has custom work that Abel did and all the memories that go with it."

"I get that, Dawn."

Yes!

"So, you need to call the mortgage company and find out the payoff amount. I'd also like a copy of the last statement they sent you."

"Will do...And it would also be nice not to have any more car payments."

"That also sounds prudent to me, Dawn."

"Good, Karen. So, I guess we just talk about what's left over, right? I mean, aside from some other bills I'll have to pay..."

"Dawn, you do understand that the balance, whatever the amount turns out to be, will not be enough to live on indefinitely...and that it would be unwise to try?"

"No. I mean yes, I understand that," said Dawn, trying to look unfazed. "I know I'll still have to work..."

"And, from what I hear, you've got excellent career prospects right where you are with Mr. Lynch..."

"That's true. But, actually, Karen, I never saw real estate as my choice for a career."

"Oh, really? Even though your future could be very promising?"

"Karen, I know that there's money to be made, but I only started working there because Abel wanted me to and because it was part-time."

"I see. Mr. Lynch did mention that you're thinking of opening up a small business of some sort...are you actually thinking of doing that right away?"

"Uh, not in like a week or two, but when I feel up to it. That's what I'd like to try..."

"Okay...do you think you can elaborate a little?"

37

"Well, if I had enough money, I'd like to open my own dance and drama studio for children. What do you think?"

"Well...I could help you on that. Have you prepared a business plan yet, with a realistic budget?"

"Not yet, but I could try."

"Have you scouted out any possible locations yet?"

"Oh, no. Nothing that far along."

"Okay. Definitely don't sign a lease until the money comes in and everything is planned out."

"Nothing to worry about there, Karen."

"Just put your plan together and we can crunch the numbers. Meanwhile, until you know for sure where you're going with all this, I'd advise you to hold off quitting your present job."

"I'm not making big decisions right now anyway, Karen, so that works."

"Great. Would you mind then if I told Mr. Lynch then that you *are* still grieving, you are *not* quitting, and that everything is on hold?"

"If he asks...But I don't want him thinking that I'm definitely coming back, because it's possible I might start looking for something else if my business plan is a flop."

"I see."

"I mean I don't want to mislead him."

"Of course not, Dawn. Call me when you're ready to talk further. And, on your way out today, my assistant should have a claim package ready for you to sign and send in."

TEN

Upon returning home from Dunlap's office, it seemed only fair to let agent Knight know of her change in plans.

"I'm going to send the claim to Aceworth by myself," she said over the phone. "And, for now, sir, I'm just not ready to discuss any financial planning."

"That's your prerogative, Mrs. Santoro, but I do want to remind you again that people have been known to make big mistakes when they receive so much money all at once, especially after a loss. I can't help but be concerned for your welfare..."

"I'm definitely keeping that thought in mind, sir. Thanks."

"Just be careful then...And I hope to see you again before too long."

"Mr. Knight, what I said about not being ready is true. But, in fairness to you, my boss set me up with his financial planner when I am ready..."

"Oh...I see."

"Nothing at all against you, sir."

"No offense taken. But please remember that I'll always be here for your insurance needs. And, by the way, I already alerted Aceworth that your claim will be coming in."

*****

After her best night's sleep since the tragedy, she lay there the next morning thinking about the last part of her conversation with Dunlap: about going back to work for Lynch.

She recalled telling Abel before her first day working there, "If you really think it's for the best, I'll do it part-time."

She recalled the half-days at work. She had handled it okay because so little had been required of her, rotating between studying for her license and doing busy-work tasks that took minimal skills.

But, despite believing that Lynch would continue to be patient and supportive, going back to work for him now made no sense. There had to be other options for which she was better suited, even if she wasn't really ready to have her own business. After all, she would have plenty of money in the bank and be debt free.

Why leave it hanging, she finally concluded. If an insurance agent deserved to know the truth about her future plans, then Lynch certainly did.

*****

When she called into the office later that morning, and revealed her decision to him, his prolonged silence began to unnerve her.

"So you're *never* planning to come back, Dawn?" he finally asked.

"To be honest, I really don't think so, sir."

40

"But didn't Karen explain that you'll still need income?"

"Oh yes, sir. She even suggested that I keep working for you, because of the great opportunities."

"But you're still not going to follow her recommendation?"

"I just don't feel I'm cut out for it, sir, as a career."

"I see."

"Mr. Lynch, I'm also wondering if it might be good for my morale to eventually have my own business. I could dedicate it to Abel..."

"Dawn. It's not going to be what you think."

"I'll be careful. And meanwhile I'll look for something that I feel better suited for."

Silence.

"Dawn, would you mind if I called upon you occasionally to see how you're doing...I mean if we don't hear from you in the meantime?"

"Sure, if you want to...But you're so busy."

"I'll fit it in."

"Okay, sir, but you shouldn't worry about me."

"Let's just call it concern over your new direction. And I'd also be doing it out of respect for Abel."

"That's kind of you, sir."

"Good luck then and good-bye for now, Dawn."

As she hung up the telephone receiver, she felt closure and freedom. It was now time to head to the library and look for books on how to start a small business.

ELEVEN

Although former cop Frank Bayardo's insurance
clients normally called upon him for property loss
investigations, such as reported thefts or suspicious fires,
this time it was a suspicious death with a substantial life
insurance claim on the line.

"We'd like you to take a good look into all the
surrounding circumstances," the Aceworth adjuster had
instructed him, "including whatever medical records you
can find using the release we have from the widow, and
whatever you can come up with by questioning her and the
truck driver."

Despite the opportunity to generate a handsome bill
on such a wide-open assignment, Bayardo couldn't resist
asking. "Any special reason why you want me to check out
the meds, I mean if the guy was hit by a truck? You think
there was some undisclosed condition, maybe?"

"Not so much that. Concentrate more on anything
suspicious after policy issuance, like maybe the insured had
a reason for the path he took that morning."

*****

While driving to Desert Meadows Memorial
Hospital—where Abel Santoro had been taken by
ambulance—Bayardo vowed to produce a first-class report.
Even if he found no smoking gun in this odd-ball case, he'd
be sure to keep Aceworth's goodwill.

Standing minutes later at the minuscule hospital records counter, with the records clerk monitoring him, something caught his eye: an emergency CT scan had been done due to the head injury.

After a call to Aceworth, he asked the clerk to keep the file handy for an expert to look at. Meanwhile, he'd be in the cafeteria.

While Bayardo sipped coffee, after eating a pre-made turkey sandwich, a fortyish looking Asian-American woman, professionally dressed, approached him energetically with a look that said she was all business, and had no time to waste.

"Mr. Bayardo, I'm assuming?"

He quickly stood up and nodded.

"That's me..."

"I'm Dr. Terri Lee, neurologist. I came over from my office across the street. I'm totally familiar with CT scans, and I can give you fifteen minutes."

"Not bad," said Bayardo.

"I beg your pardon?"

"Sorry, Doctor. I'm just impressed that Aceworth could get someone of your status over here so quickly."

"You're lucky. If they'd asked me to do this yesterday..."

Within minutes after she disappeared into the medical records room, Dr. Lee was back out and ready to explain. "In addition to the serious trauma in the cranial area, Mr. Santoro definitely had a brain tumor. Looks like it could have been quite serious, but that's not my specialty."

43

"Could it have been life-threatening, Dr. Lee?"

"I wouldn't be at all surprised."

"Would the patient have known something was wrong? I mean, not trying to ask something stupid, but would it have been possible that he was unaware of it?"

"Oh, no. He would have been very uncomfortable. In all probability, he would have sought medical help for the pain, and hopefully it would have been properly diagnosed."

"Of course," replied Bayardo, as he pondered the development. "Thank you so much, Doctor. It could turn out to be a great help. Uh, might I contact you again on this if Aceworth approves it? You'd be professionally compensated, of course."

"I suppose, Mr. Bayardo, schedule permitting. But, just so you don't get obsessed with *my* personal availability, what I just told you was pretty basic."

*****

Back in his office that afternoon, Bayardo studied the intense-looking man sitting before him.

Darren Penner was in his late thirties, had alert eyes and closely trimmed brown hair. With his disciplined bearing, he looked more like a cop than a truck driver. If he were ever needed on the witness stand, his appearance alone would likely win some points.

Bayardo considered how much to probe beyond the statement Penner gave to the investigating officer, claiming that Mr. Santoro ran out in front of him as if intentionally trying to get hit. The last thing Bayardo wanted to do was to undermine the man's confidence, given that Metro had already put all the blame on Mr. Santoro—as would usually be expected whenever a vehicle and pedestrian have an asphalt encounter outside of a cross-walk.

Still, there were some questions that could be asked in a private setting, if for no other reason than to get insight as to how he might handle them. "Mr. Penner, in light of the evidence that Mr. Santoro was listening to a portable radio with headphones on, and that it was early in the morning in a residential area, do you think it's possible that he just wasn't paying enough attention?"

"Not how I saw it, sir," growled Penner. "He sure as hell saw my truck, even if he didn't hear it. And the way he ran out from the trees right in front of me...he wasn't going to even give me a fighting chance to miss him."

Bayardo took careful notes, having been denied permission by Penner's employer to tape the interview. But, when he looked up again, he could see that Penner was patiently waiting and seemed to have more to say.

"Mr. Bayardo, I'm not in love with insurance companies, and it doesn't matter to me which one you work for. But I was the real victim here. I still wake up at night, drenched in sweat and thinking about that morning. I've even had some counseling for it."

Bayardo looked up from his note-taking and nodded, giving Penner his undivided attention and respect, and letting Penner know that he was willing to hear everything even if he did not write it all down.

"Please continue, Mr. Penner."

"Well, going back to the day after, I was starting to get a little hard on myself, like maybe I wasn't paying enough attention. But I realized that was bullshit. Nobody expects some guy to come out of nowhere and run in front of their rig like he did. My doubts are long gone. He did it deliberately, damn it."

"I believe you, sir."

"And yeah, I'll cooperate in any lawsuit, if that's where you're headed."

"We definitely appreciate that, Mr. Penner," said Bayardo as he made a quick note of Penner's offer, then promptly looked back up.

"I'll tell you what, sir," said Penner. "That widow better not even think of suing me or my company if she knows what's good for her."

"I wouldn't worry about that Mr. Penner until it happens...if it ever does."

Good luck, lady, trying to prove that your husband was less at fault.

TWELVE

After more days passed with no word on the payout from Aceworth, she saw no harm in asking Knight about it.

"It's still under evaluation," he answered. "And, unfortunately, they can't say how long it'll take."

Unease gripped her as she hung up the phone.

"Is this because I didn't go for Knight's financial plan?" she murmured. "Was I supposed to know that?"

She shook her head out of frustration.

"No, don't think that way," she told herself.

But her mind reverted back, wondering what might happen if she bought whatever he was pushing, as long as there was enough left over?

"No," she caught herself again, "that's not right."

She took a deep breath. "One day at a time."

*****

"Mrs. Santoro?" the gravelly voice said over the phone later that day, "my name is Frank Bayardo, and I'm working for Aceworth Insurance on your claim."

"Oh," she answered uneasily..."You're working on it?"

"Yes. And my sincere condolences on the passing of your husband."

"Thank you, sir."

"Mrs. Santoro, I do need to speak with you in person. It's part of Aceworth's due diligence in processing your

47

claim, and a fairly normal procedure on accidental deaths. Do you know how soon we could do that?"

How about yesterday!

"Right away, sir. You can do your interview at my house as soon as you can get over here."

THIRTEEN

Dawn greeted Bayardo in a modest knee-length dress, appropriately dark in color.

Upon sitting down, Bayardo was ready with his note-pad. "Mrs. Santoro, can you recall how your husband seemed to you leading up to that unfortunate day?"

"I'd say that he seemed pretty much like his normal self."

"Was he voicing any unusual complaints about anything?"

"No. Not that I remember."

"Were you aware of his habits when he went out jogging?"

"His jogging habits?" Dawn asked. "I'm not sure what you mean."

"Just whatever you know, Mrs. Santoro..."

"Well, I don't know. I mean, he just started jogging when we got back from our little beach trip. He said he wanted to work on his fitness. But I never joined him, if you're hoping that I might somehow know more about it. We had...I mean, our little girl sure couldn't have jogged, and she was usually still sleeping at that hour."

"Would you mind, Mrs. Santoro, if I asked what you mean by your 'little beach trip'?"

"Uh...it's not that I mind, sir, but isn't this supposed to be about my life insurance claim?"

"Certainly, Mrs. Santoro. All part of my due diligence, and I'll keep my focus narrow here. Promise."

"Well, our little family had a long weekend in a place called Laguna Beach, as I recall. It was just something special to celebrate what we had together. Abel even called it 'a little second honeymoon, complete with baby'."

"Had he taken you on many trips before, Mrs. Santoro?"

This is "focused"?

"No. Except on our real honeymoon, of course...and coming from Tucson to live here."

"I see. Was this beach trip during the same time of year as your wedding anniversary?"

"Uh, no. But, can I ask you again, what difference could any of this make?"

"It's all routine, I assure you Mrs. Santoro," Bayardo coolly replied, as he was already looking down at his notes for more questions. "Now, did your husband ever complain much of headaches, vision problems or dizziness?"

And now this?

She scavenged her memory. "He might have mentioned something like that a couple times? I do remember him saying one time that he had a headache that kept coming back. But I think he said he'd go see a doctor if it didn't go away pretty soon."

"And do you know if he did see a doctor?"

"As far as I can remember, he never said one way or the other. Keep in mind that Abel hardly ever complained or talked about himself."

Bayardo wrote for a moment. "Okay then, if that's your best recollection..."

So, am I being graded on this?

"Sir, I am trying to cooperate with you, but can you please tell me what any of this could possibly have to do with my claim?"

"Don't worry, Mrs. Santoro, the sooner I finish here, the sooner they can finish the claim processing."

Then quick answers you'll get...

"Are you sure that's all you can remember about your husband having headaches and such?"

"Basically, yes."

Bayardo stared at her, as if probing.

Dawn stared back long enough to show she wasn't happy with his routine. "Mr. Bayardo, how long will the processing take after you finish with me?"

Bayardo noisily cleared his throat while shifting his eyes back into his notebook.

So, you won't answer me.

"Now then, Mrs. Santoro, what do you personally think about your husband all of a sudden taking up jogging, and then unfortunately getting himself killed like that? Doesn't that seem odd?"

"Odd? In what way?" she crisply replied.

"Well, I'd say, like the closeness in time and all..."

She looked him straight in the eyes. "Abel made a decision to start jogging, just like a lot of people have done. And, when Abel made up his mind, he usually carried it out. Nothing odd about that as far as I'm concerned."

"Mrs. Santoro, I know how you must feel as a result of this tragedy. I lost my wife two years ago..."

51

So you say...How'd you like to be low on money at the same time?

She merely offered an unimpressed stare. But, when the silence became awkward, she decided against trying to antagonize him. "I'm sorry for your loss too, Mr. Bayardo."

Assuming...

"Thank you, Mrs. Santoro."

"Mr. Bayardo, my claim is not about being lonely. I have a small child to support, along with house and car payments to worry about. I would greatly appreciate it if you will tell them to hurry up on this."

Bayardo started readying himself to leave. "I understand, Mrs. Santoro. Hopefully, you'll hear from Aceworth within a couple weeks or so. Meanwhile, perhaps you have a friend or some other means of getting a loan, if it becomes necessary."

"Not that I know of...But, if I did get a loan, do you know when I'd be able to pay them back, so I could tell them up front? I really don't see how my claim can be that complicated."

"I understand your question, Mrs. Santoro, but I'm not the one who decides. All I do is turn in my report. Aceworth will be in touch with you some time after that. Thanks again for your time."

Bayardo stood up and handed her his business card. "If you think of anything that didn't come to mind today, don't hesitate to call me."

And make Aceworth take even more time?

She took the card.

As Bayardo started toward the door, he stopped to look at some family pictures on display. He pointed at a husky older man. "May I ask who this gentleman is?"

"That's...I mean that *was* Abel's father."

"Was he also a carpenter, like his son?"

A 'carpenter'? You moron!

"I really don't know where Abel got his artistic skills. I think his father was mostly a truck driver."

FOURTEEN

After a restless night, she thought about how she felt worse, not better, as a result of the Bayardo interview. And soon, some unknown Aceworth employee—who couldn't care less what obligations she faced—would have her future in a file on their desk.

She thought about Bayardo's advice to her, *as if* every woman whose husband died could just call upon a friend or family member for a needed loan. "Why even say loan," she scoffed. "Why not just ask for free cash?"

"No way my mother could help," she exclaimed. "Besides, she wasn't thrilled about me marrying Abel to begin with...And forget his mom: a coffee-shop waitress with her own husband out of the picture."

After eventually coercing herself to get up and dressed, she paced and fidgeted around the house for the next ten minutes, as if groping for a direction.

She finally fixated on the yellow pages book next to her telephone. She opened it and found many entries under "Loans", with some ads claiming "Fast Loans" or "Quick Loans."

"Five thousand should hold me until Aceworth finally pays up," she muttered, while copying down the telephone numbers from four of the most prominent ads.

But, after the first two lenders promptly rejected her for not being currently employed, she looked again until she found a smaller ad boasting "Easy Qualifying".

A man with a thick accent answered her call and invited her to come down to their office. "We'll do our best to work something out with you," he said.

After lining up Nanny G, Dawn fed her daughter and headed out. From Gwen's, she drove toward an older part of town where she was able to home in on the street address. She saw a *"PAWN"* sign in flashing gold, with the word *"L-O-A-N-S"* underneath it in cash-green. The location, near some older casinos, was obviously intended to pull in tourists who'd busted through their gambling budgets while searching off the beaten track for the proverbial "hot" slot-machine.

She parked at the curb and walked toward the front door, noticing as she approached that the building had apparently been remodeled from some other failed business—maybe a small restaurant. She mustered her courage and entered.

Once through the nondescript entryway, she immediately noticed a security guard behind protective glass. There were jewelry counters and shelves everywhere, with a vast assortment of other valuables on display as well: musical instruments, guns, electronic gadgets, and more.

A middle-aged couple was ahead of her. Tourists, Dawn guessed.

As soon as Dawn reached the counter and uttered the word "loan", she was unceremoniously handed a clipboard and ballpoint pen by the young Latino-looking female employee. With a minimal smile, the woman then pointed toward a nearby table with chairs.

While plodding through the form, Dawn soon noticed someone standing next to her.

She looked up to see a man in a suit and tie, with dark features including curly black hair. He looked to be in his thirties.

"Hello, I am Irwin," he said in an accent similar to the man on the phone.

She nodded and forced a quick smile.

"How are you doing with your application?" he asked.

"Working on it, sir."

"Someone will be available soon to consider you. In fact," he said, "you can just come with me."

"Uh, but I wasn't quite finished..."

"Don't worry, miss," said Irwin.

He led Dawn through a nearby door and into a conference room. There were impressive paintings on the walls, a dark wood table and an elegant set of padded leather chairs. The room appeared to be much more appropriate for a serious business meeting than to consider her loan application.

"Have a seat and relax for a minute. Can I get you some coffee or water maybe?"

"Oh, no thanks. I'm fine."

I think.

Irwin excused himself and disappeared through the other door without bothering to close it.

She could faintly hear male voices emanating from an apparent hallway or adjoining office. Then, the talking stopped.

An older heavy-set man, with similar dark features, but wearing a more expensive looking suit, stepped into the conference room.

"Hello Miss Dawn, I am Ari," the man said, while extending his hand to her. "I own this business and I am sorry you were kept waiting."

Kept waiting?

"Come into my private office, and I will see if I can help you," he said, motioning her in.

His large office was equally ostentatious, albeit with more paintings stacked next to the wall and jewelry spread out on a small side table.

Dawn nervously took a seat.

"Excuse my directness, Miss Dawn, but tell me for what reason you need a loan from me?"

"Yes sir, to help with expenses for the time being. I'm hoping I can pay it back very soon."

"What amount, and how long do you need the money?"

"Uh, would five thousand be possible, maybe a month or two?"

"Anything is possible with Ari. Are you working right now, if I may ask?"

"Not right now, no. I took some time off."

Ari gave a perfunctory smile, then raised his heavy eyebrows and took a deep breath as if dramatizing what would come next. "Okay, we will keep talking. With me, you do not have to be working full-time, but then there is usually collateral. You must have something of value?"

Dawn thought a moment, then held out her hands, palms up. "Sorry, there's nothing I can think of," she said with a shrug.

Ari stared blankly a moment as if in thought, then focused upon her left hand. "Are you still married, may I ask?"

Dawn shook her head somberly.

Guessing where he might go next, she slid her right hand protectively over her left, as if her ring would otherwise levitate off her finger and onto Ari's desk. She decided to speak first. "All I have is my one car, but it's not even close to paid for and I couldn't survive without it anyway."

Ari said nothing, but displayed apparent interest in her situation, as if wanting to hear more.

He must think I'm loony.

"Sir," said Dawn, upon gathering her courage, "I expect to get life insurance money soon, on account of my husband dying recently. I will pay it all back to you then."

"'Soon', you say?"

She nodded.

"So, then, how long have you already been waiting for that money? I mean, I have to wonder if maybe you are here because there is some problem, yes? And what if that problem gets worse for you?"

"Then, I don't know...Back to full-time work, I guess, and I'd pay you over time."

Silence followed, as Ari appeared to be mulling something over.

Though she now doubted that anything good would be forthcoming, she politely waited.

"You seem honest to me, Miss Dawn, so here is what I can offer you today," said Ari while reaching into his back pocket. He pulled out his wallet and removed a wad of cash. He then counted out ten one-hundred dollar bills on his desk."

She looked at the display, then back up at him.

"I will loan you one thousand right now, no collateral, at only two percent interest for sixty days—usually I charge much more. Would you like that?"

Dawn froze, unsure how to respond.

"I know you want more than that, so come with me tonight to a dinner party. It's at a nice restaurant and many people will be there. They will mostly be foreign like me, but I promise they will be friendly. We can even go early and relax with a drink. If you will do that for me, I will consider a bigger loan for you."

Dawn went from uneasy to positively nauseous.

What in God's name am I doing here?

"Just dinner," said Ari, his eyes like penetrating lasers.

No more eye contact.

She lowered her head. Her hands nervously roamed over her upper legs and elsewhere to confirm that she was still fully dressed.

Nobody even knows I'm here.

"I'm sorry, Mr. Ari. No offense to you, but I just can't. I just lost my husband, and I am not up for anything, uh, social yet."

"So you will let yourself default on your debts then?" he pressured her, his eyes apparently searching for any sign of weakness.

I answered him.

"I'll just have to find another way, sir."

"I understand, Miss Dawn. It's your choice. But there is really nothing special about this dinner tonight. There will be more, so I will hold my offer open for you."

"Thank you. I will keep that in mind."

As if.

"Here," Ari said, reaching over the cash for the card-holder on his desk. "Keep my card in your purse." He then rose to hand it to her, just in time for Dawn to take it in her left hand while the rest of her was already making a turn toward the door.

"Thank you Mr. Ari. I sure will."

She determinedly worked her way toward the front door, while trying to appear composed, but her mind kept flashing back to the thousand dollars and Ari's laser eyes.

With her heart racing by the time she was outside, she walked quickly to her car. She nervously fumbled to get her key into the ignition until the sound of the engine comforted her.

"Holy shit," she grumbled. "For a moment there..."

But, as she drove back toward Nanny G's home, the relief soon ended. With more bills on the horizon, not getting any loan was bad enough. But she couldn't help wondering if Ari could possibly be onto something about the delay in her insurance payout.

FIFTEEN

Within a week of sending in his report, Bayardo was re-reading it while waiting for a conference call with Aceworth.

"The medical records would help," he had written, "to prove that the insured had a brain tumor". And, "yes, Penner will testify if Aceworth wanted to argue that the insured intentionally ran in front of his truck."

But Bayardo had his doubts about what the Aceworth people might have in mind. "I know from years of work on criminal cases," he had written, "that proving someone's intent is tough. And, in this case, Mr. Santoro would have been risking the loss of two hundred fifty thousand for his soon-to-be widow, which is still an astronomical sum for that family."

Once the conference call was underway, Bayardo was happy to let the two others, both lawyers, take it in whatever direction they wanted. He had done his job and provided support for a defense that might even succeed in court if it went that far.

"Obviously," remarked Aceworth's assistant general counsel, Lindsay Noveder, "we never want to recklessly subject the company to potential bad faith claims. But we also can't be quick to pay double when we've got arguable grounds to deny all of it. Besides," he added with a hint of sarcasm, "It's not like we collected much in the way of annual premiums."

"Don't sell that last point short, Lindsay," said local insurance defense attorney Ken Tilden, of Smith & Tilden. "I could easily see a jury taking that into consideration."

"Totally fine with me," replied Lindsay. "So, that's about the size of it, gents. We're going to try to save as much as we can on this one. Start out nice and low."

"Will do," said Ken Tilden.

"And, if we can't settle it quickly, we'll deny coverage based on the truck driver's statement and medical records. Hey, I've denied claims on less in good faith. That's assuming, of course, that you would have alerted me if there was any new Nevada case law that dooms us."

"None up to today," said Ken.

"I wouldn't think so," said Lindsay. "Even on a national level, we're not aware of any bad faith findings on analogous facts."

"But if it drags on too long," replied Ken, "a case like this could go into uncharted territory. So we'll try to see that it doesn't."

"If the landscape changes that much, let me know Ken and we'll re-evaluate," said Lindsay. "But for now, if Mrs. Santoro rejects our offer, go ahead with the declaratory action. You know the drill."

"Backwards and forwards."

"And Ken, use Frank as needed on this. He's talked with the widow and has a good feel for the case."

With the conference call ended, Bayardo was happy for the endorsement, but he understood that his "good feel for this case" included his awareness of another reason for Aceworth's low-offer strategy. Whether or not the husband actually committed suicide, the widow seemed to be getting close to desperate.

SIXTEEN

Dressed in her best professional attire, Dawn nervously waited outside the entrance to Lou Lynch's office.

"Mr. Lynch," the assistant stepped in to announce t him, "a woman is here asking if she can work for us."

"A woman?" Lynch grunted.

"It's Dawn Santoro, sir," the assistant cheerfully replied.

"Oh, that's terrific. Show her in right away."

The assistant passed Dawn on her way out, giving her a quick wink.

Despite the playfulness of the lead-in, it did not erase Dawn's feeling of awkwardness.

She sheepishly entered the room, and was immediately struck at how much more intimidating Lynch seemed to her now that she was in need of a job. In his fifties, well-tanned, with closely-trimmed gray hair, a strong chin and piercing blue eyes, he had the looks of a big-time football coach or maybe even a former astronaut.

She instinctively hesitated before speaking, hoping he might somehow give her a hint as to where she stood with him.

He flashed just enough of a smile.

"Sir, I apologize for staying away as long as I did, but things have been crazy for me. Is there any chance that I could have my old job back, or is there any other job you might have for me?"

"No apology is called for. We hoped you'd eventually return."

"Thank you, sir."

"You're sure that you're ready to work?"

"I need all the hours I can get, Mr. Lynch."

64

"I see. When do you want to start?"

"Now, sir. I'm ready."

"Well then, welcome back," said Lynch, extending his hand.

"I do have one appointment tomorrow, though," said Dawn, as her hand was finally released from his grasp. "Now that I'm working again, the loan companies will consider me for what I need until the insurance finally comes in."

Lynch stared at her as if evaluating a science experiment. "So, I take it that you're having trouble getting your life insurance money?"

She nodded.

"Have they completely denied it or..."

"No, God forbid. They say they're still evaluating, but it's taking forever."

"Evaluating...I see."

She nodded again with a shrug of her shoulders.

He stared at her some more. "Listen, how much of a loan do you need right now?"

She looked down and thought. "I guess whatever I could qualify for, Mr. Lynch. At least five thousand, if I could get it."

"Cancel your appointment, Dawn. I've got something better for you."

Lynch reached into his desk drawer, took out a sheet of personalized stationary and began writing. "Just go next door to the mortgage company, and tell them I sent you."

"Really, sir?"

"You mentioned five, so I'm going to assume that ten would do, especially with you working again." He put the handwritten message in an envelope and sealed it. "Just go on over there around three today, and give them this."

"Ten thousand! You can really have them do this for me?"

"It's as good as done. They'll require a second mortgage on your house because that's just part of the lending business. But don't worry. You can just pay it back whenever you're able."

"Thank you so much, sir," said Dawn, unabashedly rubbing her hands together in relief. "Now I can totally focus on my work."

"Uh, that's fine, Dawn, but one more question before you get started..."

"Yes sir?"

"Would you mind if I asked how you're holding up these days...I mean, other than financially?"

Although she couldn't help but feel more positive with the loan coming in, his question put her off balance. "Uh, as far as my loss, I am definitely still grieving...if that's what you're asking, sir."

"Completely understandable, Dawn. We all miss Abel very much. But you hang in there and I'm sure good things will come your way."

"That would be great, Mr. Lynch. But, right now, I'll just feel better getting back to work."

*****

On her drive home at the end of the day, Dawn rejoiced at her decision to go back to work for Lynch, even to the point of singing along with radio.

She could hardly believe how easy the ten-thousand-dollar loan had been. The loan officer had even giggled as she rattled off all the normal requirements that had been waived. "Wow," she had remarked, "I hope you realize how unusual it is to issue the check without even a preliminary title or appraisal? Oh well, it's his money."

Dawn did not need to ask who she meant by "his" money. Of greater importance, however, was the knowledge that, with her check from L&L Mortgage Co., combined with the resumption of her work income, she could now patiently wait for the Aceworth payout.

And, meanwhile, she vowed that, when that payout did finally come, she would still keep working for Lynch until some unknown date, far enough into the future for her not to feel that she had taken too much advantage of his generosity.

SEVENTEEN

With still no news from Aceworth after ten more days, Dawn called Bayardo, only to reach his answering machine. No call back came in the ensuing days.

Eventually, upon returning to the office one day from a licensing class, she was given a phone message that insurance agent George Knight had called and had asked for her to stop by his office today after work, saying he'd be open until 6:00 p.m.

"Yes!" Dawn shrieked with a fist-pump.

No wonder Bayardo didn't call back.

In response to the commotion, the receptionist pointed toward Dawn with a smile. "Wow, don't *you* look happy."

"'Relieved' is a better word," replied Dawn, blushing at the attention she had brought on. "My insurance check is finally in!"

"Well, we're all happy for you."

The clatter was enough to draw Lynch out from his office. "Would someone mind enlightening me?" he asked with a quizzical smile.

"Dawn's finally going to get her insurance check," the receptionist volunteered. "Right after work today."

"I shouldn't have even bothered you about needing a loan, Mr. Lynch," said Dawn. "Guess I just panicked."

"Uh, that's just terrific," replied Lynch with apparent surprise. "So they told you that over the phone?"

"Not exactly, sir. The insurance agent left a message for me to come in before six tonight. And I can only assume that's why..."

"Of course," said Lynch. "Why else would he be calling. Hey listen, it's already close to four. Take off now, and you might make it to a bank before they close."

*****

Sitting in Knight's office, Dawn readied herself for another sales pitch, no doubt more forceful this time. But, just in case that didn't happen, she remained poised to spring up and be on her way as soon as she had her check in hand.

"Uh sorry, Mr. Knight, but this won't take long, will it? I was hoping to be somewhere by five."

Knight raised his hand as if to slow her down, his minimal smile vanishing. After making sure he had her full attention, he cleared his throat. "Mrs. Santoro, you should not be the one saying you're sorry. I can't tell you how sorry I am for having to break this news to you..."

What?

"...You'll be receiving a letter before you leave today," he continued, nodding toward the apparent item on his desk. "I personally had nothing to do with it, but I'm the messenger for Aceworth and I'm going to first summarize it for you. Basically, they are offering to pay you fifty thousand to settle your life insurance claim."

"Fifty?"

"Although fifty is not the policy amount, Mrs. Santoro, the company believes that you, uh..." Knight picked up the letter, "that you should, quote, 'seriously consider accepting this offer in light of the evidence that the insured's death resulted from suicide. Such a finding would render the company free from any obligation under the policy due to the unexpired two-year exclusionary period,' end-quote."

69

She sat stunned, not knowing yet if there could be some correctable mistake or if she should just go straight to outrage.

"Suicide," Knight went on, with another nod toward the Aceworth letter, "is completely excluded from coverage in most, if not all, life insurance policies for a certain period of time after the policy is purchased."

He looked up at her from the letter, grimacing, then continued reading. "The lengths of time may differ with the jurisdiction, but it's two years in Nevada, and this policy had not yet reached that point."

"Mr. Knight," Dawn said, loudly enough to surprise herself, "This is crazy. Everyone knows that Abel was killed by a truck."

Knight looked at her and nodded his head, his expression sympathetic but dire. "Yes, they are well aware of that, Mrs. Santoro."

With no obvious direction to take, she groped for some way to respond. Nothing came to her. She felt her body collapse backward into the same chair she thought she would be out of by now. The idea of getting to her bank by five had turned into a cruel joke.

Knight let her have whatever time she needed.

"Abel paid for that policy," she pleaded. "They can't just make up something about him and get away with it. They have no right to keep the rest of that money."

With tears quickly forming, she accepted a tissue from Knight, who continued to wait patiently, obviously willing to hear her out for whatever good that would do.

But instead of saying anything more, she lowered her head and shook it dejectedly,

"Mrs. Santoro," Knight finally said in a softened voice, "this is very difficult for me, too. I respect your questions, but I'm in no position to defend a decision by Aceworth that I had nothing to do with. I can only say, once again, that I'm very sorry this has happened to you."

And maybe sorry you can't sell me something.

After more silent seconds passed, Knight continued, "Mrs. Santoro, when all is said and done, it's my duty to make sure you understand that I have here a fifty-thousand dollar settlement check if you decide that you want it, as long as you are willing to sign an acknowledgment that it would be, quote, 'a final settlement and expression of good faith in assuring that you receive a substantial payment as the policy's beneficiary,' end-quote."

She glared at him.

"Mrs. Santoro, I understand this has all come as a shock to you. Sleep on it. Maybe talk to someone you trust. Aceworth is giving you ten business days from today to accept."

"I won't need ten days," she said, sobbing.

Knight handed her another tissue. "Please excuse me again, Mrs. Santoro, but it's my duty to also inform you that, should you choose not to accept this settlement, the company would intend to deny coverage completely and merely return the premiums paid."

She wiped her eyes and took a deep breath.

"Mrs. Santoro...at least they came through with fifty thousand. That can go a long way for you..."

She stood up and again glared at him. "All I can say, Mr. Knight, is what good is buying life insurance if they can do this to you?"

Knight flinched.

"You can read me whatever you want or give me that letter, but I can't accept that check. I'd just be agreeing with Aceworth that Abel killed himself, and that's a flat-out lie."

"Mrs. Santoro. You know that I wanted you to get every dollar. But, even with the fifty...well, never mind. I'm not trying to force this money on you. Take the time. Get some advice. It'll be here if you decide to take it."

She snatched the letter off the desk as she got up to leave. By the time she was out the front door, she felt as though she was in a different dimension, far removed from where she'd been only twenty minutes earlier.

Upon reaching her car, she stopped a moment to think. They offered fifty thousand instead of paying five hundred thousand because they say that Abel didn't wait long enough to kill himself? She shook her head.

But, by the time she was driving, she was surprised at how much the fifty thousand had started vying for her attention. It was way more than she'd ever had at one time and far more than Abel had paid them. She could pay off the loan from Lynch and, at least, get a little ahead.

But then again, she realized, that little cushion would probably be gone before Cora was even in kindergarten. And it was nowhere near what Abel had in mind when he bought the policy.

At a stoplight on her way to Nanny G's, she found herself staring at a nearby piece of undeveloped desert land—one of many barren patches scattered throughout Las Vegas. She had noticed that, the further away you got from the Strip, the more empty spots you encountered until it eventually became completely barren. She feared that was the future she and Cora might face if everything depended upon her real estate career, which she never chose in the first place.

At the next stoplight, however, as she glanced up at a particularly glitzy casino billboard, she was taken over by a wild feeling, almost giddiness, about the bizarre city she still inhabited. She recalled an old movie scene where a desperate wretch, dying in a desert, suddenly broke into a fool's laughter when a cool running brook turned out to be nothing but rocks and sand.

She then shook her head, smirking at the thought of her own situation. Not long ago, she'd left a thousand dollars on the table at a pawn shop. Today she walked out on a fifty-thousand-dollar check.

"I may not have a clue what to do next," she said with a sigh, "but at least the amounts are getting bigger."

EIGHTEEN

At work the next day, her mind wandered toward the unanswerable questions. Hunches and thoughts emerged then faded. Then, late in the afternoon, she was called into Lynch's office.

"Is anything wrong, sir?" she asked nervously.

"Not at all, Dawn. I just wanted to say how nice it is to have you back in the office. And, if anything is ever bothering you, feel free to discuss it with me."

But it's not about work.

"Thank you, sir. I'm happy to be back myself."

"And how is everything going for you, now that you got your life insurance money yesterday?"

"Oh I absolutely did *not* get it, sir. There's trouble."

"But I thought..."

"Mr. Lynch, you wouldn't believe it. They're saying that Abel violated the policy, so they don't have to pay. They say he committed suicide, even though he got hit by a truck."

"Oh my goodness...Must have been devastating for you..."

"And it's an insult to Abel's memory, sir..."

"I can't imagine what they could base that on..."

"Me neither. But, right now, I don't see how I can fight a big insurance company. And, if I did take the fifty thousand they offered to settle," said Dawn, surprised at how seriously she seemed to be considering it, "I could at least pay back that loan you got me and have a little cushion..."

"Not much of one."

"I know, Mr. Lynch. It's only a tenth of what they should be paying me."

"So you're still undecided on what you're going to do?"

She stared at him. "Mr. Lynch, I'll be honest with you because you've been so generous toward me. Things have gone from bad to worse. So, right now, I have no idea what I'm going to do about anything, and that includes whether I'll even stay here in Las Vegas much longer."

Lynch grimaced, then stared blankly as if in deep thought. "Okay," he finally spoke, "since you're being open with me, I'm going to give you my honest reaction. You need a dual approach here..."

"A what, sir?"

"First, I'll get you a legal consultation. They might think they have evidence to support their position, but a good lawyer could evaluate it for you. At the very least, he might get you a higher settlement."

"Oh, yes sir. That's exactly what I need."

"Second, I'll set you up again with Karen Dunlap, so you can do some realistic budget planning based on whatever settlement the lawyer might help you get."

"Really?"

"Happy to. No big deal."

"But sir, you've already done so much for me time and again..."

"Dawn," he interrupted with a quick smile as he rose to show her out, "your gratitude is refreshing, but let's first see how it all works out."

NINETEEN

Days later, she found herself in the reception room of Ashe, Kramer & King, which easily outdid Karen Dunlap's. There was antique looking mahogany furniture, including chairs that looked too expensive to sit on, an exquisite *faux* fireplace, artwork that would seem appropriate for a museum and burgundy wall paper with gold aristocratic emblems complementing the gold-plated letters *"AK&K"*.

The law firm's receptionist greeted Dawn with elegant diction, matching her perfect makeup and coiffure.

As Dawn took her seat, on the verge of her first-ever meeting with an attorney, she started to feel as nervous about her own appearance as about the reason for being there. But it occurred to her that, even with her modest outfit, she had Lynch's backing for this appointment.

After a few minutes, a youngish man stepped into the reception room by way of a door that presumably led back to the lawyers' offices. With light brown hair, he was boyishly handsome in his medium-blue suit and red tie.

Although he quickly made eye contact with Dawn—the only person in the reception room at the moment—his steps toward her seemed hesitant, as if he were still somehow under the spell of other matters waiting for him back in his office.

"Good morning, Mrs. Santoro," he said with a busy smile and time-pressured energy, as he held out his hand. "I'm James Claverson. I understand that you have some legal issues to discuss..."

This is really happening!

"Yes sir, I sure do," she replied gratefully, her hand eagerly shaking his.

"Okay, then. If you wouldn't mind following me back to my office..."

As she took her seat in front of him, she was startled by the wondrous view she had of the entire southern skyline of Las Vegas, with hotel-casinos lined up one after another. It made her wonder, though, if this serious looking man ever paused to turn around and take it all in.

"So, Mrs. Santoro, I understand that you're a widow and that you work for a client of this firm."

"Yes," she nodded. "I do work for Mr. Lou Lynch."

"I've heard of him. I think he's mainly a real estate client."

"That's the one."

"Ever been involved in litigation before, Mrs. Santoro?"

"Definitely not. But I'm not in a lawsuit now, sir, just in case you got some wrong information."

"Of course, Mrs. Santoro, I didn't mean it that way. But, if the situation calls for it, I do litigate. I'm here to help any way I can."

"That's good to know, sir."

"So, may we use first names?"

"Sure."

"Good, call me James."

She smiled and nodded.

"Now Dawn, let me say first that I am not trying to be insensitive about your unfortunate tragedy, but your husband was killed as a result of being hit by a truck, right?"

She nodded again. "Absolutely."

"And you're here today because the life insurance company refused to pay up?" said James with a touch of disbelief.

"That is it, sir...I mean James."

"Okay, then. I'm having trouble so far speculating why they would do this. Do you happen to have some sort of letter from them?"

Dawn pulled it from her purse and handed it over.

He mumbled softly as he read it to himself with a perplexed expression, while using his free hand to massage his forehead and temples, as if he'd already worked a full day's worth but was coaxing his brain to press on. He then put the letter down and stared blankly at Dawn, his mind obviously still processing it all, until he finally seemed ready.

"Dawn, so far I'm not impressed with their position. I could see an insurance company trying this on a helpless policyholder...But," he said self-assuredly, "you're now beyond that."

Okay...

"It is still a new case for me," James went on, "but so far I'm thinking that I'd be very comfortable going to court for you, if that's what it takes. They're the big out-of-state insurance company who sold this policy to your deceased husband. You're a widow...and do you have any children, Dawn?"

"Yes, Cora. She's not yet two."

"So they're doing this to a widowed mother of an infant daughter. If this ever goes all the way to a trial, they'd better know what the heck they're doing."

Dawn nodded, mildly encouraged, but not yet seeing any reason to celebrate.

"Dawn," James continued, "you also need to understand that this fifty thousand would be their low-end offer anyway. By putting that figure in writing at the outset, they're actually signaling that they'd go higher."

"Wow, that's sure good to know..."

"So, it looks to me so far like we might have to fight it on the merits and see how that goes. At the worst, we should still get a better settlement even if your case later develops problems."

"So there's some hope for me?"

"Definitely. And, assuming we do have to litigate, I'll determine the best strategy. Maybe a Dec action. That means 'declaratory', which is a lawsuit where we are asking the court to confirm your contract rights, and it's supposed to get heard more quickly. I'd probably also include a claim for bad faith, which should get their attention, especially if they're relying on flimsy evidence."

"I'd have to leave all that up to you, James."

"Hey, I was just thinking. If we want to be ultra-aggressive, we could file suit before the time ran out on their fifty-thousand offer. Can't think of a better way to show strength."

Despite her cautious instincts, she could not help but feel encouraged by such spirited talk, in stark contrast to all the delays from Aceworth. But, not wanting to jinx the moment, she resisted the urge to ask how long it could be before she might get some money.

"You brought the policy with you, I assume?"

"Sure did." She reached again into her purse. "I copied it all at my office for you."

"Excellent," said James, "a well-prepared client."

After receiving the document, he stood up and started moving toward the door, as if he was resuming his clock-watching pace. "Dawn, it was good to meet you and I'll be proud to represent you. You'll hear from me soon."

As she walked into the parking garage, her steps suddenly became more hesitant. Although Lynch had talked about getting "advice" from an attorney, it now looked, for better or worse, like she might soon have a "case". And it had all happened in a blur.

"God, it sucks feeling like you're in way over your head," she murmured.

But, as she continued to walk toward her car, the massive multi-level parking structure itself seemed to bolster her confidence. The echo of her footsteps on the thick concrete reminded her that she had just come from a powerful law firm—a force normally reserved for the wealthy and elite, like her boss.

"I can actually dream again," she whispered to herself, "and also defend Abel's honor...Mr. Lynch, I owe you once more."

TWENTY

With each passing day, Dawn struggled to preserve the optimism she had upon leaving Ashe, Kramer & King, while also wishing she could better recall exactly what James said toward the end. If only she knew what to expect next, and when.

One week after her meeting with James, she had trouble thinking of anything but her insurance claim, especially on slower days at work. After telling herself that she'd been patient long enough to at least justify a call to the law firm, she found a quiet corner with a phone extension and dialed.

"I'm sorry, Mrs. Santoro," said Stephanie, the legal assistant James shared with another junior lawyer, "he's not available right now. Can I take a message for him?"

"Just, if you could tell him that I inquired about my insurance claim...and maybe remind him about the deadline in their letter?"

"Certainly, Mrs. Santoro, I'll relay your message next time I speak to him."

The rest of that day and the entire next morning passed with no word back from James.

A return call finally came late in the afternoon, but it was only from Stephanie. "Mrs. Santoro, Mr. Claverson is still unavailable, but I'm to tell you that you can expect to receive a copy of an important letter from him in the mail soon."

"Thanks, I'll look for it," replied Dawn, at a loss for anything else to say.

At least that's something...I think.

After hanging up, she tried to imagine what could possibly be accomplished by a mere letter. She wondered whether James really did have a realistic back-up plan. But, in her wondering, she realized again how helpless she was. She could fret all she wanted, but her fate, and Cora's as well, was in the hands of the busy young lawyer she had barely met.

*****

The letter from James Claverson reached her home mailbox the next day. Looking at it after her day at work, she immediately saw that the original had been express mailed to Aceworth. Although that was good to see, the letter itself was disappointingly brief:

> Please be advised that this firm represents Mrs. Dawn Santoro, the policy beneficiary, with regard to her life insurance claim against your company.
>
> With the loss of her husband, Mrs. Santoro, a mother of an infant daughter, is in financial distress and urgent need of the funds that should have already been paid to her. Demand is hereby made for immediate full payment under such policy based on Mr. Abel Santoro's accidental death. Otherwise, Aceworth Insurance Company will face allegations of bad faith breach of your fiduciary duties owed to her, with the potential for a punitive damages award against your company, in addition to compensatory damages and other relief.

Despite the minimal content, she found herself impressed by its forcefulness, especially under his law firm's letterhead.

Maybe James is tougher than he looks, she thought, but will this really work?

*****

After several more days dragged on, a telephone call finally came in from James. Because Dawn was still at work, she asked him to hold while she found a more private extension. By his initial tone, however, she was not expecting any cause to rejoice.

"Okay, I'm back on."

"Unfortunately, Dawn, I've been told by Aceworth's local attorney, Ken Tilden, that his client rejected our demand and that we might as well just file whatever suit we want. He says he's authorized to accept the summons and complaint on behalf of Aceworth and that he will see us in court."

She was speechless.

"Frankly, Dawn, I don't understand their arrogance on this one, but maybe we'll find out why in due time. Right now, though," James added apologetically, "I happen to be tied up almost every day on a new litigation emergency with an upcoming preliminary injunction hearing. I was given that assignment only a couple days after we met, and it's taking up most of my time. I'll also be out of town nearly all next week to take depositions on that case. But, I assure you, Dawn, that I will get your case moving."

So Aceworth already had its lawyer set to fight me, while I'm lucky if mine can even return my call.

"They didn't raise their offer at all, James?"

"No, not yet."

"I'm getting worried."

83

"Hang in there, Dawn. I need to meet with you one more time to be able to file your suit. I'll call you as soon as I can to arrange it. Keep the faith."

"I'll try."

"And there'll be other chances to try to settle."

"Okay, James."

But, meanwhile, I can't plan on anything.

TWENTY-ONE

At home after work during the following week, she was surprised to receive a call from James.

"I'm finally at the end of this round of depositions," he said, "and I head back from L.A. tonight. Could you come in tomorrow evening after you get off work and the partners are all gone? That way, I know I'll be free to work with you on your lawsuit."

*****

As she sat patiently and watched James work, with his office clock reading 7:32 p.m. and all the other attorneys at AK&K apparently gone for the night, Dawn wished she could be of more help. And, because he must have started early and already worked hard on other matters, she almost felt guilty. But she reminded herself that every step so far—from their first meeting onward—had been at his direction.

He finally put away some papers that had absorbed his attention for minutes and looked into Dawn's eyes. "Aceworth must think they have a motive for a suicide. So I have to ask some personal questions, starting with your marriage during, let's say, the last six months. Any problems there?"

"James, there's no reason I know of why Abel would have even *considered* suicide. As far as I knew, he was very happy with our marriage and enjoyed working for Mr. Lynch."

"You two weren't buried in debt?"

Dawn emphatically shook her head. "When Abel was alive and working, we were doing well enough to easily pay our bills."

"Dawn, I apologize, but the questions I'm now going to ask you are necessary."

She looked back and nodded.

"Okay. First of all, are you sure your husband didn't develop a gambling habit here in Las Vegas, or that he didn't get into drugs perhaps? Those things can happen to anyone."

"No way, James. Not Abel."

"Again, I'm sorry to ask again about your marriage, but was there possibly another man, or woman?"

"Oh, no. I mean, for real, no. Based on everything I knew, I thought we were faithful right to the end. Abel's death was a total shock."

After having nodded in reaction to each of Dawn's responses, as if all he was doing was ruling out things he didn't suspect anyway, James rubbed eyes, then turned and stared out his window.

Thirty seconds passed. He turned back toward Dawn and attempted a smile. "Based on everything you say, Dawn, their suicide bullshit—excuse me, their suicide *argument*—seems like a concoction, maybe even a bluff. But I frankly don't get why a substantial insurance company would even try that, let alone do it so arrogantly."

"I have no clue, James."

"Dawn, in spite of this mystery, I can give you some encouragement. If you were as credible on the witness stand as you have been with me, then they have a huge problem. In other words, if Mr. Santoro's wife honestly did not think it could have been a suicide, then how are they going to overcome that? And there's no suicide note, at least as far as I've been told."

"You won't get any argument from me, James."

"And you really do need that money now, to get by, just like your husband intended when he purchased their policy."

She met his eyes and nodded, as if a battle bond was being forged.

"Okay, so here's what's next. I'll draft and file the complaint. Then, I'll ask for an early case conference and we'll stipulate to any immediate discovery they want as long as we can get to trial quickly."

She nodded again. Although his legal jargon was over her head, he seemed to be confident enough.

"Can you meet me here again Saturday before I file this thing, say 10:00 a.m.? I can focus more on your case on the weekend."

Again with the off hours...but at least he's trying.

"I'll be here," she said with a smile.

TWENTY-TWO

"Dawn, how are things going now for you?" Lynch asked at her work desk, after returning from an out-of-town business trip.

"Okay, sir, thank you. Did you have a good trip?"

"Yeah, but always good to get back...So, did that loan help?"

"For sure, sir. That and being able to work for you again. But I'm fighting the insurance company. I'm actually meeting with my attorney this weekend."

"Really?" Lynch snickered. "I thought those of us in real estate were the only ones who worked weekends. I guess that's good for you then, that he's going all out."

"Well, yes and no, sir. It seemed like, right after he got assigned to me, they put him on some big case that's taking up most of his time."

"I suppose that can happen..."

"But I like him enough so far, Mr. Lynch, so don't think I'm complaining."

"I see...good. Keep me posted on it, Dawn. I care about your welfare."

*****

On Friday afternoon, a call from Stephanie came in for Dawn. "Sorry to bother you at work, Mrs. Santoro, but Mr. Claverson cannot meet with you tomorrow after all. He wanted me to tell you that he has to prepare for more depositions starting Monday morning. But he also said that he'll still be filing the complaint on your case soon, and that you'll receive a copy."

"Okay...He can do all that without us meeting again?

"That's what James said," replied Stephanie, "and he wanted me to assure you that he'll still try to move the case along as quickly as possible."

Although disappointed, Dawn didn't dare risk her good relations with this woman. "Thanks, Stephanie. I trust James and know he's busy. I guess it's all just so new and confusing for me."

"Well, I've got some time right now, Mrs. Santoro. Maybe I can help if you have any specific questions..."

"Oh," exclaimed Dawn, "well, I guess the main question I have is whether there will be another time soon when they talk about a settlement? I was hoping James might be able to convince them to go a whole lot higher and get this over with."

"Of course. There'll be many chances to talk settlement. There's the case conference, which will be coming up soon, and then anytime later right up to the day of trial—even 'on the courthouse steps' as the saying goes."

"Uh, do you think we have a chance for a good settlement at the...case conferring, or whatever it's called?"

"Oh, sorry, Mrs. Santoro, but that's not for me to say. But I'm sure James can go over that the next time he talks to you. It's actually called a 'case conference' and it's probably several weeks away."

I guess that's supposed to be soon for lawyers.

*****

On her way to Nanny G's home after work to pick up Cora, she stopped at her bank to make a withdrawal. Once back in her car, she sat and stared at her account balance on the tiny receipt.

Her mind uncontrollably projected ahead. Weeks. Months.

Things are either happening too fast or too slow.
Should I have asked for an even bigger loan?

TWENTY-THREE

Two and a half weeks later, in the middle of her workday, James Claverson unexpectedly called.

"Dawn, are you still managing all right?"

"As best I can, James, but hearing again from you helps."

"Good. I need to meet with you. Any chance you can make it in this afternoon? Otherwise, it might be awhile."

"I think so. I'll call you back if it's a no."

*****

From the looks of his office, with files and papers spread all over his desk, and even more stacked on one of his chairs, there was no doubt he was inundated. He also looked exhausted, but he still managed to stand up quickly to greet Dawn when she was shown in by Stephanie.

James pointed to the one empty chair. "Thanks for coming in on such short notice, Dawn. You're just going to have to ignore this mess."

"I'm sure it's not a mess to you."

"Dawn, I asked you to come in because I had the initial case conference with Aceworth's attorney this morning. The good news is that they are very conscious of not delaying things due to our claim for bad faith. So I was able to get the conference completed even before their deadline to file an answer, which is highly unusual. They'll also agree to a joint request for an expedited trial date, if it does go all the way."

"Okay, I guess that's good."

"But there was some not-so-good news," said James, as his expression turned somber.

"Uh oh..."

James looked intently at Dawn, seeming to force aside his fatigue. "Their lawyer absolutely insists that he can prove your husband's death resulted from a suicide."

She looked back then shook her head in disgust. "James, this is getting crazier all the time...is he sure he's got the right person?"

"Unfortunately, he'd say 'yes'. For starters," said James, handing her a set of papers. "For starters, here's the police report on the accident. As you'll see where I've clipped it, there's a statement from the truck driver. Look at the sentence starting on line eighteen."

Dawn found the line and read: "The jogger who was injured that day intentionally ran in front of my truck just like he was trying to get hit."

She looked up. "But that's just his version, isn't it? He didn't know what was going on in Abel's mind."

"Right," said James with a nod. "But Aceworth's lawyer said that the truck driver will be a solid witness. And, they have an additional reason to take that position—at least for now."

"What?"

"A motive, according to them."

"That can't be?"

"Dawn, I'm sorry, but they have medical records from before the accident. And they're saying that Abel was dying anyway, from an inoperable, advanced stage brain tumor."

Dawn's mouth gaped. Tears formed, then fell.

James handed her a tissue. "Nobody ever mentioned that he had a tumor?"

She shook her head.

"Maybe at the hospital, the day of the accident?"

"It was such a god-awful day, James, but I don't remember hearing that."

"Maybe, if they spotted it while trying to save him, they might have figured you already knew—to the extent they would have even had time to bring it up."

"I just know that I was going out of my mind from the moment I heard that Abel got hit."

"In any event, they say they can prove that your husband sure knew about it."

She looked up at the ceiling as tears continued to flow. She took a deep breath, trying not to sob. "The investigator for the insurance company asked me about Abel getting headaches and I think I told him that he did sometimes. But, typical of Abel, he really didn't talk much about it."

"Nothing else?"

"I swear, James, if Abel really did have a brain tumor, he kept it from me up to that point—up to his last day."

"I believe you," said James. "But, let's back up to something you previously hit on. For them to actually win the case, they have to prove that Abel intended to commit suicide. It's not enough to just speculate based on a disease or on what that truck driver says."

She wearily nodded.

But that doesn't seem to bother them.

"I'll even go you one further," said James enthusiastically, as if trying to uplift them both. "As far as the policy's face amount—the two-fifty—I'm not so sure your claim would fail even if they could convince a jury that your husband absolutely intended to get hit. If he was terminal anyway, like their lawyer is now saying, they may be making a quantum leap. I'm going to research that as soon as I can. Do you follow me?"

"I think so. You're saying that he would have just been speeding up the insurance payout because it was going to come anyway?"

"Exactly...In fact, you just said it in a way that I didn't think of," said James. "Maybe all Aceworth should get, at most, is the right to sit on the policy face amount until some date that the jury figures your husband would have died naturally. That would still be two hundred and fifty thousand, which I suspect you would gladly take."

"For sure."

"I think they might be overlooking this whole argument."

Or intentionally ignoring it?

But James unexpectedly looked cautious again, shaking his head as if to restrain the optimism. "Dawn, my talk is cheap until I do the legal research. And, for all I know, they may have already done it."

"And you have the time for that?"

"I'll make time, Dawn. It's too important."

"Thank you *so much*, James."

He nodded, but held up his hand. "Switching gears again, Aceworth's lawyer wants to depose you. And, as part of our agreement to expedite everything, we tentatively scheduled it for Thursday of next week, assuming you are available..."

"Depose me?"

"Yes, take your deposition. Dawn, I know I'm moving fast, but can you be here by one? We scheduled it for two and that'll give us time to prepare and walk over to their office."

She nodded uneasily. "As long as you explain enough to me so I can avoid making stupid mistakes."

"Of course, that's part of my job. And I'll even start right now, by telling you about one angle I expect them to try."

"Angle?"

"Dawn, try not to let it bother you, but I think they're going to grill you on whether you and Abel, quote, 'conspired to defraud them,' unquote. Their words, not mine."

"That's total BS, James," she said angrily, while rising from her seat as if there were someone she could physically confront. "God, they're full of it."

"It's okay, Dawn," he replied. "Get it out now, if it helps you, but keep your cool later. And, as long as you've got an idea what's coming, their lawyer can't trip you up as easily."

She stared back, disturbed that she even had to compete in such an arena. But knowing what was at stake, she resigned herself to the challenge. "I'll try my best."

"Good. I think you took that pretty well under the circumstances."

"James, would you mind explaining more to me about depositions? I'm clueless."

"Sure. Most people never even need to know."

She nodded.

"It's like testifying in court. You'll be put under oath, and every word will be taken down so it can be used later. But we'll be in Ken Tilden's office...I'm guessing for about three hours, including breaks."

"I hope that's all."

"He can ask you about a wide range of things, including what you knew about Abel committing suicide, like I already told you."

"And I'll just say that's a lie..."

"Uh, that's a touch overboard," said James. "You don't have to prove anyone is lying. Just saying that you don't believe it is enough."

"Obviously, I don't. Anything else?"

"Yeah, their lawyer will seem completely insensitive with some of his questions...even heartless. But, it's just the way attorneys can be. So try to be tough and hang in there. You have nothing to hide," added James with a reassuring smile.

She tried to smile back, while searching her memory for anything she could be accused of trying to hide.

"And, oh yes," added James, "this goes against human nature, but you have to put it completely out of your mind that you could ever convince Aceworth's attorney of anything important."

"Okay..."

"He might even secretly believe you, but he could still pretend that he thinks you're lying to him."

"I understand, James."

"Just answer his questions, but don't think about him as a person."

"I will try my best, James."

"Good. When we meet next Thursday, I'll go over more. Meanwhile," James smiled again, "I'm an attorney who does believe you."

"Thank you James. Sorry to be so difficult; it's just that..."

"Don't apologize, Dawn. This is all normal stuff to go over with anyone who hasn't had the fun of being deposed before."

"Some fun."

James sat all of the way back, as if satisfied that the most intense part of their meeting was complete. But he still showed a look of concern. "We need to switch topics one more time today."

She braced herself.

"Unfortunately, their settlement offer is now down to forty-five thousand. I didn't want to tell you that right away because I had to cover the other things."

"Well that's just great. And to think that I was looking forward to you having settlement talks with them."

"I know, Dawn. They're being arrogant...at least so far."

She shook her head wearily. "First I lose Abel, and now all this. I don't know, James. If they're that confident and determined, maybe I should just make it easy on everyone..."

"No, Dawn..."

She looked down and continued to shake her head.

"Dawn," James said more sternly than she'd ever heard him speak. "I need you to be strong for me so I can do my best work for you."

Surprised by his intensity, she looked up and into his eyes.

"I know you can do that," he said.

"I will, James. I'll be as helpful as I can for you. You're my lifeline."

"Okay, I put you through enough for today."

TWENTY-FOUR

Still reeling from her meeting with James as she climbed into her car, and in no mood to go back to the office for the last part of the day, she needed a destination.

As she started to drive toward Nanny G's, she realized that she needed a break before picking up Cora. And if relaxing was going to be possible at all, she knew one person who might be able to make it happen—the one friend who would listen to anything and everything.

She drove to the nearest convenience store to buy a small carton of milk for her churning stomach and made the call.

"It's Dawn, Jewels. Any chance you could join me for an early dinner, mainly to talk...like me talking and you listening?"

"Sounds okay to me, Dawnie...but could it be a little later, like six? I'm with a client."

"Sure. Any particular place you'd like?"

"Hey, how about that Mexican place: Santana's? It's friendly and reasonable—not that we don't deserve gourmet."

Though Dawn was ready to drive away from the convenience store, she again pondered where to go with the dead time she still had. There was no way she was going to show up early at Santana's as a single woman. She had no interest in drinking at their bar, and the last thing she wanted was to have to deal with any guys trying to pick her up.

"Someplace I can be alone, like maybe a library...or better yet, a church...Might even try saying a prayer."

Despite over a decade since she disassociated from organized religion, she recalled going to a wedding with Abel at a quaint little church in the downtown area.

She found her way there and eased into a shady spot in the church parking lot, which was completely empty on this weekday afternoon.

As she approached the main entry, however, she saw the door closed and a notice encased in weather-worn plastic. Through the dust and smudges, she read the message:

GREETINGS FAITHFUL: DUE TO THE ONGOING RISK OF VANDALISM, THIS CHURCH IS ONLY OPEN FOR SCHEDULED SERVICES AND BY PRIOR ARRANGEMENT. PLEASE CONSULT THE SCHEDULE IN THE WINDOW TO THE LEFT. GOD BLESS YOU.

She stared at the notice, partly in disbelief, but also secretly hoping that someone might appear out of nowhere and make an exception for her on the spot.

But nothing happened. She really was locked out.

The more she thought about it, the more she felt angry as well as humiliated. "How dare I think that I could just show up to pray on a weekday?"

With still over an hour left to kill, she couldn't think of anything better than just sitting in her shaded car. Staying nearby, she figured, would also remind God that she really did want to go inside.

She sat back and started to roam the FM radio dial for whatever sounds she could tolerate to pass the time. But, after more minutes lapsed, she became increasingly self-conscious. Whoever had locked up the church, and refused to come make an exception for her, could also be watching out for suspicious-looking people hanging around.

What would I tell them? I'm just sitting here praying in my car?

As she turned on her ignition, she felt a final urge to protest against being denied access on the one occasion in the last ten years when she came to God seeking help. She rolled down her car window just before exiting to the street and yelled out: "You'd probably just do what you want anyway, God, like with Abel."

Driving away, she had no desire to search for another church that might actually be open. She navigated instead toward the freeway for a short drive to the Practica Mall.

*****

Walking into the enclosed environment from her parking spot—which was much closer than she could have parked on a weekend—she tried to recall the last time she had come to any mall just to hang out. It had to have been as a teen.

God, if you're still listening to me, at least don't let me spend any money here.

101

Once inside, she started strolling and looking, not so much at the store displays but at the people who seemed to be real shoppers. Though she was close to them physically, she thought about how far away from them she was financially. They not only had money to spend but probably didn't carry any comparable burdens to cramp their shopping pleasure.

As she continued to meander, her mind unintentionally reverted back to the truck driver's statement. She loathed his brash words about Abel, who was not alive to defend himself. It was all she could do to fight back tears in this public setting.

But, just as unexpectedly, the tears turned into a half-smile. Even while obsessed by the threat of a horrid injustice, her body had been hypnotically drawn to the mall's cookie shop. And, with only two shoppers ahead of her, she was close enough to be staring at the double chocolate-chips.

She apologized to the lady behind her and stepped aside.

Even half of one would ruin what little appetite I still have.

TWENTY-FIVE

Sitting together in Santana's, Julie listened to all of it, giving unblinking attention other than to take occasional sips of a strawberry margarita.

Dawn finally laid it all out, shaking her head in disgust at her predicament.

Julie, after waiting a moment, as if to ensure Dawn had finished, gave a nervous smile as she begun to speak. "I can't really say that I know what you're going through, because I've never had a family to complicate my life, not that I didn't want my baby because you know I did..."

"Of course I know that, Jewels."

"So...is it all right if I just focus on Dawn Santoro, the individual?"

"Sure. I'm open."

"Okay then. At this moment, I think you're in the middle of some dark and gloomy trees, with no view of the forest..."

"Okay..."

"...But you don't have to panic because you're not next to any cliff-edge. You've got some income, some bucks in the bank still, and it sounds like your lawyer is really trying for you. So, why don't you just let the professional do the worrying?"

"If only, Jewels. With Abel, I never had to worry about just being able to survive. But, right now, I feel so exposed, even with a lawyer."

"For sure, it rocks to be spoiled by a good man. Who wouldn't miss that?"

103

"And that's not all, Jewels. This insurance company is attacking Abel's memory and my child's future. I think that's downright cruel..."

"And I can see how deeply that hurts you, especially with all the stress you've already been under. But you're taking everything these a-holes are doing way too personally. You have to go easier on yourself..."

"Maybe so, but I'm not sure I'm even capable..."

"Trust me, Dawnie, you have no choice but to ease up on yourself because the law suit could drag on and on."

"For all I know..."

"Besides, the ultimate outcome— whenever it does get decided—is not really in your control."

Dawn stared back, then reluctantly nodded.

"So try to relax and also have some fun to offset the agony."

"If you're suggesting a vacation, then sure. All I need is the money to pay for it and the time off work."

"Hey, time out, Dawnie. How about no more talking about money tonight because it'll just depress you."

"Okay, Jewels," said Dawn with a smirk. "But, given how important the M-word is to me right now, what else *can* we talk about?"

"Well...for starters, how about getting back in touch with being a woman?"

Dawn laughed. "Why am I not surprised you'd go there, Jewels?"

"Seriously, Dawnie, we need more in our life than worry and work. I know you've got the mother side too, but, no matter how many sides you have, you're still a woman on one of them, and an attractive one at that."

"I love this, Jewels," said Dawn with a shake of her head. "You've flat-out detoured me, just as I hoped. But, seriously, I don't see myself dating again for who knows how long...It would seem so strange and I wouldn't be ready yet for it to go anywhere."

"Who said anything about dating," Julie crowed. "I'm just talking about getting a little vitamin F."

"Jewels!" exclaimed Dawn as she quickly looked around and covered her blushing face. "Now you've really done it."

TWENTY-SIX

Despite welcome distraction that Julie had provided, her overall stress was reignited the next morning when she was unexpectedly summoned into Lynch's office.

She meekly stepped in.

He stared at her for a long moment, with an indiscernible look in his eyes. "Dawn, you like shopping malls, don't you?"

Holy...Is this about yesterday: not coming right back to the office?

But softening her inner panic was her perception that Lynch's tone of voice seemed cordial, almost affectionate.

"Uh, yes, sir. Who doesn't?"

"Good," Lynch replied calmly. "I have a professional interest in the future of one particular shopping mall project. I'm saying 'project' because it's not even in the construction phase yet."

Whew.

"Up to now," he continued, "I may have been a little remiss in not including you in some of the more interesting parts of my business. So I've decided to do something about that."

"You're building a mall, sir?"

"Oh no," he chuckled, obviously flattered that she would even consider that a possibility. "This involves the pre-construction planning, not the actual construction."

"Oh."

"Here," he said, handing her a folder. "This has the basics of the proposed mall site, with some preview renderings of the actual structure that you might enjoy looking at if you want."

She cautiously extended her hand to receive the folder.

"The project is going to occur in stages at a fairly slow pace," he said. "So take your time and familiarize yourself. Even drive out there and look around when your schedule permits."

"I sure will, Mr. Lynch."

"Soon, there will be meetings of the county commission on variances and use permits for the project, and I might take you to one of them. They're fun to watch," he said smugly. "We'll have an opportunity to work together closely on this."

She smiled and nodded, suppressing her urge to ask what in the heck she might be expected to do.

He has to know better than to rely on me for anything important.

"I'll definitely look forward to that, sir."

Meanwhile, my paychecks keep coming.

TWENTY-SEVEN

Days later, while reading a story to Cora, she realized that her dramatic delivery was not all there, but also felt that there was little she could do about it. Tomorrow was Thursday, the day of her deposition.

I can't even relax with my child, and Jewels thinks I could handle casual sex?

Despite her mediocre performance, Cora seemed happy enough just to have Mommy's company, right up to the time a telephone call came in from James.

"Dawn, sorry to bother you, but there's something that can't wait."

"What, James?"

"I need you to listen and not overreact, if at all possible."

"Not overreact? Hang on just a minute..."

Dawn put the television on for Cora, promising to be back to the story soon.

"I'm back, James. Could you start over?"

"What I'm saying, Dawn, is that I can't be at your deposition tomorrow. But I'm also telling you not to worry because another lawyer from my office will cover it. His name is Harold Dibbs."

Dawn was stunned. "Why James...if I'm allowed to ask?"

"It just can't be helped."

"But James, what about just rescheduling? I wouldn't mind a week's delay, or even two. Honest."

108

"Stay calm, Dawn, and please listen carefully. I profusely apologize, but I can't even be your attorney on this case anymore. You need to just go to your deposition and tell the truth. You convinced me that you have nothing to hide, and that's what I told Harold."

"But James, this makes no sense! You started this case and we worked together on it. I relied on you to be my lawyer."

"I understand how you feel, Dawn, but you just have find it within yourself to accept this change and go forward."

"But you convinced me that you wanted to help me fight them—up until now at least. Does this really mean that I should just take whatever they offer? I need to know the truth, James."

"No, not at all, Dawn. I briefed Harold on everything and he'll meet with you before your deposition just like I was going to. Don't give the other side any excuse to delay."

As if it would be all my fault!

"I'll keep in touch and we'll talk again, I promise. I'm not leaving the city or anything like that. Meanwhile, you'll do fine at your deposition with Harold there."

TWENTY-EIGHT

While being escorted into the office of Harold Dibbs, Dawn wondered whether James was in his own office at the moment, but she wasn't going to ask. She felt self-conscious enough about being handed over to Harold.

As she took her seat, she felt out of place, recalling a similar feeling she once had in middle school when she accidentally walked into the wrong classroom and drew dozens of stares before realizing her mistake.

Nevertheless, Harold, a short and pudgy young man with a beardless face that made him look even younger than James, was all business. "Dawn, we have about twenty minutes before we need to leave for Smith & Tilden. I understand that James already prepared you to some extent…do you have any specific questions right now?"

Feeling rushed, as well as disoriented, she couldn't think of anything to ask, let alone try to guess what James had not covered.

"Uh, nothing right now, sir."

"Okay, then," he replied as he pulled out a sheet of paper and held it in front of him. "I'm now going to go over a few specific things before we head over there."

"Okay, sir."

He made no attempt to hide that he was simply reading from the sheet. "Just answer the specific question they ask you and then stop. You don't get points for saying more, and the more you talk, the more likely you will slip up or give him ideas for more questions."

Dawn offered a guarded smile, now fearing more than ever that her case might heavily depend on her performance this afternoon under less than ideal circumstances, and also that James might have sugar-coated what she was up against.

"Next, don't expect me to say very much. But," Harold read on while holding up his index finger, "if I do start talking, you have to listen to me because I might tip you off that the question is unfair, or maybe even a trap. Got that, Mrs. Santoro?"

She gave a quick nod, sensing he was quickening the pace as their departure drew near.

Whoa, my heart's already racing.

"Good," said Harold, "but also don't assume that a particular question is safe just because I might not say anything. You need to listen to the wording and use your common sense."

He then paused to look at her with a quizzical expression as if she were some troublesome mechanical device that he had just finished tinkering with.

Use my common sense on questions from a lawyer?
"Okay..."

"Most important of all, Dawn," said Harold, raising his voice for emphasis, "don't forget that the lawyer asking you questions is absolutely, positively, not your friend, no matter how he tries to come off. He's trying to see that you get as little recovery as possible, and he couldn't care less how badly you need the money."

Oh my God.

111

Her stomach instantly churned, to go with her frayed nerves and racing heart.

One of those times…Be brave.

He put the paper back into a folder, peeked at his watch, and forced a smile as if that could somehow encourage her. "One final thing, Dawn. Don't be concerned if you see me working on something, because it won't pertain to your case. I have a tight deadline in another matter, but I'm quite capable of doing two things at once."

Oh really? Did James know that?

She said nothing. The last thing she wanted at this late moment was to cause friction with her lawyer, especially when it would be pointless.

TWENTY-NINE

With her deposition about to start, in a modest conference room, complete with drab walls and functional furniture, she already felt intimidated by Aceworth's attorney, Ken Tilden, who looked like he could have been a football player and had greeted Dawn and Harold with a condescending smile, all-the-while brimming with self-confidence that seemed all too real.

Once everyone sat down, however, the man sitting next to Tilden began to bother her even more without speaking a word. Tilden had introduced him as a defense consultant and potential expert witness, and his name somehow seemed vaguely familiar. But he seemed to be staring at her, apparently with an attitude about something, which only added to her redlining stress.

Even when Tilden started asking "preliminary" questions about her background, she could tell by quick glances that the other man's staring wasn't going to stop. She looked toward Harold to see if he might have noticed, but he was already absorbed in whatever else he was working on.

Minutes later, during her response to Tilden's first question specifically about Abel, Dawn detected that the man had gone beyond staring to a cruel, and almost sadistic-looking, glare.

"Excuse me," she finally said to Tilden, upon finishing one of her answers. "Could I talk to my attorney in private? It shouldn't take long."

"Certainly, Mrs. Santoro," said Tilden. "It looked to me like you finished your answer, right?"

Dawn nodded meekly, then turned toward her own lawyer. But seeing that he was oblivious, she implored through her teeth, "Harold...please...can we step outside a minute to talk?"

Visibly surprised, he quickly shuffled his papers together and stood up.

Tilden stayed seated as he watched. "Let the record reflect that there will be a short break at the request of the witness."

Once in the hallway, Dawn tried to calm herself while making sure that she had Harold's full attention. "Harold, that man in there is constantly glaring at me. I don't think I can stand it anymore."

His eyes widened, as if having been abruptly awakened. "I'm sorry, Mrs. Santoro. Do you mean the one asking you the questions?"

Dawn couldn't believe she had to spell it out further. "No, Harold, the other man. I don't remember his name, but he's supposed to be an expert."

"Okay, him...You say he's glaring at you. Let's go right back in and I'll bring it up."

"Wait, Harold. I don't really want them to know that I..."

But Harold was already on his way back into the conference room.

Dawn followed just in time to hear Harold say that he "wanted to go back on the record."

Tilden nodded to the court reporter.

"Ok," announced Harold, "we're all back in the room again after a very short break. My problem is that this gentleman seated next to defense counsel, who was described as an expert, is constantly glaring at my client, whether he realizes it or not."

"Counsel," Tilden immediately replied, "are you sure about that? Might it be that your client is just nervous or something?

Dawn looked down, wishing she could disappear.

"Yes, we're sure. And, with all due respect," continued Harold, "what's his purpose here today? What kind of expertise are we talking about?"

Before Tilden could respond, the man glared at Harold this time. "I'm an expert all right, about the best damn rig driver in town. Never..."

"Hold on a minute, Mr. Penner," Tilden said, with his hand raised. "Let me handle this..."

Penner, his face turning red, turned back toward Dawn. "I never had a problem before. I've even won safety awards. But that husband of yours ran right in front of me from out of nowhere..."

"Okay, Mr. Penner," Tilden interrupted more forcefully. "That's enough. You're talking on the record and it's not your deposition. As attorney of record for Aceworth, I don't want any more of that, sir."

"I still might have missed him," Penner rattled on defiantly, "if he hadn't been so determined to get himself killed. But he didn't give a damn about me now, did he? If

115

I'd been fully loaded, I might have rolled it and got killed myself trying to avoid him."

When Penner finally paused to take a breath, Dawn noticed Tilden nodding toward Harold, as if acknowledging the extent of the problem. Tilden then turned back toward Penner. "All right, everyone, we're going off record now."

After Tilden eyed the court reporter to verify that her hands had stopped, he looked directly at Dawn. "I apologize, Mrs. Santoro. This honestly wasn't supposed to be part of your deposition."

Darren Penner, however, didn't seem to care whether he was on or off the record. "Why would you apologize to her? She wants to make money out of what her husband did."

"Okay, you've said enough for now, Mr. Penner. We understand that you're unhappy. But you might be deposed yourself in this case, or testify at trial if it goes that far. So, for now, I'm going to have to ask you to kindly exit this room and wait in the reception area until we take the next break here. I'll confer with you later."

Penner remained seated, but, for the first time, seemed to be defensive. "Mr. Tilden, I promise not to say another word if..."

"Sorry, Rob, it's already gone beyond that," said Tilden, who then stood up and opened the door.

Penner shook his head, got up and walked out.

When the door was closed, Harold sighed. "After that moment of tension, Ken, let's take another short break if you don't mind. My client was justifiably rattled as a result

116

of having to endure such conduct when we're supposed to be here for a deposition."

"As you wish," said Tilden, who then stood up and politely smiled toward everyone. "As a matter of fact, I'll make use of the time and excuse myself for a couple minutes."

When Tilden was out of the room, and only the court reporter left, Harold leaned toward Dawn and whispered, "Mrs. Santoro, I have no doubt that he was bothering you, but now you should be able to relax and just answer the questions."

As if.

She gave Harold a noncommittal look, then turned her head toward the window, not for the view—because there was none—but so that she could simply stare and try to process what Penner had just been railing about. He was out of the room for now, but it would only be a matter of time before he might have his full say in front of a judge or jury.

THIRTY

Upon his return, Ken Tilden first looked around the room, as if to confirm that order had been restored, while also showing a look of disapproval, as if Penner's outbursts had been an unpleasant surprise for him as well.

In Dawn's eyes, this conduct by Tilden led her to suspect that Penner's performance had actually been scripted. Although she didn't know if such antics were normal at depositions, she had taken enough drama classes to know bad acting when she saw it.

"Okay," Tilden announced, "We can now resume. If I need to consult with Mr. Penner, I'll take another short break and do so in my office."

Again, Dawn wasn't buying it. Why would Tilden need to consult with Penner about questioning *her*?

She peeked at Harold, but he was already absorbed in other work. She was on the verge of concluding that he had done zero preparation for her deposition and that the earlier warnings he read to her were all written by James.

"We're back on the record," Tilden announced. "Now, Mrs. Santoro, did you and your husband discuss which means of suicide he would utilize in order to try to collect on the insurance policy?"

"We never discussed that."

"So he decided what way he was going to commit suicide all by himself?"

"Sir, I had no advance knowledge about his decision. No wait, what I meant is..." She looked toward Harold, but he was zoned out again.

"Mrs. Santoro," Tilden persisted, "you need to finish answering my questions, please, instead of looking to your attorney for help."

As if.

"Did you know when your husband went out running that morning that it was the day he chose to run in front of a truck?"

"No sir, but the way you're wording everything..."

"He was depressed wasn't he, Mrs. Santoro, before he ran out in front of the truck?"

Feeling under attack even more than when Penner was in the room, she thought briefly of asking for another meeting with Harold. But, upon glancing over at him again, she sensed that would be futile.

Probably thinks he's already done more than enough.

She vowed to just answer each question as carefully as she could.

"You're delaying, Mrs. Santoro. Please answer my question: wasn't your husband depressed before he ran out in front of the truck?"

"All I can say is that the last time I saw my husband alive, he seemed to be his normal self."

"If the truck driver, Mr. Penner, who was here in this room earlier, were to testify under oath that your husband had a clear view of the oncoming truck, even though it was

119

early in the morning, would you have any reason to dispute that?"

"I wasn't there, obviously, but I don't believe that Abel ran out in front of the truck on purpose."

"But you have no *personal* knowledge to dispute Mr. Penner on that..."

"I guess not, but I still don't believe it."

"Isn't it true that your husband would not have been the type of person who could tolerate being incapacitated and in pain?"

"He was never incapacitated, to my knowledge. But, as far as pain goes, how much pain?"

"So, you're saying that your husband was not able to tolerate significant pain?"

"I did not say that...Can I ask you a question, sir?"

"No, you may not, Mrs. Santoro," Tilden snapped back.

But, sensing that she had ruffled him—even a little—her instinct was to stay with it. "Mr. Tilden, how could anyone possibly know what was going on in my husband's mind?"

"Mrs. Santoro," Tilden bellowed, "this is your deposition. As I'm sure your attorney explained to you. I ask the questions, not you. That's the court's procedure under the rules that govern this case that you filed against my client."

But, knowing full well that his questions were twisted, she couldn't stop. "I'm sure there are rules, sir," said Dawn, raising her voice as well, "but there must also be rules against asking confusing questions that you know I can't answer. Besides, I'm wondering why Mr. Penner was operating his big truck so early in the morning in a residential area."

Tilden's mouth opened and his eyes widened.

Harold somehow came to life, grabbing a legal pad and making notes.

"Mrs. Santoro!" Tilden growled, "I've been patient with you, but the legal system absolutely requires you to cooperate and answer my questions. So, I'm asking you and your attorney right now on the record: Are you going to stop quibbling with me and answer my questions or do we have to contact the discovery commissioner and seek sanctions?"

She looked over to Harold.

With a look of dread, he nodded toward her, confirming that she had no choice. He then turned toward Tilden. "Ken, keep in mind that it's her first time being deposed and she's been under a lot of stress. I'm sure she'll try to do better."

What about him!

"Okay, then," said Tilden, not waiting for any confirmation from her. "With my clear warning given, I'll expect nothing but answers, unless you did not hear the question or need it rephrased. And, above all, no arguing or asking me questions."

So, as one-sided as possible.

"I'll try, sir."

"Now, Mrs. Santoro, your husband had just taken up jogging before he died, hadn't he?"

"Uh, for all I know, he may have done it earlier in his life. But the answer is 'yes' for the time I knew him."

"I'm just asking what you know personally, Mrs. Santoro."

And whatever else you can trick me into saying.

"Did you support your husband's decision to commit suicide by jogging right into an oncoming truck?"

Back at it again...

She turned toward Harold and tapped his arm.

As Harold looked up, she grimaced toward him.

He scrambled. "Uh, excuse me, Miss court reporter, but what was that last question again, please?"

The woman fingered through her notes. "Did you support your husband's decision to commit suicide by jogging right into an oncoming truck?"

Harold smiled smugly, as if he were preventing a petty crime. "I'm sorry, counsel, but I object to the form of that particular question. It sounds like the proverbial 'when did you stop beating your wife?'"

Only that question?

"Counsel," Tilden retorted, "she's the plaintiff in this case, so this is the equivalent of cross-examination. Therefore, I don't see any problem with my question."

"Well," Harold sheepishly replied, looking at Dawn as if annoyed that she got him into this clash, "my objection is of record."

Tilden turned back toward Dawn, showing no further concern about Harold. "Did you discuss with Abel Santoro anything about his decision to commit suicide?"

122

How many ways can he ask this?

She looked back again at Harold, only to see that he had escaped back into his other work.

Tilden grinned.

"No," she replied wearily, "we absolutely never ever discussed that."

Tilden's following parade of questions gradually became a blur to her. She heard her own voice offering answers, but it was as if she were responding from another dimension.

"What was your husband like in his final days?"

"I didn't know they would be his final days."

"Well, you know now and you were living with him, so you must answer, Mrs. Santoro."

"I never noticed anything different."

"Did he have much pain the day before, or even the week before, he died?"

"Not as far as...he didn't say that he was in much pain."

"What was your marriage like during his final weeks?"

"'What was our marriage like?'...I thought it was very good."

"What did you know about his medical condition and when did you learn it?"

"Only whatever I've been told after I made a claim on the life insurance."

"Now that you do know that your husband was terminal, with an inoperable brain tumor, doesn't that make you realize that he had a motive to commit suicide?"

"Sir...I honestly don't understand what you're asking me."

"Well, Mrs. Santoro, with all that you know now about your husband's condition, and how he died just after he started jogging, doesn't that at least make you suspicious as to what happened on that final day?"

"Suspicious? No, I'm not."

Tilden relentlessly continued, as if she was all his to be abused. In her semi-detached state, she started wondering what would happen if Tilden, instead of just forcing her to answer his questions, simply rose from his seat, came around the table with the same arrogance, and started undressing her. Would Harold even notice?

Meanwhile, she worried about how long she would be able to even endure the ordeal, let alone keep some presence of mind.

"Mrs. Santoro, I'm still waiting for an answer to the question I just asked you."

"Uh, I guess I lost concentration, sir. Can you ask it again?"

He nodded toward the court reporter, then sneered while the court reporter looked for the question's starting point.

The court reporter read: "What kinds of things do you remember discussing with your husband about his terminal condition during the weeks prior to his death?"

"I didn't know about his condition. I thought I already said that, sir."

"So, you're saying you didn't know any details about your husband's terminal condition right up to his death?"

"No sir," Dawn barely muttered, furious as to how many times and ways Tilden could re-ask the questions. "I mean, yes sir, I did not know that he had a terminal disease."

As his questions droned on, she sensed that her brain was slowly becoming mush and that she might not even be able to detect when she crossed over that line. And, for an unknown amount of time that followed, uncertainty and worry gnawed at her after each answer she gave. But, ready or not, the next question came at her.

At about the point when Dawn felt like the questions would *never* finish, Tilden surprisingly paused and took a long look at her. "I think I've covered it," he smugly announced. "But I'm going to check my notes one more time while you relax a couple minutes."

"Relax"?

Despite her weariness, Dawn noticed that the intervening silence itself somehow caught Harold's attention, enough to make him raise his head and look around.

Tilden closed his folder and again confronted her. "Just one more question, Mrs. Santoro: When all is said and done, you're still asking everyone to believe that you had no advance knowledge whatsoever of your husband's intent to commit suicide, and also that you never discussed that with him?"

125

Dawn hesitated, unsure that this was a real question or some kind of lawyer's tricky gambit. She thought about looking to Harold, but he'd already had enough time to speak if that was going to happen. "Sir, I have no way of knowing what you or Aceworth Insurance or anyone else really believes, and you told me earlier that I could not ask you anything."

"Well, then, Mrs. Santoro," Tilden said gruffly, "I guess we'll have to take that as your answer."

"I'm afraid so, sir. You've worn me out today with all your questions."

"So you're done then, Ken?" said Harold, eagerly jumping in.

Tilden turned toward Harold, as if about to reprimand him for not really participating. "That completes all *my* questions for now, Harold. I don't suppose that you have any...it's almost five."

Harold made a show of putting all his papers back into his briefcase, while offering a mild sneer of his own in return. "We're all done then, Ken. I'm not going to depose my own client."

On hearing Harold's words, Dawn wanted to bolt straight out of the building.

Before anyone could even stand up, however, Tilden re-seized control. "Just one thing before you both depart. I have something to serve on the two of you."

He placed a legal document in front of each of them, with an additional receipt page for Harold.

While Harold signed, Tilden kept talking. "This, Mrs. Santoro, is called an 'Offer of Judgment'. Normally you get ten days to accept it, but I'm expressly giving you thirty days in the interests of getting this case settled."

"But, it's only for forty thousand," said Harold, upon handing over the signed receipt.

"Right," said Tilden. "Frankly, as result of today's deposition, I was tempted to not even serve it without talking to my client about lowering it further. Therefore, Mrs. Santoro, I respectfully recommend that you take it or you could actually face financial liability if you fail to do better at trial. You might even be ordered to pay my attorney's fees, as well as your own. I'm sure Harold will explain all that to you."

At this moment, as far as she was concerned, thirty days seemed like an eternity. Whether to accept or not was another day's problem.

Just get me the hell out of here.

THIRTY-ONE

As she walked out of Tilden's office, escorted by Harold, she realized that she'd endured over three hours.

She then caught herself starting to wonder what ever happened to Penner. But, even though mentally drained, she was able to push the thought out of her mind.

Who in the hell cares.

"Mrs. Santoro," said Harold, "you should just try to relax this evening. Later on, when you feel up to it, go ahead and give serious thought to their offer like he said."

"Harold, I'm sorry, but right now I can't think clearly about anything. I feel like I'm the one who just got run over by a truck."

Harold motioned her to a stop and looked her in the eyes, as if to confirm that he still had at least some remnants of her beleaguered attention. "I understand, but maybe you can keep this in mind: whatever their reasons, they seem determined to fight you all the way to the end."

She forced a nod, hoping he was done.

But he obviously wasn't, as he grasped her forearm. "To be completely honest," he confessed, "I'm not in a position to give you a final recommendation on whether to accept their offer."

"So what exactly are you saying, Harold?"

"I mainly do transactions, not litigation. And, beyond that, I've never researched the effect of a suicide on a life insurance claim when the insured was terminal. I mean *if* they could actually prove suicide."

128

Then I'm guessing James told you zilch about his research, if he ever started it.

"That's okay, Harold, I don't need any recommendations tonight. I've got thirty days he said."

"Dawn," Harold meekly continued, "you know that I was simply asked to take over because James Claverson couldn't continue."

"May I ask why James couldn't continue?"

"They just gave me your file and said it was now my case. They didn't explain why."

So you say.

"Feel free to get an opinion from another attorney before you decide whether to accept. But, if your case goes ahead, and if they want me to stay on it, I assure you that I'll do my best."

"That's good to know, Harold."

"Well then, good night for now, Dawn."

"Good night, Harold."

Finally free from the lawyers!

As she maneuvered her car into the still sluggish after-work traffic, she could not avoid thinking about how vulnerable her future was. Even keeping Harold as her attorney depended on whether "they" would allow it—the same "they" who took James away.

But, then again, all that wouldn't matter if she just took the forty...before the number got any lower. Then there would just be the rest of the world to deal with.

THIRTY-TWO

Driving from downtown toward Nanny G's, she couldn't help thinking ahead to a long hot shower at home, intending to scrub away at the day's harassment and humiliation. But, as had happened before, she knew she needed some down time before picking up Cora.

"Relax," said Harold...So, okay, just one drink.

She noticed the "Frontier Barbecue" sign up ahead, which would probably just have couples and families who were there for dinner—about as safe as it could get.

Once inside, she decided to call Julie.

"Jewels, can you talk?"

"For a little...Hey, I hear noises; are you at a party?"

"Not quite...Listen, I hate to bother you again, but..."

"But what...cough it up."

"I need your ears once more, Jewels. I had a deposition today in my life insurance case and it was absolutely horrible. I feel like a total piece of crap."

"Ouch! For sure, let's get together. But, unfortunately, I have a prior commitment tonight. Hey, I'm going to the lake tomorrow. Call in sick and ditch work. We'll have plenty of private time to and from, and you can go water-skiing with us. That'll chipper you up."

"Wow. Never expected an offer like that."

"Dawnie, it sounds to me like you really need tomorrow off. Besides, I think that Charlie—this guy who owns the boat—is bringing a buddy named Joe. That would make four and it would be easy practice for you. It wouldn't be a real date and I'll be there, too."

"I don't know, Jewels. I think it's still too soon for me. And, the way I feel, I might ruin your fun."

Julie remained silent, as if waiting for more.

"Jewels, I'm not disagreeing with your idea. But there are just too many things on my mind at this moment. Could you call me when you're completely free? I'll buy you lunch or dinner, whichever."

"I tried," said Julie. "But if that's still where you're at, let's shoot for lunch on Sunday. Meanwhile, lighten up if you can, Dawnie. Have a little fun, rather than just brooding over your lawsuit. I guarantee you that the other side isn't."

*****

That night, despite having had a hot shower and a long hot soak in the tub, she lay awake in bed, unable to keep from reverting back to Tilden's relentless grilling as if she were a criminal.

She thought of good times she'd had with Abel, hoping to then fade into sleep, but that did not work.

Still tormented, she vowed to all gods of slumber that she would accept the worst nightmares imaginable as long as they would have nothing to do with depositions.

"Bring 'em on," she whispered as she tried to surrender herself to whatever sleep she could get.

But that failed as well for another hour, until total exhaustion finally won out.

THIRTY-THREE

At 7:00 a.m., her alarm clock played with no regard for the prior night. She rubbed her eyes and foggily remembered her nightmares vow. "The gods must have taken a pass—would have been overkill."

"Oh crap," she mumbled. "It's Friday."

Without extended thought, she got out of bed to call the office number, figuring it would still be early enough to just leave a message on the answering machine.

At the beep, she garnered her weakest voice: "I'm sorry, but could you tell Mr. Lynch that Dawn cannot make it in today. I feel absolutely awful."

True enough.

She got back into bed and lay there staring at the ceiling, trying to savor every minute of the respite before Cora made her wake-up noises which would start the day for real. She thought about Cora's normal morning routine, waiting there happily in her oversized custom crib that Abel had made, knowing that Mommy would soon come in.

Have I ever had such faith in anything? Maybe in Abel...

But I won't let my problems harm her little world—at least as long as I can help it.

Minutes later, she could hear Cora's room come to life.

Dawn rose from bed and put on a smile. "Here comes Mommy," she said in a high-pitched voice, first from the hallway, then while sneaking up playfully toward Cora's crib, and finally from the end of the crib while holding up Cora's stuffed panda bear as temporary cover.

"Hi, little precious. Did you sleep well? Let's get you some num-nums."

As Dawn carried Cora to the kitchen area, she continued her playful chatter as if it would somehow be good for both of them. "You know what tomorrow is, sweetie? It starts the weekend and we'll do something fun, okay?"

Cora gave a quick smile.

"How about the children's zoo? We'll see ducks and rabbits and other fun animals."

Cora nodded, mimicking her wide-eyed mother.

"But today, we eat first and then off to Nanny G's. She always likes to see you."

*****

After dropping Cora off, she reentered her car as if it were a normal work day. As she sat behind the wheel, however, edgy and worried, she was at a loss as to her next move. She feared she'd go stir-crazy if she went back home. But she sure couldn't spend the day in her car in front of Nanny G's house.

She slowly drove away without a destination.

A few blocks later, an idea came to her. "The way I'm feeling, I might as well let it all hang out...as the saying goes."

*****

On her first time back since the funeral, she scanned the tombstones as she slowly walked, while embracing the quiet pause from the rest of the world. The warmth of the morning sun, as it broke through an opening in the trees, was surprisingly pleasant. With no time constraints, she stopped and stretched her limbs, selfishly absorbing the rays.

Strolling further, it began to seem strange that she hadn't already reached his gravesite, but just then, then she happened upon him. Her husband—the man she committed herself to for life—lay under the ground before her. On this day, however, it was all so different. His site was like all the others. His moment to be special here was long gone, until now when he was special just for her.

She felt guilty in not having thought to bring flowers. All she had to offer were her time and thoughts. "I promise to do better next time, my love," she whispered.

The grass next to him was dry enough to sit on. As she eased herself down, she recalled that the very spot she was lowering herself upon was to be her own final resting place, having been hastily reserved during those heart-wrenching days when death was in full command.

For now, this adjoining plot patiently waited. In the grand scheme, there was only her lifetime—however long or short it would be—before this spot be the grand stage for her own final act.

"So what," she scoffed, certain nobody could hear her. "I've got more than enough to worry about while I'm still alive. Take a number and get in line...Besides, I think

134

the peace and quiet here is very nice, so deal with that too, while you're at it."

Having said her piece, she thought again of Abel and the real reason she came. She edged even closer to his grave and let loose a long sigh.

For some unknown reason, however, she then started to wonder how long it might be until Cora accompanied her here. And, thinking of the two most important people in her life, while reclined in the middle of a graveyard, brought on tears.

She quickly pulled her head back and wiped her eyes to make sure no tears fell upon him. Besides, these tears were not the same as those she had expended in the hospital, at his funeral, and at countless other times at home or even in her car. These tears were for what was left of their family, his memory, their daughter, and her troubled self.

She thought of the men in her life who had been taken from her. Her father, who left home for good when she was so young she could barely remember him. Her husband, just when their future was brightest. Even James, her lawyer, whom she had begun to trust.

She stared at his entrenched tombstone. He might be here a thousand years, she thought, or even longer. She seemed to recall hearing of graveyards in some countries that were already much old than that. These stark thoughts made her feel more alone than ever.

She peered about to reconfirm her privacy, then turned back to him. "Yes, I'm proud to have been your wife, Abel. And I will do all I can to fight for your honor and for

Cora's future. But I can make no promises that I might not be able to keep. Any decisions will have to be mine, for better or worse...for richer or poorer."

She looked at her watch, as if to show Abel that time still had control over her, if not over him. "That's all I can do for today, love," she whispered. "I'll be back soon."

She stood up to leave, but immediately realized that doing so would only change her anguish, not eliminate it. While the empty plot next to Abel waited patiently for her death, the world outside the cemetery walls stood at the ready to battle her in life.

"Me, of all people," she said with a shake of her head, "with no choice but to go back and fight. Somehow, I'll have to find a way to win. But I know it won't be today."

By the time she reached her car, for lack of any other ideas, she decided to join up with Julie if there was still time.

Changing my mind like this, she'll know how badly I need her company.

THIRTY-FOUR

Having melted into the front seat of Julie's Audi for the drive to Lake Mead, and with the radio volume low enough to allow a yet to start conversation, Dawn could have easily dozed off. But she did not want her temporary escape to pass in a nap. She was going to savor every minute.

"Jewels," Dawn finally moaned, "let's just drive around for the rest of the day. I'll pay for the gas."

"No way," Julie laughed. "That might solve this moment, but what about tomorrow and the next day? At the risk of repeating myself, you're all tilted inward right now and you need to venture out before your shell gets too hard."

After another couple miles, Julie pointed. "That up ahead is the site of the proposed mall site, if the project ever gets approved by the county commissioners. It's another clash between some private citizens and developers."

Her comments reminded Dawn that she was supposed to be at work, maybe even reviewing maps and plans for the very same project. But, then again, he did say to take a drive out there.

"Jewels, as long as we're this close, would you mind taking the exit and showing me whatever you happen to know about this new mall—if we have the time, that is?"

"Can do. You'll get the grand five-minute tour. And I think there's a mini-mart we can hit nearby. I'll bet you could use a donut or something."

"Awesome, Jewels, as long as we won't be late. I don't want to make the guys upset with you..."

"Wow, you really are out of practice," Julie cracked, as the mini-mart came into view. "Waiting a little would be good for them. Anyway, they'll probably futz around with the boat for half an hour no matter when we get there, just to show us how important they are."

*****

As Dawn nibbled on an apple fritter, Julie drove by a large section of vacant land she described as "the main part, if the developer gets their way".

The area, from what Dawn could see, was bordered by various parcels containing some unfinished homes and vacant lots, all of which Julie described as a mostly abandoned housing development.

"So, what I think they're currently fighting over," Julie elaborated, "are planned routes for the high volume of mall customers to be able to ingress and egress. The county commissioners seem to be split so far, but it's still way too early for shopping plans anyway," she quipped.

"Shopping, what's shopping?" replied Dawn.

"Huh?"

"Jewels, with my budget right now, shopping's not even on my radar. But, thanks to you, I can at least pretend like I know something about this site. My boss is involved, but don't ask me how."

"Glad to help. And, have faith, Dawnie. You'll be shopping again. It's your entitlement as a woman."

THIRTY-FIVE

When Julie finally reached the access road to the lake, Dawn started feeling edgy about the upcoming encounter. But, as the two women walked down the long gravelly traverse to the marina, the sight of Lake Mead unexpectedly captivated her, with its abundant blue water reaching out into the vast wasteland like a life-giving hand.

If nothing else, I couldn't be further away from yesterday.

When the pair finally reached the docks, Julie led the way until she was able to point to a cabin cruiser with an enormous outboard motor. "Good, we're just a few minutes late," she said as they approached. "I mean good that we're not right on time," she added with a laugh.

They could see two men sitting leisurely on the *Cummin Tru*, both appearing to be in their thirties. One, with a baseball cap pulled low over his face, seemed to be listening to the other and nodding in agreement.

"It's a killer boat," Julie told Dawn. "Roomy, awesome power, a nice cabin, and guess what...it looks like they're actually ready to go."

As Julie and Dawn prepared to board, the man wearing the ball cap stood up at military attention and ceremoniously removed it for the women. His action was a comical sight in Dawn's eyes, given that he was wearing pink and blue swim trunks that came down past his knees and a sleeveless shirt. Dawn could see that he had an athletic build and just the start of a paunch.

"Welcome aboard, ladies, and good morning to you both," he said gregariously. "It is still morning, isn't it?"

The man's taller and leaner friend, who had long dark hair, bushy eyebrows and an over-sized mustache, was standing and smiling as well. He was dressed in knee-length dark blue trunks and a red T-shirt with something on the front about car racing.

To Dawn, the second man had the look of a nineteenth-century southwestern desperado. And, with his glistening white teeth peeking out though his mustache, she figured his smile might make him attractive—in a somewhat sinister way—*if* a lady happened to be up for that.

"Gimme a break, Charlie," Julie shot back at the pink-trunked man with feigned indignation. "I figured you'd still have lots of prepping to do, like last time when I actually got here early."

"It don't make no never-mind, Julie," Charlie chortled. "We still have enough time for some drinking, even if it's too late now for skiing."

"Yeah, Right!" retorted Julie. "With this kind of harassment, you're obviously forgetting Charlie that I'm only fifty-one-percent nice."

"Meanwhile, everybody," the second man interjected through an unbroken smile, "we're neglecting the intros."

"Well, that's very gentlemanly of you," said Julie. "Guys, this is my friend, Dawn. And Dawn, the one with the attitude as big as his boat is Charlie. And his smiling friend there is...uh, Joe, right?"

Joe nodded.

"And I'm Julie, of course. Both you guys are in construction, right? At least that's what they claim, Dawn."

"That's right, Julie," quipped Charlie with a grin toward Dawn. "*C*onstruction on the weekdays. *D*estruction on the weekends, and also on any weekday we can manage to take off, like on this happy Friday."

"Don't worry, Dawn. He's not that loony," said Julie.

"Oh, yes I *am* that looney," Charlie scoffed, feigning hurt feelings, then winking toward Dawn.

Despite the levity, Dawn felt awkward, having nothing clever to say herself, and not expecting that she'd be able to come up with anything later. She merely offered a nervous smile and nod.

"Seriously, though," continued Charlie, as if wanting to negate any awkward pause, "I'm docile compared to Joe here. He's a wild man once he gets warmed up."

Joe, with a sheepish grin, threw a mock punch at Charlie. "We ain't even shoved off yet, Chuck, and you're already giving these pretty ladies the wrong idea."

"Oh, excuse me, I only meant that Joe's a wild man on the skis," replied Charlie with another wink.

Dawn managed another smile, but already realized from the interplay that her single-again status still had a long way to go. And, though the guys seem good-natured enough, they might as well have been aliens as far as she was concerned. She already missed being alone with Julie on the car ride out.

"Dawn," Charlie politely inquired, "is there anything special you like to drink? We've got quite a selection, but I don't wanna be out on the lake and find out I don't have what you want."

Doubting if she'd be drinking any form of alcohol, she gave a quick smile and shook her head.

"Ok, then. I'm sure we'll be able to accommodate you. And, as for Julie, I don't believe she'll turn down any type of drink...Just kidding. Just kidding," Charlie laughed. "Oh boy, I'm in trouble already."

Julie gave Charlie an exaggerated nod, but still with a smile.

"Ladies," Charlie barked, "grab yourselves a seat. Julie, keep above that fifty-percent nice line, and let's all boogie on out."

Dawn retreated to the seat furthest from the captain's chair, grateful she could sit and let her mind drift while the guys seemed temporarily occupied.

The sun was comfortably warm and the sky a translucent blue, with only a few wisps of clouds and a mild breeze.

This could be quite nice, if only…

Charlie steered the boat away from the dock and began heading through the marina within its low speed limit.

Dawn casually looked around. Other than the few fishermen, whose small boats were anchored just outside the marina, there was not a lot of visible activity on this weekday.

When the boat was fully clear of the marina, Charlie advanced the throttles steadily until the engine roared and she felt a slight lurch from the acceleration. Then, with no looking away from his nautical duties or any other wasted movement, Charlie's free hand accepted his first cold beer from Joe.

Joe then turned toward the women with a smile and shouted above the engine noise, "What can I get each of you?"

"A beer for me too," Julie answered eagerly, as if confirming she was ready to party. "A light one if you got it, but no matter."

"And, how about you, Dawn?" offered Joe. "We've got lots of stuff besides beer, all nice and cold."

"Oh, thanks very much Joe. For now, I think a cold water be quite nice, if that's okay."

"Very sorry, Dawn," Joe lamented, "but I don't think we brought any water."

She tried to suppress her stunned reaction, but Joe apparently caught it.

"Just foolin," he grinned. "I'm sure there are some waters hiding in there under the beers. Would the bubbly French stuff do?"

"Sure, thanks." With her first long gulp, Dawn realized she was dehydrated and hoped there was plenty more.

As Charlie's boat motored on, with the engine noise loud and steady, Dawn's eyes started to close. She tried to force alertness, but remembering how little sleep she'd had, she knew it would be a losing battle. Whether it be rude or not, she'd soon have to crash for a while.

More minutes went by until Charlie eased back the throttles in an open part of the lake, letting the boat slow down to a drift.

"Okay," Charlie announced. "It doesn't get any better than this. Dawn, as the newbie, you're welcome to go first."

"Uh, thanks very much, Charlie, but can I just watch a little first? It's been awhile for me."

"Dawn's quite athletic," Julie interjected. "She'll do fine when she's ready."

"She'll have the world's greatest boat driver," Charlie quipped.

Dawn watched with mild interest as Julie got ready to ski. But, before her friend was in the water, Dawn's eyes got even heavier and her head started dropping.

"Dawn," said Charlie, "That seat reclines. It's simple," he explained, pointing to a lever. "Or you can just rack out in the cabin if you want. We won't mind."

Dawn mouthed a "thank you" and worked her way into the cabin. After moving some life vests aside, she eagerly collapsed onto the cushion.

Indeterminable time went by with Dawn not quite able to doze off due to the changing engine noises. At one point, with the engine momentarily quiet, she couldn't help but overhear Charlie: "Hey Julie, your little friend's a real steamer. Does she actually have a swimsuit?"

"Leave her alone," Julie responded. "She didn't get much sleep last night. And, yes, I lent her one of my one-pieces. Just give her some space, if you guys are capable of that. She'll be okay."

"Hey, we've got plenty of space out here today," replied Charlie, "which beats the hell out of the weekend with a lake full of animals like us."

On overhearing these words, Dawn wondered if these two guys were really such "animals". So far, she didn't feel threatened by them.

She wrapped a towel around her head, attempting to muffle the outside noise and, though it only helped a little, she was finally able to fall asleep.

THIRTY-SIX

Waking up disoriented, she began to reconstruct where she was. The still-burning memories of her deposition. The cemetery. The long car ride with Julie. And now this boat with the two guys.

For better or worse, she was going to have to leave the cabin and socialize,. Probably for worse, she figured, given that the others have been drinking. She got up, took a deep breath, and ventured out.

"Hey, look what we have here," Charlie announced as Dawn emerged with a forced smile. "Sleeping Beauty woke up without even being kissed...Hey, wait a minute," said Charlie as he turned toward Joe with mock suspicion. "Did you sneak in there, your highness?"

"Zip it, Chuck," said Joe. "I try not to advertise my princely identity."

Charlie smiled. "You'll have to excuse us, Dawn. We're just happy to see you out here again."

Silliness I can handle.

"It's okay, guys. Just as long as nobody ever puts a frog up to my face."

"Touché, Dawn. Looks like that napathon did you good. So are you ready for something cold now?"

"Uh, sure. But do you happen to have anything with caffeine?"

"Of course," said Joe, who straightaway pulled out a can of cola and popped it open for her.

"Cheers," said Dawn as she raised it to her dry mouth. A full gulp had a quick and welcome effect. She then chugged more while watching Julie climb back into the boat.

"Hey Dawn, you're awake," Julie shouted. "Are you ready to skiing now? I've been twice and the water's awesome."

"We're not rushing you, Dawn," Charlie chimed in. "Did you ever get to see enough, or would you like crazy Joe here to demo for you?"

"No, I'll go. If I fall, I fall. Just slow and easy, please—at least to start."

She finished the cola, then modestly removed her T-shirt and jeans, which had been covering a conservative one-piece suit.

"Just lean back and keep those pretty knees bent," said Charlie. "You'll do fine."

With her vest on, Dawn cautiously jumped into the water, holding her nose in amateur fashion. As she maneuvered toward the skis, she was grateful how warm the water was. With the rope handle in a death grip, she nervously gave a thumbs-up.

The engine power somehow brought her smoothly out of the water—wide-eyed and tense as she was—until she was upright and stable enough to surprise herself.

"Oh my God...of all the things to be doing today. This is insane."

As if the boat had a mind of its own, however, her speed kept gradually increasing until she shook her head violently, while locking her legs.

147

"Come on...back to nice and easy."

The boat obeyed, causing her to smile and nod her head.

Feeling enough in control again, she gradually relaxed and glanced from side to side, as if taking in the panoramic views was a requirement of the ride. But, in doing so, she couldn't help but feel a modicum of enjoyment, at least for the moment.

Damn it, Jewels, I'm almost ready to say you were right about this.

*****

While the boat quietly drifted, Dawn sat back and actually relaxed with the others, while clasping her "skiing trophy" from Joe. But this time, part of the cola's original contents had been replaced by "only a drop of rum".

Although she politely accepted it, she intended to only take a few social sips.

"Here's to an awesome day," Charlie announced as he hoisted another beer.

Dawn raised her cola and took a cautious sip.

More than a drop there, Joe.

As they all basked in the afternoon sun, talk centered on their favorite rock concerts—meaningless conversation she could listen to or ignore at her pleasure. Time had stopped momentarily.

This is tolerable. I do owe you, Jewels.

As if reading Dawn's mind, Julie flashed a smile.

As more time passed, Dawn took more sips, shaking her head with a smile on one occasion at the rum's bold kick.

"Hey gang," announced Charlie, "this has been fantastic, but what say we head back in while we're still sober enough to find the marina?"

"No way," said Julie, "I worked hard this week and this is too much fun. Hey Dawnie, if the rest of us pass out, you can drive the boat back, right?"

Dawn shot a wide-eyed stare at Julie, on the off-chance that she just might happen to be serious.

Julie laughed. "Just kidding, Dawnie. Charlie can handle it. I'm confident in him."

"Well, fine then," said Charlie. "You two girls can say when, at least up to a point. But, eventually, I'll be wanting some restaurant chow back at the dock."

With that settled, Joe promptly took it upon himself to swap what was left of Dawn's rum-injected cola for another fresh one.

Oh my.

THIRTY-SEVEN

As the day on the lake eased along, with Dawn having sipped through most of her second rum and cola, she felt more relaxed than she had in weeks. She wondered if that was more surprising or the fact that Joe hadn't yet replaced her current drink.

Must be out of colas...

Everyone's attention then turned to the first sign of other humans in a while, as a couple on jet skis seemingly came out of nowhere and sped between the *Cummin Tru* and the barren lakeshore.

Joe immediately posed the question whether the girl was riding hers topless.

"I'm guessing 'yes'," said Charlie as he grabbed a ready pair of binoculars and started focusing in. "That's affirmative...Actually, they're nice and firmative...Oh, sorry ladies."

"Cool," said Joe as he took the binoculars and gazed for himself. "A nice little pair if I do say so myself...of jet skis, I mean. His and hers."

"Sure, Joe," said Julie.

"I'm guessing the chick lost a bet," added Charlie. "Hey, it's my turn again."

The two men exchanged the binoculars until the jet skiers disappeared around a small peninsula. The abrupt end of their entertainment left a dead moment.

"I'd like to try that someday," Julie casually remarked, then took a sip from her current beer.

"What, riding on one of those little toys?" asked Charlie, as if she was hinting that water-skiing behind his boat wasn't good enough.

"No, going topless," Julie coldly responded.

Jewels?

Charlie, showing obvious interest, nudged her arm. "Come on, Julie-for-truly, do it and make our day."

Julie, feigning naivety, pointed to her skimpy bikini top. "You mean you can't see enough as it is, guys?"

"Now, you be backing out?" said Charlie, "and after giving us the royal tease?"

Julie, unable to keep a straight face, let out a giggle.

In Dawn's eyes, Julie was just enjoying her ability to manipulate Charlie, if not Joe as well. But where was this going? That she was a free spirit was a given, but, after a few drinks, her boldness could apparently reach another level.

As the two guys awaited Julie's next move with obvious interest, Julie put on her serious face and made a show of looking in all directions, as if checking for any more intruders in the vicinity.

This was not missed by Charlie or Joe.

Why look around, with these two drooling guys right in the same boat?

Julie, having apparently satisfied herself, smugly announced to the guys: "Maybe I will and maybe I won't. You'll just have to wait and see."

"No maybes for us," quipped Charlie while holding up his binoculars. "Whatever you're willing to show us, we will definitely see."

151

"You two promise to behave?"

"We'll be good," chirped Charlie. "Joe, tell Julie she can trust us."

"Oh, most definitely," Joe said with a grin. "What he said."

"I'm serious," Julie said sternly. "*If* I happen to go that far, it'll be just like you both took cold showers when I come back in. If necessary, you can even shove a cold beer down your trow."

"Absolutely, Julie-truly," said Charlie. "No such extreme measures will be required."

Although Dawn was amazed at the exchange, she kept a poker face of her own. Secretly, however, she was impressed at how assertive Julie could be over two seemingly red-blooded beer-drinking guys.

Julie, ostensibly satisfied that the guys would behave, asked Joe to throw in her skis. She then jumped in alongside the drifting boat. "As you can see, gentlemen," she yelled up, "I have no life jacket, so I'm relying on you for my safety."

"Don't worry, you'll be watched very closely," Charlie shouted back.

Julie swam to the boat's secluded underside. With her back to the guys, she promptly worked out of her top, then scrunched it up and flipped it up onto the boat, while still covering herself with her other arm and hand.

That didn't take long.

Julie next maneuvered the skis to the rope's length, then appeared to work her way into a ready position. "So, hit it already," she yelled.

The engine noise was immediately accompanied by hollering and whistles, while Julie waved back with what appeared to be an impish grin.

After about a minute of displaying herself, she let go of the rope and sank back into the water, while coyly waving good-bye with one hand and covering herself again with the other.

Charlie, surprisingly quiet, eased the boat back toward her.

Julie, still grinning, yelled up. "Surprised you all, didn't I? Now throw me my goddamn top."

Joe tied her bikini top to a life vest and tossed it to her.

"You surprised and impressed us," Charlie commented. "But don't think that little piece of fabric is protecting you. You're safe because we're both perfect gentlemen."

Charlie then turned toward Dawn with a wink. "Isn't that right, Dawn?"

Dawn, uneasy about being included in the exchange, offered a noncommittal smile, then turned back to watch Julie get back on board.

"You're up, Dawnie," said Julie, smiling and batting her eyelashes seductively.

As if!

"Sorry, Jewels, I have a strict policy against going topless on weekdays. Besides, I don't even have a two-piece."

"I'm done with mine for the day," replied Julie.

"Uh, thanks, but that's okay...Nothing personal."

"Julie, we appreciate your efforts," said Charlie. "But I don't think she wants to..."

Thank you.

"Sure, she does, Charlie," countered Julie. "She just doesn't realize it."

I what?

Julie marched up to Dawn and herded her a few steps away from the guys. "Dawnie," she whispered, "you remember our little talks?"

"Yes, but..."

"And wasn't I right in suggesting that you come along today?"

"Well, so far it's been nice, but..."

"Dawnie, why do you think I just did what I did?"

"I was really wondering myself, Jewels."

"I did it *for you!* This is your chance to start coming out of your shell, and you'll be completely safe. So, why the heck not?"

Julie's pressure, combined with the effects of the rum, caught Dawn off guard. She felt herself blushing and determined to avoid eye contact with the guys that might reveal how vulnerable she really was. Instead of saying anything, she picked up what's left of her drink and took a gulp.

154

"I have a solution," said Charlie, almost as if coming to Dawn's defense in the awkward silence, "you can just ski in your one-piece and pull it down however little you want."

How about as little as not at all?

Dawn tried to mimic the same stern look that Julie had previously displayed. "Okay, people, absolutely nothing is promised."

"Of course," said Joe.

"So, no matter what you may or may not see," Dawn continued, "you have to let me back on this boat in peace."

"For sure," replied Charlie.

"Perfect gentlemen," added Joe, "just like with Julie."

Dawn shook her head, showing a hint of a smile. "What's with all this chauvinism, anyway? I don't see either of you guys volunteering to put on a show."

Shit, why did I say that!

"And are you saying you'd like us to?" asked Charlie unhesitatingly.

"No!" Dawn blurted back before Julie might give life to his offer. "I mean, not today, thanks." Then, to put aside his offer for good, she stepped to the edge of the boat and jumped in.

Wow, the water still feels great.

"You'll watch out for me, too, please?" she yelled up. "I don't usually drink, especially out in the sun."

"Our eyes will be glued on you," said Charlie.

That I believe...

She worked her way into the skis, then lowered her top, just enough to show what little cleavage she had.

With her thumb up, the boat engine roared again and Dawn managed to ski upright with everything intact.

After only a few seconds, however, she saw Julie signal to Charlie to cut the engine.

I would have skied longer…

She made her way back toward the boat. But, at the spot where Dawn would have climbed on board, Julie was positioned with one hand holding her beer and the other giving a "halt" sign toward Dawn.

Charlie and Joe merely observed.

"I know you can do better than that," Julie scoffed, then took a casual sip while keeping her "halt" up.

"I was promised that it was all up to me," Dawn yelled back incredulously.

"Sorry girl, but you got no promise from me," Julie replied with a fiendish smile.

So this is how crazy Jewels can get, drinking around guys…

"Come on, Jewels..."

"*You* come on, Dawnie. I *know* you can do it," Julie added, like a faith healer encouraging someone to stand up and walk.

A brief stare-down ensued as Dawn dog-paddled in place. But Julie simply took another leisurely sip of beer and waited.

As if I didn't get enough shit yesterday…

156

Dawn, while kicking more vigorously to remain upright, held up both arms as if to plead. "Seriously, Jewels—my best friend—I cannot do what you're asking..."

Julie smiled. "Seriously, Dawnie, I think you can."

Unbelievable.

Dawn looked around and, for a moment, wondered about just swimming to the rocky desert shore. But she would have no shoes, water or transportation.

"Fuck it," she whispered to herself. "Nobody important will ever know."

Grasping the rope handle and skis in water that had gotten slightly choppy from the afternoon breeze, she edged toward the glare of the afternoon sun.

By the time she had positioned herself, her anger toward Julie had started to ease.

Crazy or not, I still need her.

While still submerged up to her neck, she lowered the top of her suit enough to expose one breast into the warm lake water and then the other.

"In the fucking middle of Lake Mead..."

When she was about to put on her skis, her last bit of disgust was replaced by an insane thought—for once, she could be the one to shock her friend.

"No freaking way," she told herself.

"But they won't know what hit them," she countered.

She peeked back. They were passively waiting, with Julie having backed away from the boat edge and apparently chatting with Charlie.

Dawn stealthily slid her suit down to her hips.

157

"With that rum in me, I better not fall," she muttered, "or wouldn't I look super dumb."

She took a deep breath, then edged the suit all the way off.

"Okay, loony, now what?"

While managing to keep her movements below the surface, she wound and tied her suit near the rope handle, then carefully positioned herself into the skis.

I just wish I could see their faces close-up.

While starting to shiver—purely from nerves—she looked around again. Nobody was in sight, other than the three on the boat who were still casually talking, almost as if they'd forgotten about her, though she knew they hadn't.

She took another deep breath. "Now," she whispered, "just don't fucking fall."

She waved one hand and yelled her loudest, "Hey, let's go before I shrivel up."

Charlie waived his hand and quickly shuffled to the controls.

As the engine revved and Dawn was pulled from her concealment, her legs buckled but she managed to stay upright.

"There, Jewels," she declared against the engine noise, "is this good enough for you!"

After those on the boat got over their apparent shock, their howls were loud enough to hear over the motor.

Julie jumped up and down, pumping both her fists, including the one wrapped around her beer.

Charlie steered the boat into a sweeping turn, while Dawn continued to concentrate on just staying upright.

As the boat straightened out again, Dawn found herself skiing almost directly into the sun and, despite her rum intake, immediately figured out why.

"That's good enough," she said, while squinting to maintain eye contact with the boat. "Three, two, one...*and done!*"

THIRTY-EIGHT

Having been summoned into Lynch's office Monday afternoon, she hoped it wasn't about missing the entire day on Friday.

"Please take a seat," Lynch said crisply from his desk.

Something seemed different in his attitude; he wasn't acting like the time she took the end of the afternoon off to try to relax at a mall.

She sat down and braced herself.

To her surprise, however, he walked around his desk, apparently to sit next to her. "May I?" he asked, while he was already seating himself.

"Of course, sir."

He looked into her eyes for what seemed to be too long. "Dawn, I got your message that you weren't feeling well on Friday. I also understand that you had your deposition the afternoon before..."

Dawn winced at the memory. "Yes sir."

"Pretty rough, huh?"

She nodded.

He studied her. "But it was all over with on Thursday, wasn't it?"

"Mr. Lynch, I'm sorry but I just couldn't bring myself to come in on Friday. I was so bitter that I would have been worthless here. Even today, it's hard to get that experience out of my mind."

"I understand, Dawn."

160

"Thank you, sir, but there's something else I should tell you."

"Oh?"

"After that deposition, I needed someone talk to, so I called my girlfriend. She invited me to spend Friday with her, as long as I wasn't going in to work. I take full responsibility, but I was just trying to get myself together."

Lynch nodded again, but seemed to be expecting more from her.

"The truth, Mr. Lynch, is that, in order to spend time with my girlfriend, I had to ride with her to Lake Mead and go boating because she already had that planned...So, on Friday, I was actually on Lake Mead of all places."

"Dawn," Lynch said with a smile. "I appreciate your honesty. It counts a lot in an employee. But, to be honest myself, I already knew what you did on Friday."

"You knew that I went boating, sir? How? I mean..."

"Don't worry, Dawn," he replied with a smile, "I don't have you under surveillance."

Okay...

"On Saturday, when I happened to be in the office, some guy—I mean, some gentleman—showed up and asked about you. He wanted your telephone number."

Oh my God...where is this going?

"Do you remember if he had a mustache, sir?"

"And then some. He said his name was Joe, and that he went water-skiing with you Friday on Lake Mead."

Dawn's heart raced as she tried to picture the smiling desperado talking with Lynch about her. "I did happen to

161

mention who I worked for, and I suppose he'd heard of your company, being in construction and all."

"Dawn, I hope you don't mind, but I politely asked him if he could describe you..."

Holy...

"...And he did a pretty good job of it," Lynch calmly continued. "But I still told him that I couldn't give out your number without your permission."

As if...

"I appreciate that, Mr. Lynch."

Now, please say we're done...

"Instead, I took his number and said it would be up to you to contact him. But I also told him that personal calls during work hours were frowned upon here."

So that's all of it?

"Here's his number if you want it," Lynch said halfheartedly, putting the note in front of her.

She picked up the small piece of paper only because it seemed to be expected of her.

Right into the trash.

Lynch, however, did not seem done. His mind was obviously working on something.

No more about Friday, please...

"Dawn, I know you're going through difficult times," he finally said, with his eyes fixed on her. "If you need another day or two off in the future, just let me or my assistants know. It's really not a problem."

She started to smile, but noticed him nervously rubbing his palms together. What was coming next?

"Dawn, you don't have to tell me whether this Joe fellow means anything to you..."

"I don't mind, Mr. Lynch. The answer is no."

"Well, I'm very pleased to hear that...So, then, would you consider having dinner with me?"

With YOU?

"Oh, Mr. Lynch, I'm flattered, but..."

"I know what you're thinking," he quickly injected, "That I'm married..."

Uh, that too...

"Well I might not be married much longer. But don't worry. It'll just be dinner, nothing serious, I assure you," he said with an obviously forced smile.

"What I was actually going to say, sir, was that the thing on Friday was just so that I could spend time with Julie. I'm not fully up yet for anything social because I'm still grieving. And I'm afraid that this lawsuit about Abel's death is prolonging it."

He continued looking at her as if he wasn't taking the hint, and was still waiting for a direct answer.

She sensed great disappointment if she declined.

What the heck, I see him at the office. And meanwhile, I buy more time.

She heard herself speak. "Yes, Mr. Lynch, I'll go to dinner with you, as long as you understand my situation and don't expect me to be great company."

He was boyishly animated. "This evening would be perfect, Dawn. You can get a baby-sitter, right?"

163

THIRTY-NINE

It was impossible not to relax in the quiet elegance of Rafael's. With the muted lighting, soft chamber music, and the exquisite pre-dinner wine ordered by Lynch, it was a momentary oasis far beyond her expectations.

When the menu was presented, she realized she'd never even dined in a restaurant of this caliber, let alone been able to order whatever she wanted. She soon found out, however, that ordering would be a challenge with such tempting choices. Meanwhile, she willed herself to not appear too hungry, even though she had barely eaten all day.

"The lobster is excellent tonight," said the waiter, who introduced himself as Milo.

"Oh my," said Dawn, slightly embarrassed. "That sounds great, but I can't remember the last time I had lobster and it would be a shame if..."

"No problem, Dawn," Lynch interrupted. "Take Milo's suggestion and, if you don't like the lobster, we'll get you something else. I'll have the same, Milo."

The abrupt way Lynch took over her ordering startled her, but she easily let it go.

If that's the worst thing that happens...

The occasional conversation, always led by Lynch, stayed easy and harmless: how was Las Vegas compared to Tucson; what kind of music and hobbies she enjoyed; and what did she see in her daughter's future.

Time passed until the lobster in a garlic-butter sauce was presented, along with butternut squash and spinach soufflé.

Though it all tasted as delicious as it looked, she forced herself to take small bites and not wolf it down.

So much for a replacement order.

Though she had vowed to only take a few micro-sips of the main-course wine, along came a different bottle and new set of pristine wine glasses after the dinner plates and silverware were removed.

But, before the after-dinner wine could even be tasted, the dessert cart arrived with an array of chocolate concoctions, cheesecake varieties, berry cobblers, and other temptations.

She initially feigned being too full, but allowed a chocolate truffle concoction to be forced upon her.

When she finished dessert, Lynch looked at her with an exaggerated smile that was apparently intended to be disarming. "Dawn, you don't have to talk about this, if you don't want to, but I was just wondering about your lawsuit. After your experience last week, are you really sure you want to stick with it?"

Despite how smoothly he asked, she wished she could have finished the evening without reality intruding. Still, she hid her irritation. "I don't know, Mr. Lynch, they made another offer to settle. It wouldn't pay anything close to what I'm suing for, but I still have weeks to think about it. That's about the size of it right now, sir."

"Well, you know that I'm here to help you, just as I have before."

"You sure have, Mr. Lynch, and I can't tell you how much I appreciate your kindness. But that lawsuit is my burden to get through somehow."

*****

Keeping his promise of just dinner, Lynch drove her directly home. While his full-sized Mercedes glided over the surface streets of Las Vegas as if on a cushion of air, she thought about how pleasant and painless the dinner had been—up until the very end. But even that inquiry was only a fleeting one.

Although Lynch offered to pick Cora up on the way to Dawn's house, she felt that would be too awkward. "Thanks very much, Mr. Lynch, but she needs a car seat, and it's really no problem for me."

When he began to walk her to her front door, after opening her car door for her, she nervously wondered if he was going to ruin the evening by trying to give her a kiss.

As if reading her mind, he stopped before her front porch, apparently waiting for her to turn around and say good-night.

"That was very pleasant, Mr. Lynch," she said as she reached out to shake his hand. "Thank you."

"Dawn, I would completely echo your words but, instead, I'm asking you to have dinner with me again. I know that this Thursday might seem soon, but I'm going on a trip after that. It'll be a different location this time—somewhere very special."

As if tonight's place wasn't?

"Uh, sure, Mr. Lynch. I just need to confirm that I can get the sitter again."

"Assuming that, may I have you picked up at, say, six-thirty?"

She slowly nodded again, trying not to reveal her inner concern. It was not just that Lynch was being forward, while sparing no expense in the process. He seemed to be following some type of plan, unknown to her.

Before she could wonder what it might be, however, he reached into his coat pocket and pulled out an envelope.

"Here," he said, as he handed it to her. "I thought you might want to do a little shopping for something nice to wear Thursday evening. I'm sure you have nice outfits already, but I think most women like to shop, especially at malls."

She opened the envelope to find a gift certificate for the Inner Circle Boutique Mall for one-thousand-dollars.

Just for an outfit?

Just for an evening?

Her speechlessness seemed to be just what he expected. "Dawn, go ahead and take off work early tomorrow to do your shopping."

"Mr. Lynch, I'm in shock, as you can tell. But you really don't have to do any of this. You're spoiling me. Actually, you're overwhelming me."

"Oh, never mind all that. You'll be picked up Thursday at six-thirty. And don't be misled if I fail to

167

mention it between now and then. It's definitely on, unless you tell me your sitter isn't available."

"I think it will be all right, Mr. Lynch."

"Uh, Dawn, one more thing if I may..."

"What's that, Mr. Lynch?"

"When we're alone, I'd like you to start calling me Lou."

"Uh, sure Lou, I'll try to remember that."

But how often does he think that's going to be?

*****

Although she had merely intended a bathroom break before leaving her house to get Cora, she reopened the envelope and set its crazy contents on her dining room table. Yes, she really did possess a one-thousand-dollar gift certificate.

And, in the same house, were bills requiring minimal payments to stay ahead of delinquency notices and penalties, along with the latest statement on her shrinking bank account.

FORTY

"I was *so* glad when you asked me to lunch," said Julie, as the two waited to be served. "I was afraid you might still be simmering from what happened at the lake."

"Forget it, Jewels. I was drinking too of my own volition. Besides, I should have been ready for anything, being out with you and a couple guys I never met."

"Whew..."

"And it definitely took my mind off being tortured in that lawyer's office."

"Okay, then, you're welcome," Julie smiled.

"Anyway, Jewels, remember when I asked you to lunch, I said that Mr. Lynch took me someplace special for our second dinner together?"

Julie nodded.

Dawn reached into her purse and pulled out a gold-plated key chain with two ornate keys. "As soon we're done eating, I'm taking you there so you can see how crazy things have gotten for me right now. Only, in my case, he had me picked up in a freaking limo."

*****

Upon opening the grand front door to the immense mansion, elegant furnishings and features could be seen in all directions. There were marble floors, stained-glass windows, recessed lighting, and expensive-looking wood cabinetry, which Dawn figured had been installed by Abel.

169

"It's not yet fully furnished," said Dawn, as she punched in the security code Lynch had given her. "But you can see the high-quality stuff that's already in the living and dining rooms."

Dawn next pointed to where she said a violinist, dressed in a black tuxedo, started playing for the two of them in the formal living room, then he later followed them to the formal dining area when the gourmet dinner was ready to be served by a high end caterer.

Julie's eyes roved to take it all in until she saw a flower display, still looking fresh, and walked over to breathe in their fragrance.

"And Jewels, I was wearing a brand new seven-hundred-dollar dress for the dinner, courtesy of a thousand-dollar gift certificate he gave me to those Inner Circle Mall stores near the Strip. He insisted I buy something special just for the evening. I also had my hair and nails done there, and, just between you and me, I bought some things for Cora and a black bikini, which I'm sure you'd say is too modest."

"Holy shitoli. You've got to be kidding."

"Like I said, Jewels, it was all freaking crazy, but later it got downright scary."

"So, go ahead and spit out the rest, Dawnie. Like, did he try to show you the master bedroom after dinner?"

"Of course not. I wouldn't have allowed it. And, actually, he's been a perfect gentleman so far. He even admitted that he was being very forward, but he wanted to

make a, quote, 'favorable impression', unquote, on me
before leaving town on a trip."

"Oh my. So what made it scary?"

"Patience, Jewels."

Dawn continued the tour into the backyard, through
a covered patio area with large potted plants and a built-in
gas barbeque.

She then led Julie further back to a secluded area that
had the swimming pool. "I remember he said it's always
kept at eighty-five degrees. And, according to him, the trees
around it will allow in just enough of the Las Vegas sun."

Seeing the look on Julie's face, there was no need to
expound upon the potential benefits of the total privacy,
afforded by the high walls and mature trees.

"This is so rad, Dawnie...and to think, he just handed
you the keys?"

"Yup."

"Hey, a person could get married right here in this
backyard."

"Don't see why not," replied Dawn.

"Heck, they could even have their honeymoon here,"
added Julie with a wide-eyed grin.

Dawn motioned for Julie to sit with her on cushioned
patio chairs half-encircled by a rainbow of rose bushes.

"Jewels, he looked me in the eye and first told me
that he wanted to help my daughter Cora have all the
advantages money could buy."

"He hoped that might interest you..."

"Oh yes. I think he put as much thought into all this as he would for one of his business deals."

Julie nodded.

"But then he kept talking, and this is when it got scary crazy..." Dawn paused, with widened eyes.

"Go on..."

"He told me that he's always felt unfulfilled in life because he only had two sons, who are now grown, and never had a daughter. He said his wife insisted on stopping at two."

"Wow," interrupted Julie. "So you're saying all of this is just because you happen to have a little daughter that he wants to help support?"

"No, Jewels. He wants me to have *his* daughter, as in give birth to *his* third child."

"Oh my God, Dawn, he moves right along..."

"My head's still spinning. He offered me this house, with all my living expenses paid for, and both daughters would be treated like princesses. He even said that they'd both be able to go to Stanford or to the University of Southern California if they want, because he has the connections to both."

"I suppose he would," said Julie, who then held her left ring finger up. "Did he spell out any offer about *your* future status with him, like after the two girls would be off to college or just grown up?"

"You'd think that would be a fair question, Jewels, as long as he's making all these offers. But, all he said was something vague about him someday getting "free", he said.

But I didn't push him on it because the whole thing was so incredible anyway."

"Wow."

"Yeah, and I'm also thinking it's all crazy for another reason as well: What if the baby turned out to be a third son for him?"

"Yeah, like a reverse Henry-the-Eighth," said Julie. "But, as long as we're talking about it, you're absolutely right to be concerned."

"The closest thing he said was something like 'there are plenty of extra rooms in this house,' which does happen to be true."

"Well hey, it's only the rest of your life he's asking for. No need to spell everything out."

"What he really thinks—as far as I can tell, Jewels—is that I'm supposed to just say 'yes', and it will all work out just the way he wishes, like the baby wouldn't dare be a boy."

"No ego there."

"So then he gives me these keys—with the security code based on my birthday—and tells me he wants me to enjoy the place while I'm deciding."

"Ah yes, just like a car salesman. Take this mistress mansion for a little test drive."

"That's about it."

"So how much time do you have?"

"Do you think that really matters, Jewels? I mean, am I really so desperate that I have to be someone's mistress? I just wanted to show you because it's so far out there and you're my best friend."

"Understood, and ditto on the friend thing. But quit stalling and tell me how much time you have?"

"Would if I could, but he didn't give me any deadline. He said he hopes I'll decide by the time he gets back from his trip, but he didn't say I had to."

"Oh wow. It still sounds like he's trying to blitz you."

Dawn nodded.

"So tell me," said Julie with a wink, "how did you—the sweet and innocent one—manage to manipulate this man? Should I start calling you Dawnie the gold-digger?"

"Not in a million years, Jewels. If I did anything at all, it would have been while I was unconscious. Trust me; I'm not even close to being over Abel."

"Uh huh," Julie grinned, "it's just some hidden talent of yours. How naive of me to introduce you to those two boating yahoos when you were lining up a bigger fish."

"C'mon, Jewels...It's really *all* his doing, whether you believe it or not."

Julie's eyes sharpened. "Okay, have it your way. But you should realize that some women would be very tempted by his offer—even if they didn't happen to be a widow with a young child."

"I suppose..."

"So, then, are you actually going to think it over?"

"All I can say is that I haven't completely made up my mind to say 'no' quite yet. It's like too wild and crazy to treat like a real decision I have to make. It's just there."

"Uh huh...But, at some point, you'll have to officially decide. I mean he's your boss and you see him five days a week—except of course when you ditch to go somewhere with me."

"Tell me about it. That's the one thing that does tie into reality. What happens when I say, 'thanks, but no thanks'?"

"Hey," said Julie, while playfully squeezing Dawn's forearm, "here's another crazy idea for you. When life in the mistress mansion got too boring, you could easily fool around on the side because he'd be busy at work or spending time with his wife if he stayed married. Heck, he'd even have to expect that."

Dawn shook her head. "Right, Jewels. Here I am thinking that this is like too outrageous to even consider and you've already got me cheating on him."

"Just trying to help you look at the pros and cons, Dawnie. Besides, it wouldn't really be cheating."

"Jewels...you know I'm not that type anyway."

"Right. That's coming from someone who water-skied naked in front of two guys she just met...Oh my, look at you blush."

Dawn smiled. "You win, Jewels. Just keep being you."

"Of course. And, as long as you're addicted to me, remember that I'm your real estate agent if you ever sell your current house. Unlike your boss, I need the business."

Dawn laughed. "For sure, Jewels. But if I were you, I wouldn't go spending your commission quite yet."

"Dawnie..."

"What now?"

"No matter what you decide to do, there's one more thing I want."

"Yeah?"

"Promise me that, next time you go shopping with a thousand-dollar gift certificate, you'll bring me along."

FORTY-ONE

While driving from the mistress mansion to Nanny G's, Lynch's proposal nagged at her. Merely calling it "crazy" did not remove it from her mind. And, though she tried to think about other things, it had staying power.

"Hey you," she said while shaking her head, "it's not like you've got extra brain space to waste."

She drove on, trying to tell herself that being a kept woman for a married man was a lot closer to being a whore than marrying for money—which at least offered a cloak of respectability.

But, as she sat at a traffic light, she started feeling stupid for what she was ignoring. "Cora!" she exclaimed. "His offer was not just for me."

She thought further. "But what does that really mean? Am I supposed to say 'yes' to something I never would have dreamed of doing all for the sake of my daughter's future?"

By the time the light turned green, she couldn't resist trying to apply cold logic, hoping that the negatives of being Lynch's mistress would squelch the pesky notion. But, in no time, she could see that it was getting too complicated, especially while having to drive.

She turned into the parking lot of a fast-food restaurant and bought a small coffee. Once back in her car, she fished a ballpoint pen out of her glove compartment, then tore open the white paper bag that the covered cup of coffee had been packaged in and laid it out flat.

She first drew two vertical columns and labeled them "Yes to Lynch" and "No to Lynch."

She then drew two horizontal columns through the vertical ones and labeled them "Settle Now" and "Don't Settle Now."

She sipped her coffee for inspiration and pondered each of the four combinations, trying to imagine what life might be like right away, in a year or two, and even further into the future.

Within a few sips, however, she could see that her matrix was far from complete and that, even if she did not choose from it today, she would eventually plop into one of the many possibilities, whether it was diagrammed or not. Her current plan—to the extent she had one—consisted of winning her case, or somehow getting a settlement far larger than previously offered.

"But what if I flat-out lose my case after saying 'No' to Lynch, which might be more likely the way things look right now?"

She pondered further. "And, if I say "Yes" to him, what if I never give birth to his daughter? Or what if I just can't handle it?"

She stared at her over-simplified matrix and tried to envision how she might include any of the other variables in a way that would make sense. For the moment, she squeezed the new items into the edges of the paper so she wouldn't forget them.

Nevertheless, by the time she finished her coffee, she realized that she wouldn't be able to engineer any diagram that would be helpful. It was like trying to look through a prism of possible futures, maybe even two prisms, with one representing her lawsuit's outcome. She calmly put her pen back in the glove compartment, then crinkled up her work and stuffed it into her coffee cup for disposal.

"At least this proves one thing," she declared. "As of today, I have no way of knowing *for sure* what I should do. There is no golden pathway."

*****

"Cora is napping," Nanny G whispered, "but maybe not for much longer."

While the two visited in the meantime, Gwen showed Dawn some of Cora's artwork, done with crayons and a coloring book.

"Gwen," Dawn whispered with a full smile, "I really can't thank you enough for watching Cora extra times like today. My life has been upside down since I lost Abel, but I will make it up to you some day."

"Now just shush, Dawn. It's my privilege to watch your sweet child, so maybe I should have to pay *you* back. Besides," Gwen whispered with a wave of her hand, "if I had too much free time, I'd probably be plunking quarters into slot machines like a lot of other widows. So, watching Cora actually saves me money as well."

"No way, Gwen, I'm sure you'd be out dancing and bar-hopping," said Dawn with an elbow nudge.

"Dawn," Gwen probed, "can I ask you something personal?"

"Of course."

"You had two nights out this week with a gentleman and something special today..."

"Yes..."

"Well, if you're actually starting to get out and socialize again, may I ask why you don't look very happy...if that's not being too nosey?"

"Of course you're not, Gwen. I'm constantly stressed about my lawsuit because it's scary and completely out of my control. Everything else is kind of secondary right now. But, meanwhile, you're my absolute savior. I *know* Cora is happy when she's here with you."

FORTY-TWO

Dawn lay awake wondering how desperate things might get if the insurance money was too little, too late or—God forbid—the worst happened.

Then, seeking a momentary diversion, she allowed herself to envision life if she said "yes" to Lynch. The mansion to live in. A prime college education for Cora. The means to live day-to-day and year-to-year in comfort.

She thought about her own relatives. Working people who had to struggle for basic survival: spending their precious free time looking for discounts even on necessities; standing in lines, often with restless children at hand; and the ever-present danger of an unaffordable medical bill.

She feared that she and Cora were headed down that same path, or maybe worse. Was it somehow inevitable, like a curse that was slowly but surely playing out? How did she ever dare think that she could escape such a fate?

Maybe, she speculated, a form of peace could be found—if only for this night—by just accepting the possibility that she and Cora might be doomed, no matter what.

But Lynch's proposal wouldn't even allow her that escape. Having patiently waited for the right moment, it vied again for her weary attention.

"Who's to say I'll ever fall in love again?" she whispered into the night. "I could go on forever looking for another Abel, all the while buried in debt, and with Cora's future on the line."

"Maybe my daughter is reason enough to say 'yes'? I could always pretend to be happy for her sake...Couldn't I?"

She gave into a sudden urge to get out of bed and peek in on her sleeping child. Such a modest little room. A room infused with love, but modest nonetheless.

Not that far away, a mansion-life for her daughter was there for the taking.

As she pondered her sleeping Cora's innocence and vulnerability, she willed back tears.

Ten or twenty years from now, will I be able to look my daughter in the eyes?

FORTY-THREE

Despite Lynch's return to the office on the following Friday afternoon, it seemed like he'd been constantly on the phone or in meetings.

As the day wore on, Dawn began to wonder if his proposition was just a fanciful probe—a rich man's form of entertainment.

Eventually, however, she was summoned to see him.

As she edged uneasily into his office, he rose from his chair to welcome her with a full-on smile.

He closed the office door, and took her hand. "I missed you, Dawn, and I still want you as much as when we were last together. Nothing has changed."

Despite anticipating this very moment, she froze in response to his piercing look of expectation, with no idea what to say.

"Sorry for my abruptness, there," Lynch finally said, as if to end the awkward silence. "I set no deadline, but I hope you are at least thinking about my proposal."

Her eyes met his. She nodded.

"Excellent. I have to remember that your decision could take a little time," he said resignedly. "But, while you're deciding, don't be shy about using the house."

"Mr. Lynch—I mean Lou, since we're alone—you are definitely on my mind, but any serious thought about my future is still tough for me because of all the stress and uncertainty of my lawsuit."

"Well then," he smiled, "it seems quite simple to me. Just settle for whatever you can get and be done with it. Why aggravate yourself when I can give you everything you need? And you'll also avoid reliving those painful experiences..."

With no real question put to her, she remained fretfully silent.

"In fact," Lynch continued, "didn't you say they made an offer...a 'judgment offer'? Whatever it was, why don't you just take it?"

If it were only that simple...

"Everything you're saying, Mr. Lynch—I mean Lou—is already in my thoughts. But so are other things. I really do need more time."

A message on the intercom interrupted the momentary unease: "County Commissioner Roland Briggs is here, sir."

Dawn started to leave, but Lynch signaled her to stay. He looked at her, obviously pondering.

"Dawn, my meeting with the Commissioner actually pertains to that mall project I spoke with you about earlier. Why don't you sit in? Building and selling custom homes is great, but you'll see how I make money in other ways as well."

As he then started toward the door to greet the Commissioner, she could only hope that he didn't expect her to contribute anything to the conversation.

Roland Briggs was a heavyset, middle-aged man, with an old-fashioned crew cut and flushed face, perched

184

above a gray suit that had apparently lost some of its press during the day.

"Commissioner," said Lynch, "this is Dawn Santoro, one of my trusted assistants."

Briggs greeted her with a gregarious smile and a vigorous handshake. "The pleasure's all mine, Dawn. Roland G. Briggs at your service."

After a few seconds of small talk about Lynch's recent trip, Lynch looked at Briggs inquisitively. "So how's our little project going, Rolly?"

"Here it is, Lou," replied Briggs in a clipped voice, as if giving a military report, "and you too, Dawn. The currently pending plan is still going to lose on the initial vote, mainly due to some opposition from the local commissioner's constituents. The developer, of course, will then have to revise and resubmit."

"Exactly as expected," said Lynch, while glancing toward Dawn. "The insiders—like us, of course—know that an initial rejection is routine and we expected it. But," said Lynch, grinning, "the revised plan will essentially be what we expected all along."

Who is "we"?

Briggs gave a quick wink to Lynch then smiled toward Dawn. "My confident prediction is that the local commissioner will still vote no on the eventual re-submission, but the revised plan will ultimately pass because we'll pick up other votes along the way."

Dawn could not help but wonder how Lynch fit into all of this.

185

"Dawn," Lynch spoke as if reading her mind, "the revised mall plan is going to eventually include new access and egress, which would mean a zoning change for certain nearby property areas. It will go from residential zoning—which is relatively low in value—to high value commercial zoning."

Okay...

"It's my role to be quietly buying up parcels, or getting options to purchase in some cases, while they still have residential zoning. Of course, I do that discreetly over time and through different entities that I control. Ultimately, the net result should be some exponential returns," Lynch boasted.

With such a disclosure, she was actually bothered about the scheme rather than impressed. But she quickly decided to fake it, rather than provoke some unknown reaction from him that she wouldn't be ready to handle.

"Wow, Mr. Lynch, sounds like you can't lose."

"My favorite kind of deal," Lynch smugly replied, but he then looked at her with apparent concern.

She sensed possible trouble.

"What's the matter, Dawn," he queried, "didn't I explain it well enough?"

"Oh, you definitely did, sir. I guess I was just wondering what happens to the people you are buying out. Will they lose their homes?"

Good one.

"That's a fair question and I'm glad you asked," said Lynch, as he pulled out a property diagram from a folder on

186

his desk. "These targeted properties were mostly part of a half-baked development that some goof-balls from out-of-state came here and tried a few years ago, with the worst possible market timing. Many of the parcels have only partial construction or none at all."

"Oh, I see," said Dawn.

"Also, keep in mind," interjected Briggs, "that anyone who sells to us is going to get market value under the current zoning, and they on their own wouldn't be able to bring about the zoning modification that we're working on."

"So you see, Dawn," said Lynch with a full-on smile, "our little project is not only brilliant but fair as well. And, as long as we are discrete, nobody should make any kind of fuss."

Lynch flashed another grin toward Briggs, who had a self-satisfied look of his own.

"Okay, now I understand it better," she said with her best attempt at an admiring smile.

Briggs looked at her. "Dawn, keep in mind that this all takes time to play out, so you may be seeing more of me down the road."

She nodded, offering another smile.

Briggs then stood up. "I'll come back when I can stay awhile, but it was a joy meeting you today, little lady. If you ever get tired of working for this slave-driving son-of-a-gun, give me a call. Good assistants are hard to come by."

As if...

She stood up as well to shake his hand. "Thank you, Commissioner, but Mr. Lynch has always been great to work for."

*****

With Briggs gone, Lynch appeared to be basking in pride, knowing that she had personally observed his shrewdness and powerful connections. He smiled at her, while shrugging his shoulders in feigned humility, as if to say that he just couldn't help being rich and successful.

"Dawn," he gloated, "just in case you were wondering, it wasn't Briggs who masterminded this, but I'm sure you can guess who did."

"Oh, you, of course, sir...I mean Lou."

"So then, I hope you come away from this little meeting feeling even more confident about your future with me. I'm very good at what I do. When I spot an attractive opportunity, I always find some way to take advantage of it."

FORTY-FOUR

As she sat on her couch with Cora Friday night, watching the child's favorite animated movie for the umpteenth time, Dawn considered it a small win to have made it to the weekend without Lynch forcing her to decide.

She recalled how the arrival of Commissioner Briggs interrupted what could have become a very uncomfortable moment. Though she felt completely out of place in the short meeting, her mere presence seemed to make Lynch happy—at least for the time being.

While Cora was absorbed in the movie, thumb snugly in mouth, Dawn pondered the upcoming deadline on the offer of judgment and the prospect of Lynch ultimately losing patience with her.

She also pondered why Lynch would say that she should just settle for whatever she could get. If anything, his financial support could give her staying power to at least defend Abel's name, whether she would actually need the insurance money or not.

As another movie character sang, Dawn looked down at her daughter. She now wondered if she would actually be able to keep her daughter happy, even with all that wealth, if her only living parent was not happy. And, with all deference to Julie, Dawn doubted that she could fill a void by cheating—if that would be the right name for it.

But then again, how could she do anywhere near as well for Cora by herself, especially if she didn't manage to win her case? And, after all, who mattered most?

189

After carrying Cora to bed, she came back to the living room, planning to channel-surf for whatever might give her mind a time-out.

Well into a drama she chose by elimination, the telephone rang.

"Dawn, can you talk?"

She tried to match up the vaguely familiar voice.

"It's me, James Claverson. I apologize for calling you on a Friday night, but..."

"James, what a surprise. I wondered if I'd ever hear from you again."

"I don't blame you for saying that, Dawn. I'm sure it hasn't been easy for you."

"You could say that."

Including not even knowing why you ditched me.

"I got a copy of your deposition transcript. Pretty tough questioning..."

She stayed silent, figuring that would say enough about how horrific that day was.

James finally spoke: "I would have objected more than Harold did."

Oh, really?

"Dawn, I simply could not be there. I had no choice."

"And neither did I, apparently..."

"Dawn, this time I've got some good news for you. I lined up a potential new attorney who I think you'd be much better off with—even better off than with me. He's an experienced litigator and he *seemed* to be interested in handling your case for a third of anything he can get *beyond* their current settlement offer. So there's very little downside for you, and I think a much better upside."

"For real, James?"

"That's how I see it. Can you meet him before five p.m. on Monday?"

"I think so, yes."

FORTY-FIVE

She cringed as she drove toward downtown Las Vegas on Monday afternoon. Among the bail bond shops, banks, and government offices was Tilden's building. "Get it together, wimp; someone else's turn today."

She turned down one of the side streets that James referred to as "attorney row". Houses that used to be modest—or not-so-modest—had been converted into freestanding law offices with parking right on the street or in the driveway.

As she waited in the reception room of attorney John Natenberg, whose own house conversion seemed to have spared no expense, she browsed at the seemingly endless array of plaques, certificates, photos, and other memorabilia on the waiting room walls. From what she could tell, he was a transplanted Easterner, probably in his forties, who first worked for the United States Attorneys' office, and then went into private practice where he has apparently been quite successful.

Once invited into Natenberg's surprisingly large private office—which looked like a war room, with its chalkboard, conference table and law books—she was further impressed. But, when she then encountered his predatory eyes—permanently glaring out from under his heavy eyebrows—and his radiating aggressiveness, she was certain that she had gone from a rookie to an experienced pro. The only question was whether she could manage to

discuss her lawsuit with him without appearing to be a
bundle of nerves.

"Yes, Mrs. Santoro, one aspect I liked about your
case," said Natenberg in an effortlessly booming voice, "was
that both sides have gone on record seeking a priority trial
setting. That works for me because, down the pike, my
schedule's going to get fully inundated."

"Uh, good, sir. I'm happy that works."

"It looks like it will, but I'm telling you at the outset
that, if the scheduling doesn't go as expected, you might
have to find another lawyer to finish it. If that's not
satisfactory, then you can hire someone else instead of me."

Is he asking me something?

The eyebrows stared at her. "I'm sorry, Mrs.
Santoro, but are you with me on that?"

"Yes, Mr. Natenberg," she said while nodding
vigorously. "I sure am."

"Okay then, before I make my final decision to jump
in, I want to take a look at your deposition transcript, which
Mr. Claverson will be sending over to me."

"I'm afraid it was pretty bad, sir."

"Excuse me, Mrs. Santoro. Though I do appreciate
your candor, let me be the one to assess that."

"Definitely, sir. You're the attorney, I just..."

"Now then, Mrs. Santoro, did you happen to bring a
copy of your retainer agreement with the Ashe Kramer
firm?"

"A copy of what, sir?"

193

"Obviously, you did not bring one," said Natenberg. "Is it possible that you can remember what they put in for their fees, perhaps hourly or contingent upon settlement?"

Dawn, still baffled, shook her head.

"Maybe a couple pages long? You would have signed it, probably the first or second time you met with them?"

"I'm thinking, but I honestly don't remember signing anything like that, and I sure don't have a copy anywhere. I guess I assumed that it was being handled as a favor for my boss, Mr. Lynch, because he's a big client of theirs."

"And they never even talked about fees with you?"

"No sir. Not that I recall."

He shook his head. "Well, whatever it was or wasn't, I'm just trying to get the full picture here so you know where you stand in the context of any settlement negotiations."

She nodded.

"Did James explain my proposed contingency fee arrangement: a third of anything we recover over and above their last offer made before I entered the case?"

"Yes, and I'm fine with that, sir."

"Okay," Natenberg droned on, "if I sub-in here, we'll see if Ashe Kramer brings up anything about their fees. Meanwhile, you've told me you signed no fee agreement."

Dawn nodded, suppressing her insecurity whether she could be sure about anything these days.

He quickly wrote some notes then looked up again. "Very good, Mrs. Santoro, thanks for coming in. We'll be in touch."

That's it?

"Uh, Mr. Natenberg," she forced herself to speak, "I know you're busy, but can I please bring up one other thing? There will be a deadline coming up in my case to decide on their offer of judgment and I..."

The eyebrows rose. "Yes, James mentioned that, but, frankly, it's not my concern..."

Oh?

"I assume you would have already accepted their offer if you thought it was fair. But, instead, you're here today."

But what if you read my deposition and then decide...?

"I focus my available time on things that are pertinent, Mrs. Santoro. So, that's it for today, but you need to see my assistant on your way out. She's got papers for you to sign."

Before exiting, Dawn hastily reviewed and signed his retainer agreement and also the substitution of counsel form that his assistant said would be filed in court—neither of which had yet been signed by him.

As she walked toward her car, she tried to fend off disappointment. Maybe he's a good lawyer, she thought, but why didn't he ask me questions about the case, especially about the suicide thing? Meanwhile, until he reads the deposition, there was no certainty.

"So what else is new?"

FORTY-SIX

With her Tuesday dragging, while she wondered when she'd hear back from Natenberg, Lynch summoned her into his office. As she headed in to see him, she could only think about how vulnerable she felt.

"Dawn, I hope you don't mind if I get right to the point," Lynch abruptly began.

Uh oh...

"No, I don't mind..."

"I assume you're still thinking my proposal over?"

"Definitely sir...I mean Lou."

"Well, I was thinking, Dawn, that you might be helped if we removed one big unknown. And, by that, I'm talking about yours truly."

"Uh, I'm not sure what you mean, Lou."

"Well, I'm just saying that, so far, in spite of the two very enjoyable dinners we've had together, you still don't really know me outside the office. So you're never really going to feel comfortable about me, no matter how long you take to decide, unless we can do something about that."

She cautiously nodded.

"I mean, if I were you, I'd certainly want to know me better before committing."

"Yes, that could help. No offense, Lou."

And, meanwhile, more time.

"Good, we're in agreement. So, I was thinking that we should start by spending a weekend together..."

Keep calm.

"And it could even be platonic," he hastily added. "At least the first time—if that's what you prefer."

Still the gentleman...but what do I say?

"Uh, as long as you bring it up, Lou, spending a weekend together would make sense."

Upon hearing her acceptance—without even adopting the "platonic" part—Lynch was speechless, his eyes open to their stops as he leered at her.

"But Lou," she finally added, "I have a favor to ask."

"Oh, what's that?" he blurted out, as if fearing he was about to lose what had just been offered to him.

"I can't remember ever being away from Cora for a whole night. And I also don't know how long her nanny would be willing to watch her. I need to work that out by myself first, while I'm at home and on call. Once that works—assuming it will be okay with the nanny—we could at least do most of a weekend."

"Well, I uh..."

"Could we please try it that way," said Dawn in the most appealing voice she could manage. "I mean, if you want me to be *completely* relaxed while we're together..."

"Oh...that's fine," he conceded, "as long as it's moving in that direction."

"I really appreciate it, Lou."

"Okay, Dawn, but let me know if your nanny balks, because I'd be happy to pay for the best professional sitters."

Dawn nodded and smiled. "I will, Lou."

Holy freaking shit!

197

FORTY-SEVEN

That evening, upon hearing her telephone ring, she hastily turned off the stove burner under the grilled-cheese sandwiches.

What now?

"It's me again, Dawn," said the voice of James Claverson. "How did your meeting go with John Natenberg?"

"Oh...Hi James. I'm waiting for a confirmation from him."

"Anything I can help with in the meantime? I'm about to call it a day here."

Despite her efforts to keep James in the "possible jerk" category—at least until Natenberg actually committed—a thought occurred to her. "As a matter of fact, you might help on some decisions I'm facing. Do you have dinner plans, James? I'll treat, as long as it's not gourmet of course."

"No plans as a matter of fact, but no way you're paying."

"Let me clear it with Cora's nanny first and I'll call you right back."

*****

As Dawn partook of her won ton soup at Chan's, she couldn't help but notice James sneaking peeks at a slender young waitress who had a flawless complexion and shapely legs extruding from a black skirt that was just snug enough.

He's definitely into women, for whatever that's worth.

While James occasionally let his eyes roam, Dawn unconsciously directed hers toward his light brown hair. It still basically looked like it did in his office, and some might even say it needed a trim. Apparently, he either hadn't had the free time or he was intentionally pushing the limits on the one part of his appearance that wasn't restricted by the mores of his profession.

When Dawn noticed that the subject pair of legs had temporarily left the dining area, she seized the opportunity. "James, do you mind if I bring up what's on my mind now?"

He smiled. "Of course not. Fire away and I'll do my best."

"Well, it isn't about Natenberg. Whether he takes my case or not, I have something else entirely on my mind. It's probably bonkers, but it's nagging at me."

His lawyer eyes activated.

"I've been offered this fantastic house to live in. For me, it would be an incredible mansion. Plus, I was assured that my daughter and I would have as much money as we'd ever need to be comfortable."

"Uh huh, and the catch is?"

"Yes, there definitely is one. I'd have to be a mistress for my boss, and also give birth to his, quote-unquote, 'daughter he never had'."

"Dawn, you're not pregnant on top of everything else, are you?"

"Oh no," Dawn gasped, while feeling herself blush. "I haven't, uh…slept with a man since my husband died. And I'm still on the pill, anyway."

Why did I say that!

"Oh, that's good…I mean that you're not pregnant," James hastily added, blushing himself.

Oh my God, we're going backwards.

She took a deep breath, then a sip of white wine.

"So," said James, businesslike again, "where do you want to start on this? If you're looking for a lawyer to draw up some type of contract, it's way out of my area and I'm not even sure it would be enforceable."

"No, not that."

"Are you concerned about your mistress status if you were to have a boy instead of a daughter?"

"Well, that's one issue for sure, James, with a fifty-percent chance and all, but..."

"Hey Dawn, not to interrupt, but is this all close to a done deal for you, with the house and everything?"

"Oh no, I wouldn't say that at all. But his offer stays on my mind, mainly out of concern for my daughter's future, and maybe even my future as a last resort, assuming he keeps it open."

"Not sure I follow."

"Well, so far, he lent me some money and he's kept me working for him so I'll have some income. But things could get extremely awkward soon. Meanwhile, the time to accept Aceworth's latest offer of judgment is running."

"Okay, I think I follow you now," said James with a smile. "As far as Aceworth's offer of judgment, they'd probably overlook their own deadline if you don't drag it out too long—as in months, not just days. I think they just want to get rid of your case more than anything. After all, they gave you thirty days instead of the normal ten."

"Okay, that sounds encouraging. But what do I do if Mr. Natenberg declines?"

"There's no point in worrying about him yet. He sounded interested to me, and he's already invested some time with you."

"You think so? I couldn't read him."

"Maybe, by delaying, he's just making you appreciate him more."

She gave a puzzled look.

"Dawn, he's knows how clients can think. If you get the impression that he's overly interested and then he gets a good settlement right away—well, some people would think that he's made too much money for doing too little. I can't say for sure, but it could just be his normal routine."

"I hope so, James."

"Then again, it could also be that he's just real busy and the delay is completely legit for that reason."

"It definitely looked like he was. But how would I ever know any lawyer's *actual* workload?"

"Whoa," James sighed, "I hope that comment wasn't also directed at me."

"No offense intended, it's just my reality. And, even though you became unavailable for my case, you still care what happens, and you at least tried to get me Natenberg."

"Okay, good...So here we are, Dawn. I'm sitting here giving you my full attention."

"True."

"And I'm offering to help..."

She looked down, then back into his eyes. "If you're willing, I sincerely want your opinion on something more basic. So far, I only have my girlfriend's views and I don't currently have a large circle of friends."

"Dawn, I'd be honored if you called me your friend. I think you're one brave lady"

"Oh my gosh," she said, rolling her eyes. "I really don't think so. But, if you say so, then fine, I'm brave."

"So, enough with the preliminaries," said James, "what opinion do you want already?"

"Right," said Dawn, taking another nervous sip of wine while groping for the right the words. "It's this opinion, James: Do you think that I owe it to my daughter to be Mr. Lynch's mistress? That may sound like a stupid question, I know, but he has promised real security for her future, all the comforts in life, and a top-flight education."

"That's the question?"

"For now, yes."

"And you're asking me, even though I've never been a parent?"

"Yes I am," she smiled eagerly, "and keep in mind that I'm just a first-time parent myself."

"Okay then, here's the best way I know to answer..."

She leaned forward intently, both elbows on the table, her head resting upon her fists.

"Based on the short time I've known you, Dawn, I think that good things will come your daughter's way because she has you for a mother. So, basically, I'm saying don't sell yourself short." He smiled. "There, that's my genuine certified opinion, so I hope it helps."

"Thanks James, but..."

Just then, the waitress made her presence known with their entrees.

"Looks delicious," said James, as the waitress positioned their plates.

Despite the presence of the food, Dawn determined to press him further as soon he swallowed his first bite. Her lemon chicken could wait.

"James, would you mind if I asked you a question about your non-lawyer self?"

"Uh, no...I suppose not."

"It could help me to appreciate where you're certified opinion is coming from."

"I think you're being too analytical...as opposed to instinctual," James chuckled, "but if you must..."

"Okay—if this isn't overly prying—when you were growing up, did your family ever face potential financial disaster, which is what I feel like I'm facing right now? I'm guessing most lawyers come from pretty well-off families."

"I'd have to say no. We weren't what I'd call rich. No Porsche for my graduation or anything like that. But I always had pretty much everything I needed. And my parents did cover me through law school, which was pretty hefty."

"Uh huh," said Dawn, trying to process his answer.

"So, did that really help, or are you maybe just checking out what it's like to cross-examine someone else?"

"Yes, it helps," she said defensively. "I mean, there are no simple answers, but the fact that you're listening to me is a comfort. Since Abel died, you're the only man I've talked to who I felt I could completely trust."

"Uh, Dawn, does that even include your boss?"

"Oh...Well, he's done so much to help me so far...but I have to be careful what I say to him. He's on a different level than me, if you know what I mean. No offense to you, James."

"None taken, but you still haven't really answered my question."

"I know. I guess I trust him or I wouldn't even be having this conversation. But it's definitely easier for me to say that I trust you, James."

"Maybe that's because I care about any person who started out with me as their lawyer. But, you in particular, seem to be worthy." He smiled, slightly blushing.

She smiled back.

"Anyways, Dawn, getting an opinion over dinner is completely painless. If there's any other way I can help you, within reason, I'll be happy to do it for you. How's that?"

FORTY-EIGHT

Despite having said good night to James and having parted ways after their dinner, she found herself still thinking about his wide-open offer to help as she fell asleep that night and began dreaming.

While he stood next to her, the two looked out the mistress mansion's scenic window, just as on that earlier evening with Lynch. Fiery sunset hues, interwoven with darkening blues and the towering silhouettes of the mountains to the west, were all breathtaking.

"James," she said, pausing in the tour she was giving him, "wouldn't this be incredible for me and Cora? I mean, if this is what I choose."

He listened, but offered only a half-hearted nod.

Her tour eventually took them outside, and they reached the rear gardens. The sky displayed its early stars in the sunset's aftermath. The secluded pool once again resembled a pristine tropical pond.

"Stay right there," she said, then stepped a few feet away to activate a hidden switch.

Water instantly cascaded into the pool from rocks high above.

"It's all quite nice, Dawn. I agree."

"And get this, James, the pool stays heated and is up to ten feet deep. You could even jump in from the overhang. There are steps going up."

"I'm definitely impressed, Dawn."

She took a step toward him while holding her hands out. "So, now that you've actually seen what this place is like, does that change your opinion at all on what I should do?"

"No denying it's beautiful," he said. "I guess it would just depend on whether you think that you and your daughter would stay happy and content based on living here."

I sure feel good here right now.

"James," she said enthusiastically, "I'm sorry to ask this of a lawyer, but any chance you could get us some drinks? The bar just inside has its own fridge."

"Sure, Dawn," he said as he turned to walk back into the house. "A drink for each of us."

As soon as he was out of sight, she quickly undressed down to the black bikini she had bought with the gift certificate from Lynch.

By the time James returned, she was playfully bobbing in the warm water just outside the splash of the waterfall.

He walked to the side of the pool, eying her all the way.

"Why don't you join me?" she said, while making sensuous strokes with her arms.

He shook his head ever so slightly.

"Don't you want to come in, James? It really is nice and warm."

He just stood there.

Is he this shy?

"James, it's deep here and I don't know how long I can keep treading water," she laughed. "I might soon need rescuing."

He offered a split-second smile, but shook his head again. Then, as if to further confirm that he planned to stay dry, he walked over to the nearest lounge chair and sat down.

"Is it that you can't swim, James?"

Instead of answering, he aimed his eyes back toward the house, obviously wanting her to do the same.

She turned to look.

Oh my God!

Lou Lynch was walking toward what was still his swimming pool, holding a large beach towel with an extra one draped over his shoulder. He was stone-faced.

Holy shit! The one night I come here…

"Dawn" said James, "I met Mr. Lynch in the house and he asked if I was with you."

Her heart raced. She didn't know her next move, except that it would not be to climb out for a towel.

She gulped air and dove into the foam of the waterfall, then savagely stroked to get beneath it.

In seconds, her head pounded and her lungs demanded more oxygen, but she willed against it.

She maneuvered toward the sub-surface bubbles, where her starving lungs tried to take in what they could, but she began choking.

"Cora!" she tried to scream from the edge of oblivion.

"Cora!"

With no breath left, she awakened, still gasping.

Upon gaining her senses, she violently shook her head and then the rest of her body, trying to fully expel the vision. "Oh my God, that seemed so freaking real."

Hearing no sounds from her daughter's room, she laid back and let her consciousness slowly roam until a thought grabbed hold of her. "Judging by how I felt when I saw him coming," she whispered, "maybe it was fucking real enough."

FORTY-NINE

On Friday afternoon, after thinking that she might finish the workweek without being confronted by Lynch about scheduling their weekend together, she was summoned into his office.

"Please close the door," he said with a quick smile.

She did and started walking toward him, reminding herself that their pool encounter was only in a dream.

"Dawn, no need to sit down," he said, with only partial attention toward her. "I wanted to quickly touch base with you because I've got a lot of other things going on this afternoon. Have you tried to make any overnight arrangements yet with that nanny of yours?"

"Uh, not yet, Mr. Lynch."

"It's 'Lou', please..."

"Lou...sorry. It's harder for me to remember that during a workday."

He studied her. "May I ask if you've at least talked with her about it?"

Silence.

Say something...

"Lou, to be honest, I've had some second thoughts about..."

"Second thoughts?"

He laid down papers he'd been working with. "You mean about us spending a weekend together?"

"Well, that idea would still make sense. But I guess I'm talking more about the whole commitment you want

209

from me. I just don't think I could be sure enough right now, no matter how well the weekend went. I guess I was just hoping we could put everything off for a while."

"I see," he replied, noticeably agitated. "Frankly, I'd gotten the impression that we were beyond that stage."

She tried to appear apologetic. "Sorry, Lou, I take all the blame. I guess I'm just more confused than I thought."

He stared at her, grim-faced, as if struggling with an inner conflict. "No, Dawn, I think I deserve the blame. I've been using the wrong approach to help you see what's best for you and your child."

What?

"Uh, I don't think I follow, sir. I mean Lou."

"Well, I've been very patient here while I also gave you unrestricted access to that high-end house."

Oh wow, just get through this.

"Yes, for sure you've been patient, Lou. But I'm just hoping for more time so I can be more certain to make the right decision."

"More time; More time," he echoed.

She nodded meekly.

"While we're on the subject of time, Dawn, what about that deadline you have for accepting that offer in your court case? Isn't that about to run out, or did it already?"

"Not yet, Lou, but it's gotten complicated."

He looked toward the window. "Of course that case is your business. Hell, everything's your business."

She remained quiet, her head and eyes fixed downward, trying not to convey any clue as to his deteriorating prospects with her.

"May I ask, Dawn, if you're in love with someone else?"

That, I can answer.

"No, Lou," she said, looking back up at him and emphatically shaking her head. "I mean, you may ask and no, I am absolutely not in love with anyone...unless you count that I'm still grieving for Abel."

"Well then, are you currently involved with some other man?"

"No, I am not, Lou."

He appeared skeptical. "Well, just in case you are even on the verge of being involved, I think you should ask yourself if he can support you like I could."

"I fully appreciate how generous your offer to me is, Lou, and I assure you that I'm not even dating anyone. I just have a couple friends is all."

"Just a couple friends...Does that include that guy who came here asking for you?"

"Oh, absolutely not, Lou. I haven't seen him at all since that one day at the lake."

"But you do have other friends?"

She nodded.

Obviously perplexed, he studied her again. "This is not easy for me," he said smugly, "but you've forced me to conclude something. What you really need to help you

211

realize what's best for you and your daughter is not more time, but a dose of reality instead."

Oh my God.

"Dawn, I can't have you in my office every day unless I know you're going to be mine. I have no choice but to let you go, effective today. Besides, my business really needs career-minded people and I'm not seeing that kind of motivation in you."

Though she felt on the verge of vomiting, she willed herself not so show it. "I understand, sir," she replied, barely able to get the words out.

"But even though I'm taking these necessary measures," he said with a forced smile, "my offer stays open and I hope you'll eventually give me the right answer."

Before she could think of anything to say, he got up from his chair and walked toward her. "Dawn," he whispered, as he looked into her eyes, "you know that I'm not used to begging for anything. But I stand before you and promise that you'll never regret being mine."

If it were only that simple…

She met his eyes and nodded ever so slightly.

He stared at her, as if trying to use his personal force of his weld his promise into her brain.

She stood still, trying not to provoke him any further.

After more seconds went by, he put his hand out. "By the way, Dawn, do you happen to have the house keys with you today?"

She flinched, suddenly reminded how he looked in her dream, holding the towel for her. "Uh, no sir, they're hidden away in my house."

"That's okay; keep them as a memento. I'll get the locks changed and we'll just see what happens after you've used up all this time you think you need to think things over."

FIFTY

That evening, while one part of her brain attempted to process the afternoon's events, she looked over the newspaper's employment section until the phone rang.

"It's James, your night-time caller."

"Oh my gosh, James, you're fine. What is it?"

"Hey, I'd been out of the office and just now checked my messages. Natenberg's secretary called. He wants to meet with you on Tuesday at two-thirty, but she said he is definitely going to take your case."

"That's *super* good news, James. And anytime on Tuesday works because I'm now unemployed."

"What?"

"Yup. He didn't want to be looking at me every day while I took my time deciding."

"Oh my—just what you did not need. Will you be able to find something else?"

"That's the question. I'll just have to see."

"Good luck, Dawn."

*****

Marginally uplifted by the Natenberg news, she renewed her employment search, looking for something that would help her hang on as long as possible.

She soon found herself thinking about how good she had it while working for Lynch, and why she couldn't fault him for letting her go. After all, he was correct that she

214

wasn't career minded. And she had actually been the first one wanting to part ways—even if it only turned out to be temporary—back when she thought she was going to be flush with life insurance money.

She concluded that there would be nothing wrong with personally thanking him for all he'd done for her and her family. She could easily stop in Tuesday before going to see Natenberg. Lynch would appreciate it, she figured, especially in light of how uncomfortable their last encounter had been.

FIFTY-ONE

After being cleared into Lynch's office, Dawn was surprised to see him walking toward her, looking more ecstatic than she could ever recall seeing him.

"Dawn," he said, still beaming as he took her hands in his, "this definitely calls for a celebration; how about tonight?"

She immediately felt idiotic not to have anticipated this. "Mr. Lynch..."

"Oh, for crying out loud, Dawn," he snickered, "no more of that 'mister' stuff."

"Uh, Lou...," she said, bracing herself, "the truth is that I came in today to thank you for everything you did for me, and for Abel, too. I am so grateful and appreciative, and I just wanted to make sure you knew that."

He froze, as if unable to compute that there was no reason to celebrate.

She forced a smile, desperately trying to lighten the moment. "I'm actually on my way right now to see a new attorney who's agreed to take over my case. Then," she said with an even bigger smile, "I get to play the job-hunting game," as if that would be nothing but fun for her.

He didn't smile back, but continued to appear enraged that she would dare come back just to further disappointment him.

What now?

She quickly leaned forward and kissed him on his cheek.

He endured her gesture, making no effort to reciprocate.

When she then stepped back, he looked at her coldly. "So you're going to see a new attorney...Well, then, I have something to tell you ahead of your meeting."

She backed away another step.

"You say you're grateful, but you don't even know everything I've done for you, like even protecting your life insurance case so you could have a chance to settle."

"Protecting my case?"

"Absolutely—by not telling the other side what Abel told me before his death."

"What he said to *you*?"

"That's what I'm trying to tell you. But now, it seems like you're actually enjoying your lawsuit—with a new attorney and all. That's all you care about instead of us."

"Not really, Mr. Lynch, but I need more money than what they offered me."

"No, you sure as hell don't. I told you I'd take care of you, and I still would if you'd just wise up. You don't have to fight an insurance company for a few extra dollars, unless of course, that just happens to be your life's ambition."

Holy shit.

Feeling flustered and vulnerable, she wanted to just turn around and race out of his building. But she thought better of it.

He studied her while she stood there.

217

She put her fingers up to her lips for fear of saying anything that might further upset him.

"Why can't you just be reasonable," he admonished her, as if she were still an underling.

"I'm sorry. Maybe I'm just not smart enough to realize what's best for me. But I simply can't help the fact that I'm not fully ready to commit to you. I have no choice right now but more job hunting and my lawsuit."

"Fine, then. You'll just have to survive another dose of reality coming your way because my conscience won't let me to withhold what I know any longer."

"Honestly, Mr. Lynch, I'm not trying to fight you, or even upset you in the slightest. But, for the life of me, I have no idea what you're talking about."

"Well then listen up, Dawn," he said, staring angrily into her eyes. "Shortly before your husband had his so-called accident with that truck, he flat-out told me that he was seriously considering suicide. So your new lawyer's going to have to deal with that when it comes out."

She tried not to overreact. "Sir, hearing you tell me this for the first time...I'm sorry, but I can't believe it."

"You can believe it or not, but it's the damn truth. Abel asked me to see him at your house one day when you were out. He told me he had been diagnosed with terminal brain cancer and said he feared a long drawn-out death. Then he had me look at his life insurance policy."

So you say.

"He was concerned about the suicide exclusion, meaning no coverage within the first two years. He asked me

218

if I thought that having a terminal illness would make a difference, and I told him that I didn't think he should take such a chance. That's when I offered my beach house and told him to try to relax and not make any rash decisions."

"Mr. Lynch, I'll never forget that beach trip. Abel didn't act at all like he had that on his mind..."

"Dawn, I know this is hard for you to accept, but just think about what happened after you got back."

"I have thought about it ever since Aceworth brought up the brain cancer. Abel could have been out jogging because he thought it might have helped him live longer, or even get better. He might have read something on that."

"Dawn, when he brought this up to me, he had already accepted that he was terminal. I know because I questioned him. But he told me he was shielding you from it, including his suicide idea."

"I'm sorry, sir, but they'd have to prove all that."

"So you're back to your lawsuit again..."

This is just getting worse.

"Well then, Dawn, you'll just have to wait and see how Aceworth's lawyers use what I tell them."

She started edging toward the door. "I'm sorry, but I need to get to my appointment."

"Go ahead with your pointless priorities," he snapped back, spraying out bits of saliva. "But you're just going to find out that it doesn't matter who your new lawyer is. Keep turning me down and you're going to have to find one hell of a new job to be able to even survive, let alone support that little daughter of yours."

FIFTY-TWO

Still reeling from the Lynch encounter, she stopped at a convenience store on the way to Natenberg's office to get a soft drink and to try calling Claverson. Fortunately, he was available.

"James, I'm on my way to Mr. Natenberg's office, but I have a quick question..."

"Sure..."

"I'm trying not to panic yet, but Mr. Lynch just told me that he was going to tell Aceworth's lawyers that—get this—Abel told him before the accident that he knew he had a terminal condition and was thinking of suicide."

A prolonged silence.

"James, are you still there?"

"I am, Dawn, and that *is* quite significant, assuming Lynch really means it. But I wanted to think it through before opening my mouth."

"Okay..."

"Listen, Dawn, no matter what Lynch might threaten you with, your concern right now is Natenberg. I say don't mention it because, for all you know, his willingness to represent you might be tenuous and Lynch might just be bluffing."

So my former lawyer is telling me to keep a secret from my new one?

"Hey," James added as if trying to change the subject, "how would you feel about trying to stall Lynch?

220

You know, string him along while you keep going after Aceworth?"

"James, it's way beyond that point," replied Dawn, not hiding her unease. "He was already pressuring the heck out of me for a commitment."

"Okay, forget that," said James. "Go ahead and cooperate with Natenberg, but still leave this out, at least for now."

"If you say so, James. And sorry to keep stealing your time like this, but I'm starting to feel a little less brave right now. First, the truck-driver helps Aceworth and now Lynch says he's going to."

"Dawn, back up a second. How did Lynch tell you this? Did he just call you up out of the blue?"

"No. Actually, I stopped in just now to try to personally thank him for all his help."

"Ah yes, no good deed goes unpunished...But he could have just been responding to you on the spot. Talk is cheap, so don't overreact just based on that."

"I hope you're right."

"Try to forget about Lynch for now and stay completely away from him. Maybe he'll forget about you."

"Will do...Can I ask you one more thing?"

"Go ahead..."

"Even if he does stay out of it, he's one more person claiming that Abel committed suicide."

"So it appears..."

"But James, even though I don't believe them, it doesn't seem fair that Aceworth could avoid paying on life insurance based on suicide if doctors were telling Abel that he was going to die anyway."

"That's exactly what I was researching early on..."

So, you did get around to that?

"...and, unfortunately, it looked to me like courts would still just apply contract law—which is what insurance basically is—and I couldn't find an exception. Just leave it at that and try to stay focused and brave."

"If you say so...but I think it's crazy that fairness doesn't matter on contracts."

"I understand Dawn, but as long as you're talking about fairness, give Natenberg a fair chance? He's good, but he'll need your full support."

FIFTY-THREE

Sitting back in his large black leather chair, John Natenberg seemed more relaxed this time. "Mrs. Santoro, you'll be happy to know that I've formally substituted in as your new attorney. So we're a team now."

"Absolutely, sir. Thank you."

He nodded. "Despite my normal reluctance to take over someone else's case, I see a clear trial strategy for this one and it's worth a little time to explain it."

"Yes sir."

"Mrs. Santoro," said Natenberg, pointing his right index finger up, "even though the truck driver's testimony will allow them to *argue* that your husband intentionally ran in front of that truck, a jury would find it counterintuitive to deny a widow the insurance proceeds, given that your husband was going to die anyway. Your husband merely cut short the agony and expense."

"Uh, counterintuitive means unfair, right sir?"

"Close enough, yes...And guess what," he paused for emphasis, "Aceworth's lawyers are going to help us by proving that your husband was terminally ill as part of their defense strategy."

She forced a nod, trying to appear as if she completely followed him.

"Mrs. Santoro, jurors take an oath to apply the law to what they determine to be the facts. But, if one party happens to look more worthy to them, they'll usually try to rationalize in that side's favor."

"I get it now, sir."

"Good, because that's the core of our game plan."

"Okay..."

"So, then," he went on, again pointing his finger, "I believe we could still win even if the jurors really thought, deep down inside, that your husband *was* trying to get himself killed. They wouldn't be rewarding *him*, because *you're* the one who has come before them. And you are innocent and much more in need of the money than Aceworth."

"I just hope you're right, sir...I mean that I'll look that way to the jury."

He looked at her with a knowing smile. "You don't seem to be hiding anything, Mrs. Santoro..."

Ugh.

"...and James Claverson spoke very highly of you."

"Nice of him..."

"We'll make sure that your appearance for trial will be fitting for a widow in need. Excuse me a second."

Natenberg hastily wrote some notes. "And, oh yes," he nodded as he kept writing, "I'm going to ask Judge Borgivan to remove any religious zealots from the jury pool for cause due to the suicide issue."

"That all sounds great sir, but I have to confess that I'm still worried about my deposition answers. He kept twisting things and putting words in my mouth..."

"Mrs. Santoro, any person would have trouble answering confusing questions from a lawyer. The jury will forgive your prior slip-ups as long as you appear to be speaking the truth *to them...*"

"I sure hope so."

"...And, because we go first, we'll see if we can take the wind out of their sails by explaining how they confused you, even before they can get started."

"Oh my God, you can do that?"

Instead of answering her, something in the room caught his attention. Without a word, he got scissors from his desk drawer, got up and walked around his desk.

As she watched him out of the corner of her eye, he stopped at a display table holding a small plant. He trimmed off one leaf that had seen better days and carried it back to his desk where he unceremoniously dropped it into his wastebasket. He then sat back down, meticulously put the scissors away, and looked again at Dawn as if nothing had happened.

She instantly wondered whether James knew enough about this man, but determined not to reveal any concern. She stretched out her arms and yawned, as if what just took place was boringly normal.

"As long as we're talking like this," he resumed, "let me go over some other things that fit in with our trial strategy as I see it."

She nodded eagerly.

"I read their truck driver's statement," he said with a subtle head shake. "Being able to tell, with certainty, that someone *deliberately* ran in front of you while you were busy driving a large truck would seem to be quite an accomplishment, even in broad daylight. Yet, this man, Penner, tried to double cover his ass—excuse me, tried to avoid exposure—by saying it was not even full daylight. Do you see that?"

"Oh, for sure, sir. I was bothered by his story, and you've now clarified why."

Showing no reaction to her praise, he methodically continued. "Penner also has to absolutely admit that he wasn't *expecting* anyone to run in front of his truck..."

"Uh-huh."

"So he first had to overcome his complete surprise. And, by then, the contact was already made or was only a millisecond away. Got it?"

"Totally, sir."

"Meanwhile, every day of the year, somewhere in this country, a person mistakenly runs or even walks in front of a moving vehicle."

"Right; I sure like what you're saying, sir," said Dawn, nodding vigorously. "Hearing this means so much to me, even beyond winning my case."

"For that, I am pleased, Mrs. Santoro. But, what I would like now is for you to tell me where all this gets us in your case?"

She felt a twinge of nerves, afraid of giving the impression that she hadn't listened closely enough, or was just too dense. "Uh, that Penner could be wrong, and that maybe Abel was not trying to get himself killed?"

"That's close enough, Mrs. Santoro."

Whew.

"Aceworth will prove the terminal illness, but that will only get them so far. The jury would still have the freedom to conclude that Aceworth did not sufficiently prove that Mr. Santoro actually *intended* to get hit by Penner's truck."

"Okay..."

"And that's all we need. The jury is then also free to consider your situation, as compared to Aceworth's, and do justice in your favor."

"Wow, it's like a chess game that you're getting ready for way in advance."

"That's what trial work is all about, Mrs. Santoro, if you know what you're doing."

Although elated by his analysis, it made the threat from Lynch seem all the more ominous. She agonized, avoiding eye contact.

Natenberg seemed oblivious. "So, that's it from me for today, Mrs. Santoro. Do you have any questions?"

After a long moment, she determined she had no choice if they were to really be a "team".

"Just one thing, sir—and maybe nothing will even come of it—but Lou Lynch, my former boss who my husband also worked for, said something to me just this morning that you might want to be aware of."

Natenberg wrinkled his eyebrows and gave her a doubtful stare. "You're telling me that your former boss said something about this case?"

"Uh, yes sir...about revealing what he says that Abel told him before the accident."

Natenberg showed more interest, making her instantly queasy. "Continue, please."

It was too late not to. "Mr. Lynch told me that my husband said he didn't want to just wait to die and was thinking of killing himself."

"Lynch said that to you just today?"

"Yes sir. But isn't that just like the other evidence you said the jury could disregard if they wanted to?"

"Well, uh," he smiled nervously, "I don't think Mr. Lynch is even on their witness list. So it could be just loose talk on his part."

Whew.

"But Mrs. Santoro," he added sternly, "if they do add him to their list, we'll talk about it then. It *could* be problematic, depending on exactly what he's going to say."

"Oh."

"Do you think he might have just made it up, Mrs. Santoro? I mean, why would your husband say something like that to anyone?"

"I don't know, sir, and I'm not saying that I even believe Mr. Lynch. But he also said that my husband was asking him about the Aceworth insurance policy."

"I see...And what do you personally think of all that, Mrs. Santoro?"

"Uh, I definitely have my doubts that Abel would have done that. But it's hard for me to read Mr. Lynch. He's very sophisticated."

Natenberg stared blankly at Dawn for a little too long.

228

She waited.

He got up and walked toward the door. "Okay, Mrs. Santoro, thank you for coming in today and for that last information...I wish I'd known about it before I substituted in..."

She instantly felt sick.

"...but you're telling me you didn't know then either."

"Only got it today, sir," she quickly replied while shuffling toward the door, feeling like a family mutt being put outside for misbehavior.

"We'll be in touch, Mrs. Santoro."

Oh my God...

FIFTY-FOUR

She headed straight from Natenberg's office to a downtown employment agency spotted on her drive in. She was already dressed for it and, despite being upset at herself, now was as good a time as any.

Inside, she encountered well-worn office furnishings quite appropriate for the currently unemployed. According to the sign-in sheet, dozens had come before her that day. And a few of them seemed to be patiently waiting ahead of her. Feeling down, she figured that one of them would probably take the only job that would have been right for her—if it ever existed in the first place.

The receptionist, without looking up, handed her a clipboard with an application form. Cheap pens with the agency's logo were abundant.

She sat in one of the few empty chairs and started inserting her personal information until she came to a line asking for her most recent employment.

Great reference; he wants me desperate.

Though she felt stupid for not anticipating this, she resisted the urge to just walk out.

Geez Louise, just put him down. I'm doing exactly what he told me to do.

With her application completed, she took a seat again and waited. She thought about how things had come full circle since Abel died. First was the loan application in a pawn shop. Then she was told she was going to receive a half-million dollar insurance payoff, which was followed by a meeting with Karen Dunlap, who made her feel so valued.

Now felt almost like she did when she walked into that pawn shop.

When her name was finally called, she rose quickly, only to feel dizzy before she could take her first step.

Whoa, forgot to eat today. Nothing like a face-plant to start off an interview.

Fortunately, the assigned counselor did not yet get there to greet her until after Dawn steadied herself.

"Rosemary", as she introduced herself, was matronly looking, seemingly about fifty, with an immense silver crucifix on her necklace.

As Dawn followed her back into the cubicles, Rosemary trudged along wearily like someone who had already put in more than a full day's work.

While Rosemary reviewed the application, Dawn perused the cubicle, trying to get a feel for who she was dealing with. Numerous snapshots indicated that she was probably a grandmother with a sizable extended family.

"Dawn, we're informal here and I try to be efficient. From what I see, it looks like I will have to categorize you as 'unskilled', or am I missing something?"

"Honestly, I wouldn't know. I've mostly been a mother and housewife except that, during the past few months, I was basically a trainee for a real estate company—a paid trainee."

"And what happened with that?"

"Oh boy."

"You can tell me."

"Rosemary, can we just say that it was a 'personality conflict' with the boss? It's messy."

"I see..." said Rosemary as she looked Dawn over. "An older male boss, perhaps?"

"Yes...but I never really wanted to work in real estate anyway."

Rosemary gave another long inquisitive look, inviting further explanation, but Dawn merely offered a half-smile and a shrug.

"Okay then," said Rosemary, obviously less than happy with Dawn's secrecy. "We'll keep your application, but don't expect anything right away."

"I understand," said Dawn, as she started to rise from her chair. "I owed it to my daughter and myself to at least give it a try."

"You're not married?"

"Not any more. You're looking at a widow with no job and not much left in savings."

Rosemary motioned for Dawn to sit back down. She then re-examined the application.

Dawn waited.

Rosemary finally put down the paper and eyed Dawn as if she were a doctor trying to diagnose some mysterious malady. "I'm going to try to help you, with your being a widow and all."

"I appreciate whatever you can do, Rosemary. Sorry that I don't have much going for me."

"Maybe you do. You put down that you've had interests in drama and dance."

"I took classes, but I haven't yet had a job in those fields," said Dawn, more than ready for any leads.

"All right then, but this is going to be off the record, not an official recommendation by my agency."

"Yes, I understand."

So what the heck is it?

"Mrs. Santoro, you're still young and attractive, and this is Las Vegas, after all. Would you consider putting your dancing to use if the pay were really good?"

Like something R-rated?

As Rosemary waited for a response, Dawn couldn't help imagining that the eyes of Rosemary's crucifix—or at least where the eyes would be—were also interested in her answer.

"Uh, thanks Rosemary, but, if you're talking about being an exotic dancer—or something like that—just so you know, I'm not quite *that* desperate."

"Hun, I didn't know if you'd even considered it."

"Things have been happening to me so fast, but no, I hadn't so far."

"Dawn, can I tell you something? I've got a niece whose no-good husband left her and she supports two children by working as a stripper in one of the clubs here. It was either that or God knows what for her and her kids."

Fine, but how did Jesus not at least look up on that one?

"I never could have put her in a job that came close to paying what she makes. It's just a different economy here."

"Rosemary, no matter what those dancers make, I'm not so sure I even have the body for it—if you know what I mean." She stood up from her chair and held her arms out to reveal her figure, knowing that she was on the lean side as opposed to voluptuous.

"Excuse the heck out of me, Dawn, but you're probably fine just as you are. But any girl who lacks the confidence can get that taken care of. Even women who aren't in entertainment get it done."

"I'm sorry. Get what done?"

Rosemary leaned forward and whispered, "get their breasts enlarged, if that's what's concerning you."

"Oh."

"In fact, I've been told that most dancers who've had it done don't even feel like they're revealing themselves. It's just what the doc put in, not them."

"I appreciate your concern, Rosemary, but I came to Las Vegas as a regular person, with a husband, just like I could be living anywhere. And, even though he's gone now, I'm not yet ready to get anything put in or take anything off in order to make a living."

"That's your choice, Dawn. But, just for the record, Las Vegas didn't invent showgirls or exotic dancing. They just perfected it here."

*****

As Dawn brought Cora into the house, along with some essential groceries and a newspaper, she wondered if anything would come from the employment agency, especially given her "unskilled" classification. That is, if Rosemary didn't just give up on her completely for being stubborn.

The message light on the telephone answering machine caught her eye.

By eerie coincidence, the first voice was Rosemary's, saying she was "excited to have found an opening as an office assistant in a real estate company, starting at minimum wage but with long-term prospects".

"Incredible," Dawn murmured, careful not to use a bad word in front of Cora. "What would they have found for me if I'd actually asked for that?"

She turned to her daughter. "Sweety-kid, after I look at the help-wanteds, we'll watch a TV show together."

Cora's eyes lit up as she smiled.

Dawn returned to the answering machine and started the second message. On hearing Lynch's voice, she froze.

"Dawn, I'm calling because I don't think you realize what a mistake you're making. I will soon be meeting with the insurance company's attorney. Call me by tomorrow."

Though even less willing to call Lynch than to call about the real estate job, the thought that he was actually going to help Aceworth was gut-wrenching.

She pushed the erase button.

FIFTY-FIVE

Two weeks later, she rested at home after her early shift as a sales associate at a membership gym. As a former dance student, she thought she'd feel much more comfortable talking about aerobics and even muscle-toning machines than she ever did working for Lynch.

Although she appreciated the availability of on-site child care, and had been told she could make good money selling memberships based on her "tight" looks, it wasn't going well for anyone on her shift.

"Just hang in there," said another single mother who'd also been hurting for prospects. "It's bound to pick up. And even our shift should eventually do well when the New Year's resolution crowd comes in."

But New Year's was still a long way off and the fitness club had turned out to have its own issues. A co-worker had commented that most new sign-ups didn't last more than a few weeks. She'd also heard it said that, "if they all stuck with it, we'd need a gym ten times bigger."

She put down the newspaper's employment section, disappointed again. Was it really asking too much, she wondered, to have a job where you felt like you were doing good and helping people?

The thought of having her own drama and dance studio tried to creep back in, but she resisted. "As if, dumb-dumb...and ask Lynch for the start-up money?"

Within seconds of the mere thought of Lynch, the telephone rang.

"No way", she growled, her body instantly tense.

"Hello, Mrs. Santoro," said John Natenberg.

"Oh...Hello sir."

"Got a free moment?"

As if anything's more important...

"Of course."

"We received a new disclosure from Aceworth's lawyers today. Unfortunately, Mrs. Santoro, it's worse than you indicated. Mr. Louis Lynch has not only been put on their witness list, he's already signed a sworn statement for them..."

I did sense him!

"...And, according to Lynch's statement, Abel Santoro not only discussed committing suicide with him—as you related to me—but the statement also has Abel saying that you personally approved the idea."

His words pummeled her already queasy stomach. It was too outrageous to respond.

"Dawn, you don't have to comment right now, but you do have to understand something. If he gave this testimony at trial, it could undermine your innocence, especially when Tilden ties it into some of your deposition answers."

"But Mr. Natenberg," she implored, "that *has* to be a lie. And it makes me think that he's lying about everything. Abel didn't even tell me he was dying, so how could I have discussed suicide with him?"

"Uh, personally, Mrs. Santoro, I accept your denial. But, as far as calling Lynch a liar, just remember that his statement is about what he claims that Abel said to him

237

privately...and, most unfortunately, your husband is not around to deny it."

She was now dumbfounded as well as nauseous.

"In any event, Mrs. Santoro, the problem is that he's a neutral witness and we have to assume that he would testify. So I need to meet with you again to go over his entire statement. How's tomorrow for you?"

"Uh, would four be okay? I'm working now and I have to drop off my daughter."

"Come down whenever you can and I'll work you in. Good evening, Mrs. Santoro."

She stared at the telephone receiver before hanging it up, as if hoping it would turn into something else and make the call just a bad dream.

She went back to the living room couch, sat down and put her head in her hands.

Knowing that Natenberg might now have doubts about her—doubts she might be powerless to overcome—she started to question herself. She wondered if she could still appear innocent in court with both Lynch and Tilden against her. She also wondered if she could even sit still in court listening to Lynch saying such things without becoming so angry that the jury might question her sanity.

FIFTY-SIX

Natenberg's office was now beyond cluttered, with anatomical models and other medical paraphernalia intermingled among files and books that seemed to be just strewn around. She could barely see the tip of the plant that he had so meticulously manicured during her last appointment.

She took a seat, sensing that he was more than ready to begin.

"Mrs. Santoro, as you can surmise, I now have big concerns about your case. Here's a copy of Aceworth's supplemental disclosures that includes Lynch's sworn statement. It's quite wordy, but I want you to read all of it. I marked the starting page for you."

She flipped to the tabbed page and carefully began.

"As I told you on the phone," said Natenberg only seconds later, breaking her concentration, "Lynch swears right there that your husband met with him and basically said that he was terminal, that he faced a slow death, and that his idea was to commit suicide and make it look like an accident so that his wife would get double the life insurance."

"He says all that?" Dawn responded, racing ahead in search of such wording.

"Then", Natenberg continued, oblivious to her efforts, "Lynch says that your husband asked for his opinion in case the insurance company challenged the accident. He says that he told Abel Santoro that he could not provide any guidance on legalities, but told him that he'd try to help the

239

surviving spouse no matter how or when Mr. Santoro might happen to pass away."

"Oh my," mumbled Dawn, still searching.

"Lynch then says that he gave you a job to help keep his promise."

Sensing that Natenberg now wanted eye contact, she looked up from her hopeless attempt to read.

"If that weren't enough, Mrs. Santoro," added Natenberg in his full lawyerly voice, "the next part bothers me the most. According to Lynch, Abel Santoro said that you, quote, 'had approved his suicide idea because you thought it was making the best out of a nightmare with a chance for a double insurance payment.'"

Holy shit!

Natenberg put down the statement, looking at her as if he had handed her a coat made of guilt to try on for a fit. "That could be poison for our case," he said gruffly, as if to imply outrage if she'd been wasting his time.

"Uh, sir, can I say something now?"

"That's why you're here today, Mrs. Santoro."

"Well, would it be important that this written statement is different from what Mr. Lynch personally told me?"

"It's what?"

"Different. When he recently spoke to me, he never even hinted that I knew that any of this had been going on. He was actually trying to scare me with things he said that I did *not* know."

Natenberg looked sternly at her.

240

She stared back.

A long moment passed, but she held her ground.

He took a deep breath and noisily exhaled. He then picked up Lynch's statement with a look of disdain. "If your memory is right, Mrs. Santoro, then Lynch is flat-out lying...or he's at least embellishing—no doubt at the urging of their attorneys to try to implicate you."

"I know I'm right, sir. I don't think I could forget his words if I wanted to."

Natenberg put the papers back down and folded his hands together on his desk. He scrutinized her. "Can you shed any more light on this Lynch character?"

"Yes sir," she replied.

Oh my God, where do I start?

"Go ahead, Mrs. Santoro."

"Sir, after Abel died, Mr. Lynch was a godsend to me and a perfect gentleman. He'd already given me a job, and he paid me well considering my qualifications and how simple the work was."

She looked pointedly at Natenberg to confirm that she hadn't lost him already. "He even encouraged me to work on company time toward getting a sales license. But I honestly had no interest in a real estate career. I've always wanted to work with children, sir..."

"Never mind that for now, what next with Lynch?"

"Well, he also lent me ten-thousand dollars on my house and referred me to my first lawyers to help with my insurance claim."

"Okay, but I take it something happened?"

"He gradually got more forward with me until he eventually asked me to be his mistress and have his child. He offered me this beautiful custom house to live in and he kept pushing all this on me. It was a little tempting when I was really down, especially for the sake of my daughter's future and the opportunities he said she'd get. But I never said 'yes', and he eventually got impatient."

Natenberg's eyes widened.

"That's when the real trouble started, sir. When I didn't give into him, he terminated me. He said I was too much of a distraction to have around the office every day, but that he still hoped I would give into him after I had a taste of reality."

Natenberg continued listening intently.

"Then, sir, when I stopped by his office on my way to see you—just to thank him for all he had done for me and Abel—that's when he first said that he knew things about Abel's death."

"So you're basically saying that he fired you, a recently widowed mother of a small child, because you wouldn't be his mistress?"

"Absolutely, sir."

Natenberg made notes.

"His conduct sounds actionable to me. If I had the time, I'd explore that further with you, but you already know that I can't. You might want to consult a plaintiff's employment attorney..."

Though not thrilled with the notion of a second lawsuit, she saw a chance to further elaborate. "Sir, he also

242

tried to convince me to just forget about this lawsuit because he'd provide me and my daughter with everything we needed anyway."

"So was he keeping tabs on your lawsuit all along?"

"Very much so...And now he's saying my life insurance claim is defective, as if his urging me to settle had nothing to do with him wanting me to be totally dependent on him."

"You may be onto something there: at least a theoretical motive for him to give a false statement in this case."

"Because he still hadn't given up on getting me..."

Natenberg nodded for a couple seconds, but then shook his head as if aggravated for allowing the discussion to drift out of his control. "Right now, we've got to consider *our* downside with this new development. Let me think a minute."

He removed his glasses and rubbed his eyes. He looked down, running a hand through his dark hair, then looked again at Lynch's statement. "I'd sure like to depose this Mr. Lynch..."

"So, uh, can't you just go ahead and do that, sir?"

"I wish it were that easy, Mrs. Santoro, but they're being cute. They say they just learned of this evidence, knowing that the limited discovery schedule cuts off our right to take his deposition. So I'd have to go to court for special permission. If I do that, the defense could then ask for discovery to be completely reopened. You'd be talking about a six to twelve month trial delay."

"Oh my."

He put his glasses back on and gave her a long thoughtful look. He then leaned back in his chair, maneuvering a black pen between his fingers, while his eyes remained locked on hers. "That's it, Mrs. Santoro. We have serious decisions to make. Would you be open to settlement if I could get you something above their last offer?"

And if I say no?

"Sir, in no way would I try to tell you how to do your job, but could we ask the judge not to allow Lynch to testify because they came up with him too late?"

"That's a very astute question, but the more you litigate, the more you'll learn how much defense attorneys get away with. It just goes with the territory. So, for us to even bring such a motion could likely result in a trial postponement so fast, you'd wonder what hit you."

She let his answer stand, hoping that he wouldn't return to his settlement question.

He looked at her, obviously pondering. "Listen, Mrs. Santoro," he said in a subdued tone as if momentarily disinclined to engage in a battle of wills with a beleaguered widow, "you don't have to decide anything right now, and neither do I. If I decide to opt out as a result of this new evidence, I would first *try* to get you an acceptable settlement. So, how about we just call it a day for now?"

Though his words allowed for hope, she feared that he just didn't want to say it to her face. "I'm all for calling it a day, sir, but I sure hope you stay on as my lawyer."

"Thank you for your confidence, Mrs. Santoro."

FIFTY-SEVEN

She left Natenberg's office feeling more vulnerable than ever, as she drove south toward Charleston Boulevard.

"I've tried my hardest," she murmured, "but maybe Aceworth wins no matter what I do."

Just ahead, she saw a tree-lined parking lot offering a shady escape from the Las Vegas sun, and she eased into the entrance.

With the chance to sit quietly and think, it immediately occurred to her that it was a mistake to let Natenberg think that she would only accept a quick trial. She needed *him* more than anything else.

She thought about driving back to his office, still only blocks away. "I could tell him that I'll find some way to survive, no matter how long it takes to get my trial."

She tried to picture how he'd react if she went right back and insisted upon seeing him. If she were permitted into his office again, which was no sure thing, it was hard to envision the discussion going well. He might even start questioning her sanity and really seal her fate with him.

The urge to return to Natenberg's office started to fade out. "Get real," she muttered, "Lynch made my case more difficult and Natenberg's got other work that means a lot more to him."

She then thought about Lynch. Right now, he might not even be thinking about her, let alone what could happen to her and her child. Either she'd come back to him in desperation or she wouldn't.

She grew angry, but not just at herself for botching the Natenberg meeting. Fate itself was the culprit. A series of random and seemingly bizarre events had teamed up to seriously threaten the only future she and her child had: Abel getting cancer and then getting hit by Penner's truck; water-skier Joe coming to her workplace on a Saturday and talking to Lynch; Lynch determining that she should be his mistress; losing James as her attorney; Natenberg getting too busy; and whatever else had contributed to her mess.

She took a deep breath and shook her head. "All true, but so what! I have no choice but to keep trying, whether it looks hopeless or not."

FIFTY-EIGHT

Having Saturday off from her still-disappointing job at the gym, and with Cora playing in her bedroom, Dawn sat alone trying to relax, up until the doorbell rang.

The regular long-haired mailman was visible through the window, but it seemed strange that he held no package to deliver.

"Mrs. Santoro?"

"Yes."

"I need you to sign for certified mail, please," he said as he handed her a thick envelope, receipt card and pen.

"Oh my," she said as she signed the green card. "What in the heck is *this* going to be about?"

She tore into the contents to see that the first page was entitled "Notice of Default and Acceleration of Note." Based on the monetary amount, she quickly surmised that it was for the home loan that Lynch got her. Her heart started pounding, but she noticed that the mailman hadn't budged.

"I've got two of those for you today, Mrs. Santoro."

"Oh! Sorry; this is so unusual for me."

"Not rushing you at all, ma'am."

She signed the second green card, expecting that it would probably contain more trouble of some kind.

"Good-day now," he said as he handed over the residual items, then turned to be on his way.

Looking quickly at the second certified letter, and seeing that it came from James Claverson's firm, she sighed in relief as she headed back into the house.

"Probably just some lawyer-talk saying they're out of the case...as if I didn't know."

She went back to the first certified envelope, which had many pages of small print, and some things in bold. It referenced her home address and stated in part: "Pursuant to the terms of the Note, the principal loan balance is now accelerated and due...Foreclosure proceedings will be initiated if the entire balance is not paid within thirty days."

"You damn well know I can't pay this, Mr. Lynch...Oh, excuse me, you damn well know, *Lou*."

She threw the contents onto the carpet.

Still reeling, she opened the envelope from Ashe, Kramer and King. Its title exploded out at her: "Statement of Amounts Due for Legal Fees and Expenses."

She skimmed through the pages of details. By the entries and dates, it appeared to be a record of work by James Claverson and Harold Dibbs, all billed at $180.00 per hour. There were additional entries for court costs, couriers, copying at twenty-five cents per page, and other expenses. Her deposition transcript alone was almost a thousand.

With her initial shock supplanted by outrage, she hunted for the total balance owed until she found it on the last page in bold print: $18,432.69.

Just below that figure was more verbiage: *NOTICE: A COLLECTION ACTION MAY BE BROUGHT IF THE BALANCE DUE IS NOT PAID IN FULL WITHIN THIRTY DAYS.*

"Of course," she mumbled. "I'll just take it out of the same pot of money I use to pay off good old Lou's loan. And thank you, James, for not warning me that this would happen if I switched lawyers, especially since you were the one who caused the switch."

She threw the statement in the general direction of the other papers, not caring if the two toxic sets intermingled.

She looked around her living room and shook her head. She thought about how her house had been a place of happiness not long ago. The center of her life. Now, the question seemed to be how much time she and Cora still had left to even live in it.

She felt an urge to just bolt out and hit the road, like a tourist leaving Las Vegas after being fleeced by the casinos. But she instead coaxed herself not to panic.

Gradually, she felt an inner toughness somehow taking hold, almost as if she were a wild feline creature that had finally been cornered and had no choice but to fight. She figured it was the same survival mode that her mother must have had to keep going in the most difficult times.

"Now all I need is for Natenberg to confirm that he's dropping me," she scoffed, "then I'll know for sure that it can't get any worse."

Her thought of Natenberg, however, made her wonder how long before she would hear from him.

"Screw him, if he dumps me. I'll find someone else if I have to knock on every one of those downtown doors...Tucson, you're just going to have to wait until I've had it out all the way with this town."

She reached out her arms in a *bring-it-on* challenge to the outside world, offering her entire self—all one hundred twenty pounds of single mother.

Then, with a sly half-smile she recalled Rosemary's advice to her. "Maybe she didn't know jack about me," said Dawn with a shake of her head, "but she might have been right-on as to what I should do. Even Mr. Lynch said I'm going to need one hell of a new job. And, tonight's a Saturday night, so why wait."

FIFTY-NINE

She motored east on Sahara Avenue, then turned right onto Industrial Boulevard, where multiple adult establishments were within easy range of the major casinos. Beyond nervous, she worried, above all, that her chosen outfit— which ended up being her tightest fashion jeans, black high heels and a red halter top—would somehow be an embarrassment.

"God, I feel strange," she had mumbled when trying to put together what she hoped would be the right look for a first impression.

Her outfit had been sexy enough for Nanny G to ask if she had a hot date. The path of least resistance was to just smile and wink, which produced a giggle from Gwen. But Dawn knew that the only "dates" on her mind were payment deadlines.

Upon scanning the lurid signs and gaudy lights of the adult clubs, with no idea what might even be asked of her this evening—or what she'd actually be capable of doing—she also started worrying that she lacked the right body or wasn't young enough.

"I sure hope you know what you're talking about, Rosemary," she murmured, "or I'll look like a total fool and maybe even get laughed at."

She cautiously pulled into the parking lot of the Flashery—the first so-called "Gentleman's Club" she saw that didn't look too foreboding from the outside.

251

She turned off the ignition but remained anxiously in her car, slinking down to avoid attention while trying to muster her courage.

So how freaking crazy is this?

After minutes of wasted time, she told herself that she should either be brave or just go home.

She forced herself to exit her car and walk into the entrance, making sure that she entered alone, which she figured would minimize the risk of embarrassment.

She was mildly encouraged by how easily she got into the place. Two large men standing inside the door gave her nods and guarded smiles as if thinking she was someone they should already know.

She stepped further inside to better view the operation, and maybe even get a clue as to what might later be expected of her.

A dancer was performing on a small stage, accompanied by a sassy R&B song from a few years back. At the moment, the girl had on a tiny bikini-top, a G-string bottom, sheer mesh from her neck to her butt and stiletto heels. She sensuously rotated her hips a foot away from two men who had secured front row seats. Although her movements were not to the music, the men didn't seem to care, as they both had cash at the ready for her.

Dawn saw enough in these first few seconds to realize it was not what she had expected. There was supposed to be an energetic audience of men, cheering and whistling like in a movie scene. By contrast, this seemed bleary. The men exuded loneliness and defeat, resigning themselves to being teased and titillated for a price, rather than pursuing women in the real world.

Dawn wondered if it was still too early, or if it was an off-night for some reason. She turned away from the stage and, trying to appear nonchalant, scouted around for the manager. But, with no quick luck in her search, she soon started feeling self-conscious.

For lack of a better idea, she headed back to the entryway to ask the bouncers, who both seemed to have plenty of time on their hands.

She chose the less-barbaric looking one, who was also shorter, though he still towered over her. "Excuse me, sir, I'm looking for the manager, please."

The man leaned his thick neck and broad shoulders down toward Dawn until his face was only inches from hers. "Tony don't like being bothered with just anything—what the fuck you want to see him for?"

She forced a smile, wary of showing any disrespect, while trying not to become nauseous from the man's onion breath. "About applying to dance here?" she asked.

"Just as I thought," he barked back in another foul stream. "You're damn lucky I didn't bother Tony. That shit goes down on Wednesday nights. This is fuckin' Saturday. Have your ass here on Wednesday at seven, as in PM, sweet-cakes. That is, if they're hiring, which Tony will decide at that fucking point in time. Comprende?"

She nodded, trying to stay composed, but the man had already switched from reprimanding her to brazenly examining the front of her from the chest down, with a sadistic looking grin.

Though startled by his leering, she avoided making any sudden move that might somehow violate the culture of this world she had chosen to enter.

One-thousand one. One-thousand two…

"What the fuck is this?" said the bouncer. "You think you're going to dance here wearing a goddamn wedding ring?"

Despite initially keeping the ring on as a tribute to Abel, she realized that she just never got around to removing it, having no desire yet to be viewed as single anyway. "Uh, no...I, uh..."

"If your hubby comes in here pissed because you're tight with some customer, it's going to be a bad scene."

"Yeah," the other bouncer jumped in, "bad for your fuckin' husband if he tried to start any trouble. And all because of you."

"No, sir, I'm not married anymore."

"Well then take off the goddam ring-a-ding if you want to fuckin' dance. And I mean before you come in these doors again, not as part of your fucking act," said the first bouncer as he elbowed the other and broke into laughter.

In the bizarreness of the moment, Dawn determined not to let them know of her widowed status, having no idea how the two men would react. She instead tried changing the subject. "For sure, I'll leave my ring at home. And, just so you know, I do have a background in dance."

As soon as her words were out, however, she realized it was a blunder.

"So, *you* have a *background*, do you?" the taller man replied. He then stepped next to her and leaned his head around to shamelessly examine her backside.

She remained still and looked blankly ahead.

One-thousand one. One-thousand two...Relax, you're still dressed.

"I tell you what," the man said, after bringing his eyes back to within inches of her face. "Come by this Wednesday night and Trevor and I will check out that background of yours, and everything else ya got, even if Tony ain't hiring." The man roared again while playfully jabbing back at Trevor.

Dawn gave a fake smile, as if she actually enjoyed their humor. But, from what she could sense, it seemed to be their last round of fun with her for now. It was her chance to slink out of the place.

On her way back to her car, she thought again about Rosemary. "What the heck; at least nobody told me I was too old or unattractive...But, all the same, that's enough of this for tonight."

SIXTY

Early Sunday morning, she put her barely awake daughter into her stroller. Upon locking the front door, she couldn't help but wonder how many more times she would be able to open the door and enter her home.

On her way along the tree-lined sidewalk, in the cool early morning air, it was comfortably quiet, with only sparse traffic. She took advantage and sang softly to her child.

By the time they arrived at her destination, Cora had fallen back asleep. With no immediate time pressure, Dawn looked around and studied the area.

"He ran into the street just about here," she whispered. "But, it was probably darker than this, and whatever sun there was would have been rising from behind him..."

After confirming that Cora was still asleep, recollections came forth. There was the getaway weekend on the coast, then the jogging he had just taken up, which also seemed to come out of nowhere.

"If they are right, then it would only show how brave Abel was."

"But, just a minute," she said, as she studied the area. "With all these shadows here, Mr. Natenberg had a good point: How could that truck driver know Abel's intentions if he could barely see him in the first place?"

Seeing no people or traffic around, she pushed the stroller into a safe spot in a nearby grassy alcove. She then turned and walked the few steps needed to reach the approximate collision spot in the street that now blended seamlessly into the asphalt.

She checked again that she was alone and, with her chin up and shoulders back, raised a clenched fist as she shouted into the air: "I will not sell you out, Abel."

As she then walked back to Cora, however, she saw a lady running with her dog on a leash. She had appeared out of nowhere and was quickly approaching. Judging by her gliding strides and competition outfit, she was a serious runner.

The lady stopped nearby, her muscular legs still moving in place, and looked at Dawn. "Is everything okay?"

"Oh yes, thanks," uttered Dawn, once over her initial surprise. "This spot just brought back some emotions."

"Oh, I see." The lady smiled and nodded, while reaching down to scratch her dog's head. "So everything is all right then?"

"Yes, we're fine, but sorry I made you stop."

"Don't be, I have no deadlines," said the lady, with a continuing look of concern as if inviting more from Dawn.

If only you could really help us.

After silent seconds passed, the lady seemed to conclude that she had probed enough. "Okay then," she said, as she resumed her run, swinging well wide of Dawn and Cora. "Enjoy this beautiful day."

Thanks, runner-lady, but it's our tomorrows that I fear.

SIXTY-ONE

Later that Sunday afternoon, while Cora napped, Dawn sat quietly, trying to gather her nerve for the coming week. But her house no longer comforted her as much. The very things she had loved most about it, Abel's woodwork and all the happy memories, taunted her. It was as if the house itself knew that she was losing control over it.

Despite her grim thoughts, she tried to resist despair, knowing that, in the days and weeks to come, she might have to think fast at her peril.

When Julie answered the phone on the first ring, Dawn took that alone as a small victory. That Julie didn't sound preoccupied was all the better.

"Jewels, how would you like to sell my house?"

"What in the heck did you just say?"

"It looks like I have no choice; sell it or lose it anyway."

"Hey, slow down to Mach speed please. I've been wondering about you, and now this?"

"Everything's going against me. They're trying to foreclose and I don't see how I can do anything about it. Meanwhile, I'm barely making anything at my new job. I'm so desperate, Jewels, that you, especially, would get a kick out of one job I looked into."

"That I want to hear, but didn't you have a decent paying job working for Lou Lynch...and wasn't he crazy about you?"

"Long story, and it isn't even over with."

"Okay, let's slow down again. You are basically correct that a quick sale could avoid foreclosure, because foreclosures take time. So, unless you delayed for weeks after the first notice, you've got some breathing room."

"No, it's pretty recent."

"All right. Next, if you're really serious about selling, then I need to come over and get all the listing info. And, for you, I'm available right now."

"Then come right over and you'll hear the whole twisted mess."

*****

On Julie's entry, Dawn held her arms out to embrace her friend and let her know she was wide open to any support she could get.

Julie put down her leather portfolio and hugged Dawn. "Hey, just relax, okay? We'll find a way to sort this out."

Dawn forced a weak smile.

"I promise we'll deal with it, Dawnie. I even keep a shit-shovel in my car trunk. But first, got anything to drink?"

Dawn couldn't help but chuckle. "Wine okay?"

"You know me."

The two sat on the sofa, glasses of Chardonnay at the ready.

"Okay," said Julie, "let's start with the slightly lesser emergency: you're not making much at your current job?"

"I've got the worst shift at a fitness club. It's usually dead and I don't really like selling memberships anyway."

"Okay. Could I ask why you quit your job with Lynch? I'm sure you had your reasons..."

"Uh, excuse me. Try asking why I was let go, as in 'you're fired'."

"Oh my God...because you rejected his mistress offer, as in 'nobody says no to me'?"

"You could say that."

"Wow."

"As you'll see, I didn't bring any of this on myself."

"I bet I could find you something salaried in the real estate biz, Dawnie. Of course, the work might not involve exciting big deals like you probably saw with Lynch..."

"No offense Jewels, but I don't think I'm cut out for real estate, big deals or little deals."

Julie paused to sip more wine. "It's your life, Dawnie, but I think it's a great career under the right circumstances, such as having a good broker. Mine gives me all the support I need and there's nothing she doesn't know how to do. But I still think it would be kick-ass to be in on mansion sales and other big stuff like Lynch does."

"Actually," replied Dawn, "what I saw there on one deal was a bit too much for me."

"So you weren't just buried in a back room?"

"Lynch invited me to sit in on a meeting on that new mall project we looked at on that drive to the lake. It'll be a big deal for Lynch someday, but I got turned off by what he was planning with one of the county commissioners..."

"Okay, I'll bite."

"How about secretly scheming to get zoning rearranged on certain nearby properties that Lynch was slowly buying up so they could make some easy money? And I'm sorry, Jewels, but I felt insulted."

"You mean personally?"

"Yeah, because, after Lynch told me to familiarize myself, he included me in one of their meetings and just assumed that I'd have no concern about their ethics. He was in cahoots with a public official, but he just figured I'd go all gaga over his shrewdness and connections."

"Okay...it doesn't *have* to be that way in real estate, but we'll come back to your job situation," said Julie, obviously trying to preserve some teamwork. "Meanwhile, how about that job you *almost* applied for?"

Dawn, still irritated about Lynch, ignored the probe.

"Okay," said Julie, "maybe later on that, too. Let's look at your foreclosure notice."

Dawn went to the kitchen and returned with the two envelopes she'd been keeping on top of her refrigerator.

"First," said Dawn, holding up one of the thick envelopes, "these are the papers I just got from the loan company that Lynch set me up with—which I think is his company anyway. He actually urged me to take the loan, which was on top of the original house mortgage that I'm probably not going to be able to keep up with either."

Julie reached for the envelope but Dawn pulled it back.

"Not yet, Jewels."

Julie picked up her glass and took another sip, while keeping her full attention on Dawn and the second envelope.

"On the very same day, Jewels, I also got this bill by certified mail from the law firm that Lynch set me up with. First, they rotated lawyers on me and then they sent me elsewhere. Now, they want close to twenty-thousand dollars just for starting my case, even though nobody ever mentioned paying by the hour or anything like that."

"Holy Crap!"

"Hold on, Jewels. Still not done."

"Next, I find out that I'm probably going to lose my newest lawyer because Lynch gave the other side a sworn statement that Abel told him he was going to commit suicide and that I approved of it."

"He did *that*?"

"So, now you can see how I'm getting dumped on from all directions."

"Oh my God, yes."

"And I'm trying not to get too panicky, Jewels, but it looks like I need you to put my house on the market."

"That, I can do, Dawnie. But first, humor me a little and take another sip of your vino."

Dawn grabbed her glass, which still had most of its contents and gave a mock toast, with a trusting nod toward Julie. "Consider yourself humored."

"Good. We'll eat these elephants one petite bite at a time."

"Yuck," Dawn grimaced. "Go ahead, I'm listening."

"So, we first see how much equity is in the house," stated Julie, as if leading a military mission. "I'll run some comps, but I need you to get me the loan balances. If there is equity, we can try to sell before any foreclosure, so you'll come away with something."

Dawn nodded dejectedly, then got up and migrated toward the custom mantelpiece that Abel had installed and ran her hand over it. "I'm sorry to be such a wimp," said Dawn in a broken voice.

"Hey girl, I know this isn't easy, but just try hanging in with me," replied Julie. "If keeping the house is what's really most important, we may still be able to pull that off. Filing bankruptcy stops everything and that could give you enough time to get your life insurance money."

So we're back to that?

"Like I said, my broker knows more about all that than most lawyers. But she's also got a business attorney who's supposed to be terrific."

"That would be incredible," said Dawn, trying to at least show enough enthusiasm to keep Julie motivated.

"We'll fight it all the way, I promise."

"Look at me," said Dawn, as her suppressed tears finally started to show. "You're trying to help me and I'm blubbering. But I don't have anyone else to let it out to, Jewels...Don't you feel privileged?"

"Forget it. I think you're doing pretty damn good just to keep fighting these bastards. But, enough of that," said Julie with a smirk. "*Now* you're going to tell me about that job you *almost* applied for."

263

SIXTY-TWO

Dawn dragged herself toward the summoning telephone late Tuesday afternoon, hoping it would be Julie and wary of a call from anyone else.

"Hello, Mrs. Santoro," said Natenberg in a less-than-encouraging tone. "I would've called you this morning, but I somehow had the idea that you work nights."

"No sir," she replied, bracing for what she expected to be told next. "Not yet, at least."

"Okay then, I'm letting you know that I'm filing my motion to withdraw. No point putting it off much longer with a trial date on the horizon, and I'd also like to give your replacement as much preparation time as possible."

Right, my new mystery lawyer...

"I *could* combine it with a motion to postpone the trial date, but I didn't think you wanted that."

"I don't think so, sir. Things have suddenly gotten even more urgent."

"Your decision. You'll have a few weeks before I'm formally out, and nothing much should happen during the interim. So, if you change your mind on postponing the trial, I could still ask for that. But, either way, you really need to be looking..."

"I understand, sir. I'll just have to find someone."

"Would you like me to try for a settlement before I file my motion? I previously offered to do that for you."

Uneasy seconds passed. "I just won't accept anything low from them. So, it's 'yes' if you think there's a chance at a *fair* settlement, but otherwise you'd probably be wasting your time, sir."

"Dawn—if you'll permit me—in my professional opinion, I just don't see how you're going to get what you seem to want with this new evidence from Louis Lynch."

But I fucking don't believe him...

She said nothing.

"Listen," Natenberg finally said, after waiting in vain, "I'll hold off until Thursday to file, assuming I don't hear from you by then."

"I appreciate that, sir, but you don't have to delay on my account. I'm not ready to surrender to what I think are lies."

More loaded silence.

"I'll file it Thursday, Dawn. And I sincerely wish you the best of luck in finding new counsel...and in winning your case, of course."

SIXTY-THREE

Before James Claverson could say anything in his phone call the next afternoon, Dawn cut him off.

"James! How could you do that to me?"

"Do what? I'm being blind-sided here."

"You're blind-sided? How could you not tell me that you were running up a huge bill, and that I'd have to pay it even if your firm didn't get me anything?"

"Wait a second," James sputtered. "What huge bill?"

"It's right here in black and white if you want me to hold it up to the phone...But, then again, I'm sure you could get your own copy—assuming you don't already have it."

"Dawn, I swear I knew nothing about you getting billed for my work."

"Most of the time entries have the letters 'JC', so who in the heck do you think that is?"

"Well, yeah, it could be my time entries, but I didn't..."

"You didn't tell me this was going to happen. That's what you didn't."

"No. Please, Dawn. Listen..."

"I can't listen to you right now, James. I've got too many disasters going on, including your firm's bill no matter what story you try giving me." She hung up and walked away from the phone, trying to calm herself.

*****

A half-hour later, her telephone rang again.

"Dawn, don't hang up! The break let me think and I swear I can explain."

"Explain? What good would that do?"

"Please Dawn; it's very important to me."

"Go ahead if you must, but there's no way you can talk this bill into disappearing."

"Dawn, my firm makes all the associates write their time down no matter what the billing situation might be, so that the partners can keep track of how much work we're putting into each assignment. I'm low on the totem pole here, so I basically do what I'm told, but I *never* over-bill."

"So, which is it, then? Are you now saying that you didn't think I'd get *any* bill or just that it wouldn't be an *over-bill*, because you never mentioned *any* billing to me?"

"Dawn, can you please ease up a second? You never did get a bill until just recently, right?"

"Yes, to my complete surprise."

"Well, think about that. They changed their policy on you. Otherwise, you'd have gotten monthly bills like most clients."

"How do you know they didn't just overlook me until I got a new lawyer?"

"No way," James said forcefully. "When it comes to AK&K, overlooking bills doesn't happen. Besides, I was told we were taking your case because you were a friend of a longtime client..."

"I *was* sent to your firm," noted Dawn.

"...And I figured it was supposed to be a confidence builder for me, even if the firm wasn't charging."

"But you seemed plenty confident already, the way you marched us right into battle..."

"Part of that was an act, but I always thought I was taking the right steps for you, just like in any of my cases."

"Fine, go ahead and feel better now because you explained all that to me. But I'm still getting billed for not getting any results and without me ever agreeing."

A long silence.

"Dawn, are you absolutely certain that nobody at my firm ever went over billing with you...maybe even before you saw me?"

"Absolutely. Mr. Lynch arranged it, then I just showed up and the receptionist directed me to...Oh my God, how stupid of me James."

"What, Dawn?"

"I shouldn't have given you such a hard time."

"That's agreed, but what?"

"It was all him. I got your bill the same day as the notice from his loan company about foreclosing on my house."

"That could be...If he could get the firm to *not* bill you, why not the opposite?"

"Apparently so..."

"But that doesn't change the fact that I'm extremely ticked off that this is happening to you, Dawn."

"I believe you James, and I need to ask you something."

"Yeah?"

"Would your firm really go after me like they are threatening?"

"To be honest, that decision would be way over my head..."

"Okay, but can you tell me what you think?"

"Well, I guess I'd say that, if you got a nice recovery in your case, they wouldn't be at all bashful about demanding their fees for getting the case started...But, as far as going after you right now, I think that's unlikely."

"Really?"

"Well, it's one thing to just shoot out a bill—even by certified mail—but to actually sue a former client who's a widow, with no written retainer agreement...That would be on another level...Still," he hesitated, "with Lynch being an X-factor, who knows."

"So, you think it might depend entirely on whether Lynch tried to push them to do it?"

"It might."

"Holy..."

"Dawn, as a precaution, you should send my firm a letter saying that you dispute all of it. And you might as well use certified mail yourself."

"Okay, but writing that kind of letter is not something I'd be very good at."

"Dear AK&K, I dispute your entire bill for multiple reasons. I owe you nothing. Signed, Dawn Santoro...Dawn, you do realize I could get fired for telling you this?"

"Telling me what, James?"

269

"*Touché*."

"Hey, I'm not a *total* basket case, yet."

"Dawn?"

"Yes?"

"I know you're still in the fight of your life, but can I now ask you one selfish question?"

"What?"

"Am I back in your trust again?"

"I'm sorry I went off on you, James. It's just that..."

"No need," James interjected, "I'm hearing 'yes', so here's my next question."

"Yeah?"

"Can we play 'go-back'?"

"Play what?"

"As in *go back* to why I first called you today."

"Oh, right. Sure."

"Good. So, hello there, Dawn, what's this I hear about Natenberg withdrawing?"

"Oh, yeah. He's filing his motion like tomorrow. So, as long as we're on that subject, got any other lawyers in mind? At this point, I'll even take an inexperienced one, as long as they'll hang in for the duration."

"Yeah, I'm disappointed in him," James commiserated. "I'll definitely look around for you, but did he explain why he's bailing out? The only message I got from his office was that 'it got too complicated'."

"Too complicated?" said Dawn. "I guess that's one way to put it. As far as I know, it was because of a sworn statement the other side recently got from...well, I'm sure you can guess who."

"Lynch?"

"Yup, that man's been busy. Natenberg gave me a copy...a great memento to go with his loan notice and your firm's bill."

"Dawn, would you mind reading Lynch's sworn statement to me right now, if it's not too much trouble?"

"Sure. Hang on, James."

Upon her return, James listened, only interrupting occasionally for her to repeat certain verbiage.

"That's it," she added, "Lynch comes into my case and my second lawyer goes out."

Silence.

"James?"

"I've got an idea, Dawn," James finally said with a curious energy.

"On my next attorney?"

"No. I want to show you some papers pertaining to Lynch that you've never even heard about."

SIXTY-FOUR

At eight-thirty that evening, with Cora sleeping as Dawn had hoped, there was a soft knock on the front door.

"Made it," whispered James, as he hastened into the room holding a thin folder.

The two sat down next to each other, and she waited for whatever presentation he was about to make.

"Dawn, check out the top page first and I'll tell you where I'm going with this."

She examined what appeared to be a copy of a letter from Ashe, Kramer & King, marked *"PRIVILEGED AND CONFIDENTIAL"* and addressed to "Mr. Louis Lynch".

"As you can see," said James, "it's dated not too long before Abel's death and it indicates a hand-delivery."

He then pointed to the text and let her read, which she did, just loud enough for him to hear:

> The enclosed memorandum is based on legal research you requested on the issue of the suicide exclusion from coverage in a life insurance policy where the insured had a terminal disease. I hope that you find it to be both clear and responsive, however feel free to call me if you wish to discuss any aspect of it.

"Oh...my...God," she gasped, as she put the letter down and started to reach for the accompanying memorandum.

James gently stopped her hand. "I'd just as soon you *not* read the memorandum—at least for now."

Though still stunned, she could tell he meant it.

"So," he said, "having read my firm's cover letter to Lynch, I want you to assume that the research concluded that there was not—I repeat, *not*—any *established* exception to enforcing the suicide exclusion in a life insurance policy, *even if* the insured happened to be terminally ill. In other words, the researcher didn't find any court precedent where being terminal made a difference."

"Oh, that's just great," Dawn groaned. "What good..."

"Hang on," he interrupted, "because it's not the memo's conclusion that I'm here about. It's the very fact that it was provided to Lynch—at his request no less—well before your husband committed...I mean, before he had his accident."

"Okay, but what does..."

"It directly contradicts Lynch's sworn statement you read me earlier where he claimed he told your husband that he knew *nothing* about the law. Putting it bluntly, Lynch is caught flat-out lying over something that goes right to the heart of his sworn statement."

Though starved for anything promising, she was confused more than anything else. She gave him a blank stare and shrugged her shoulders just enough.

273

"Dawn," James persisted, "if Lynch is shown to be lying about this, then he can be disbelieved on what he claims that your husband said to him. It's a certified monkey wrench into their case. *Now* are you with me?"

"Oh," she replied guardedly, "that does sound like something John Natenberg would say...But how strong is it?"

"How strong?" he echoed with a smile. "I think it might even persuade John to stay on as your attorney."

"Seriously?"

"Definitely worth a shot."

"But what if Lynch just denied getting the letter?"

"I don't see how. A couple minutes of testimony by a subpoenaed secretary from my firm, whose initials are on the bottom of the letter, could blow him out of the water. Heck, I'd even be willing to testify that it wouldn't even be in the files of AK&K, where I found it, unless it had been delivered to him."

"Uh, as long as you bring that up, James, I'm getting a little curious about how you did find it..."

"Oh boy," he remarked sheepishly, then took a long slow breath. "Do you really have to ask that?"

She met his eyes and nodded.

"But you might not like where it leads..."

"It's a *personal* need to know, James."

He gave her another look. "Then don't say I didn't warn you."

"I can't imagine why, but yes, you did."

274

"Okay, then," he said with a shake of his head, "I'll just flat-out say it. I wasn't completely honest with you when I was still your lawyer, but I had my reasons."

"I'm listening."

"Dawn, some very unusual things happened and I had to make decisions that I thought were best for you at the time. For starters, this letter is the real reason I got out."

"What? But it was written way before I ever met you..."

"Obviously, but while I was still your attorney, I did some research in our firm's law library, just like I said I would."

That's nice to hear...

She nodded.

"I began looking for cases where a terminally ill person committed suicide within their life insurance policy's exclusionary period. No surprise that I couldn't find Nevada case-law on the subject. But, as I expanded into other jurisdictions, I started seeing book marks and pencil notes right where I was looking. Someone else had already researched the question."

"Wow..."

"At first," James continued, "I thought maybe the litigation partner who assigned me your case had taken an initial peek for himself. But, as I kept looking, there just seemed to be too much work done on it..."

She nodded again.

"...So, on a hunch," he said, looking intently at her, "I checked the computer in a spare office that had been used by a temporary intern, and that's where I found a draft of the memo. From there, I was able to track down the cover letter sent by the partner Lynch uses for real estate deals, Andy King."

"And, while you were doing all this for me, I was wondering if you'd completely forgotten..."

"Yes, but it actually turned into a big problem..."

"Oh?"

"...Well, I was representing a widow against a life insurance company apparently because the decedent had close ties to Mr. Lynch, and yet I now knew that Lynch himself had this very issue researched and, as far as I knew then, could have talked to your husband about it."

"Oh my."

"Yeah...I didn't know if anyone else at AK&K was fully aware of this mess, but I sure as heck was."

"So you were secretly in a bind?"

"Yeah, but then it occurred to me: If I could somehow extricate from your case, the letter and legal memo *might* not even surface...at least the way things seemed to be going at the time."

"So *that's* why you disappeared on me?"

"Right, but getting all the way out wasn't going to be so easy."

"Okay..."

"Promise to keep my entire predicament in mind, Dawn?"

"For sure, James."

"Then, here goes: I told the litigation partner that you kept coming onto me because you were lonely and knew I was single."

She stared at him in shock. "You couldn't come up with anything else?"

"Not at the time."

"But I had just been widowed..."

"Hey, bad idea or not, it worked."

"If you say so..."

"The important thing, Dawn, is that, even though you *thought* I was too busy for you, I'd have worked nights and weekends knowing your future was on the line."

"And you're even here right now..."

"That I am," he smiled. "And I've never suspected one iota that you were keeping any secrets from me about your husband's death."

"Thank you for that, James."

He nodded and smiled again.

"Wait a minute," she said, "you didn't have any ethical duty to see that this evidence came into the case?"

James stared as if in disbelief. "Are you serious?"

She calmly nodded.

"You amaze me, Dawn."

She waited.

"Well, I guess I'd argue that, once I was out of your case, any such duty ended at that point—if it ever existed to begin with."

"As long as your conscience is clear, James."

"Dawn, my conscience hasn't bothered me one bit because I was simply trying to help you get justice."

"That's all I've *ever* been after. But, what about now...is John Natenberg free to use the letter?"

"Dawn, let him handle that, after I show it to him."

"Hey, I'm just trying to survive here. That's why I'm asking all these questions, even though I *do* trust you."

"I understand," he assured her. "For now, I strongly doubt that Lynch can assert the attorney-client privilege on that letter in order to shield a lie in his sworn statement."

"Okay, good."

"Besides, the legal memo was *supposed* to be for your husband's benefit, not his."

"I like that one too."

"I'm glad you're happy."

Finally satisfied for the moment, she couldn't help but perceive the depth of his concern for her. She felt a rush of relief and gratitude where there had just recently been disappointment and distrust. "James, what about your career if this all comes out...Lynch is a big client?"

"Yeah, I'd probably be toast if I was planning to grind it out at AK&K. But, just between us, I'll be opening my own office soon."

"Oh my God, James, that's great...Isn't it?"

"Time will tell. All I know is that I've got the urge."

"That's brave..."

"Maybe, but can I tell you something?"

She nodded.

"When you asked me whether you should accept the offer from Lynch to be his mistress, with all the comfort and security he promised you, I saw myself in a similar predicament."

"Seriously?"

He looked into her eyes and smiled. "Your courage helped inspire me, Dawn."

At that moment, with Cora sleeping in her bedroom, Dawn sensed a vulnerability she was not prepared for. And the suggestive silence between them did not help at all.

But James did not make a first move—whether out of professionalism or his own fear of the consequences.

Though the moment tried to linger, she knew, deep inside, that it was not yet her karma. Some cosmic punishment would surely follow if she tried to interject sex—let alone romance—into her struggle. Maybe someone like Julie could pull it off, but not her.

Feeling enough in control of herself again, she fashioned her most grateful look. "James, no matter what comes of this new evidence, thank you for being so human and treating me like I'm a worthy person."

He smiled, but then his eyes widened as his face turned weirdly serious again. "Dawn, I think it's time that I reveal something else to you as well."

"Uh oh...Not sure I can handle anything else tonight, but go ahead."

"I'm not really human like you say," he announced. "I came from the planet Legalzop; so how are you going to deal with that one?"

She smiled and took a mock swing at him, which he playfully ducked.

Their smiles then melted away while their eyes remained locked into each other's. But, she caught herself again and rose to show him to the door while she still had the self-control to do so.

SIXTY-FIVE

After thirty minutes in Natenberg's reception room on the following Monday afternoon, Dawn was finally permitted into his still cluttered office. Just as she was seated, however, he took an incoming phone call, with no apology to her.

Figuring she was probably lucky to be there at all, she patiently waited.

Upon finishing his call, Natenberg refocused. "Mrs. Santoro, I first want you to know that I listened to James Claverson about his firm's letter and the memo sent to Louis Lynch, and I even reviewed copies that he later sent over..."

While Natenberg then paused to apparently locate the copies on his desk, Dawn grabbed the opening. "So now you'll stay on my case, sir?"

"Pardon me?" he said with a callous look, as if she had just wandered into his office unexpectedly. "That's still out of the question, Mrs. Santoro. I'm fully committed to other things. I thought you understood that."

Oh my God...Breathe

"But, sir, isn't our case stronger now, and we could maybe go to trial at a later time, couldn't we?"

He stared at her, apparently perplexed, if not annoyed as well.

"I mean whenever you *do* have an opening, sir. And meanwhile I'll try to sell my house before Mr. Lynch can foreclose..."

"Uh, I'm sorry, Mrs. Santoro," he finally interjected. "Your situation is unfortunate, but you must remember that these new challenges were not caused by me. And the matters I'm now committed to could control my schedule for years to come."

As if on cue, the intercom announced another incoming call.

He started to reach for his phone, but apparently thought better of it. "Barbara," he replied to the receptionist, "could you just hold my calls until we're done, barring any real emergency."

He turned back to Dawn, looking as if he had more to say, but she sensed that he couldn't recall where he'd left off.

"Sir, James never told me that you'd refuse to change your mind. Now, I'm wondering why I came all the way down here today."

His blank stare remained but his jaw slowly dropped.

Seeing him off balance, she sensed it was no time to become passive. She abruptly rose from her chair, gave a frustrated head shake, and started toward the door.

"Wait a minute, Mrs. Santoro. I'm sorry the way this meeting has gone so far. Could you please sit back down for me?"

She stopped and looked at him.

He stood up and, with pleading in his eyes instead of his normal aggressiveness, invited her back to her chair.

She sat down again, but kept her steely-eyed look of doubt.

He studied her, apparently still uneasy as to whether she was in the mood to listen. "Mrs. Santoro, I'll be honest with you. Mr. Claverson caught me in a moment of weakness, so to speak, when he talked me into having this meeting. But, after your appointment was made, and I looked over the papers, I concluded that he was expecting too much out of this new evidence."

So now where are you?

She continued to give him a look that said his words were falling short.

"Hold on, Mrs. Santoro. I didn't say that it was *completely* useless. James is right that it contradicts what Lynch swore to..."

But here it comes...

"...But Aceworth's lawyers could merely view it as Lynch's problem. He's got his professional licenses at risk if there were perjury allegations. I'm sure, however, that Attorney Tilden covered himself and would still defend Aceworth."

"But Mr. Natenberg, even if that were true, I still have a question."

"Certainly," he replied, obviously looking for any way to appease her. "What is it?"

"You said in our first meeting that I'm the key to this case, right?"

"I don't recall specifically, but I may have."

"Okay then, if they can't use Lynch's testimony now to argue that I was part of some scheme, doesn't that mean that my case is strong again, like before when you said the jury would probably want to help me in order to do justice?"

He stared at her, as if momentarily speechless.

She returned the stare.

"You really listened, Mrs. Santoro."

"Of course, sir, and you were convincing when you said it."

"I understand, Mrs. Santoro, but can you now understand that there are practicalities on my side?"

Am I being asked to agree that his profits matter more than me and my daughter?

She just stared at him, not dignifying his query.

He gazed toward the window for a long moment then back toward her. "Let me do this much, Mrs. Santoro," he said in a softened tone. "The other side doesn't know that I can't get back into your case full-force. So perhaps, before I formally withdraw, I could try to parlay this new evidence into a high enough offer for you."

She thought.

He gave her time.

"Sir, you would know best if that could be done, but my first lawyers are now after me for almost twenty thousand dollars in fees. So, go ahead and try if you're willing, sir, but 'high enough' means even more now..."

"I said I would try, Mrs. Santoro."

"Then thank you, sir."

"Just don't expect anywhere near the full policy amount," he said with a stern look. "And I'd say that even if I weren't about to withdraw."

284

SIXTY-SIX

On an afternoon during the following week, knowing that space would be much tighter if she were soon required to move, Dawn forced herself to work on sorting out which household items could be given away and which of Abel's things should actually be kept.

"Just make the darn decisions," she whispered aloud during her second hour of drudgery. "This was long overdue anyway."

But one item among Abel's personal things stalled her. It was a bare invoice-receipt from some business called "VAMS", which apparently stood for "Vegas Accu-Men Services". Abel had paid them "$1495.00" for "Services: as discussed".

She vaguely recalled seeing it before, when she had looked through papers pertaining to the sale of Abel's pickup truck. But things were different then, and Abel's conduct had not yet been put under a microscope.

"Who in the heck are they, anyway?" she mumbled. "No clue from their stupid invoice."

She went to her telephone and dialed their number.

A man's voice answered: "Vegas Accu-Men."

"Uh, excuse me sir, but I wanted to ask what exactly your company does? Someone at work mentioned you..."

"We're a top-tier private investigative firm, miss. We've been in Las Vegas since 1978."

"Investigative? Okay, thank you," she said, then quickly hung up as her stomach tightened.

Disoriented by the answer, a thought intruded: Did Abel get suspicious of her going out to dinner with Lynch?

"Hold on, you air-head," she muttered in disgust, "that's backasswards."

She looked at the invoice again and pondered. What in the heck investigation could Abel have spent that kind of money on?

She re-dialed the phone number, wishing that she hadn't fibbed the first time. "Hi, you probably recognize my voice from a little while ago, sir, but..."

"Yes, lady. Please tell me what you need?"

"Um, yes, I'm asking about one of your past jobs."

"Excuse me, but you're not the one who hired us?"

"Uh, not exactly..."

"Well then, I'm sure you can understand that our investigations are completely confidential unless a client instructs us to disclose to somebody else, which we would have already done by now. Unfortunately, I don't see how I can help you."

"I understand, sir, and I'm not trying to waste your time or break any rules, but my husband hired your company and he's now deceased. So whatever it concerned might..."

"Your husband hired us? His name please?"

"Yes, Abel Santoro."

"Just a minute, while I just look it up."

As if I needed this drama.

"Hello, ma'am, the investigator on that one had to take a leave of absence due to a family medical emergency

286

and he's still back east. Unfortunately, I can't even access that file right now merely in response to your call."

"I see..."

"But I will pass it on for you to the powers that be. And we've already got your contact information, as long as it hasn't been recently changed."

"Not yet it hasn't, sir. And I'd really appreciate whatever can be done because I'm frankly stumped, and even worried, as to what it could have been about."

SIXTY-SEVEN

She approached her ringing telephone, surprised at how quickly VAMS was calling her back.

But, instead, she heard the voice of John Natenberg. "Mrs. Santoro, glad I caught you. I need you to come to a special meeting this evening concerning your case."

"Uh, this evening? You mean like sometime later on?"

"Well, not *that* much later on."

"So you're asking me to come now, sir?"

"That would be ideal, if you can. It's for your own benefit."

"Oh, then I guess I will. But I'll need just a little time to arrange the nanny. Would you mind telling me, sir, who will be there and what's going to happen?"

"I was getting to that. I'll be at Panatta's Restaurant, downtown near Fifth and Huntington. In about thirty minutes or so, I'll be meeting there with a very important person in your case—if you know who I mean—along with his lawyer."

"Important person?"

"Your former boss, Louis Lynch."

"Oh my God."

"It'll be okay, Mrs. Santoro, I don't anticipate any misbehavior."

"I understand, but meeting with him is the last thing I expected right now."

"Nevertheless, I asked for this meeting with the hope of getting you more settlement potential. And tonight just happened to work for everyone."

"I'm not fighting you, sir, I just..."

"This could be the only time we'll get this opportunity."

"Okay sir, but please don't expect too much from me. I'm about at my wit's end."

"They'll be the ones on the defensive, trust me."

"I sure hope so, sir."

"Your job will pretty much be to just listen."

"I will, sir, but..."

"And, just between you and I," said Natenberg, "I let them think that I'm about to retract my motion to withdraw based on the new evidence, so I need you to work with me on that tonight."

"Huh? Oh, I get it...And I'll head right there as soon as I can get my daughter situated."

"Excellent. But there's one more thing you should understand *before* you get here, Mrs. Santoro."

"What's that, sir?"

"I'll be aiming toward a package deal for you, including compensation for the way Lynch terminated you. It won't be limited to talking about your life insurance case."

"But sir, I didn't really want to keep working..."

"Mrs. Santoro..."

"Yes sir?"

"For your own sake, work with me. Would you please."

As Dawn drove toward downtown, she felt guilty for imposing upon Gwen on such short notice and for yanking her child out of her normal schedule again. But, soon enough, her guilt was overshadowed by dread.

"'Just listen' means just that," she voiced sternly. "And I'm going to hold him to it."

As she headed eastward on Sahara Avenue, she recalled a fairly recent drive toward the Strip when she felt almost as desperate—and almost as anxious, though for entirely different reasons.

When the time came to turn left toward downtown, the thought of actually heading in the opposite direction toward another one of the local gentleman's clubs intruded, but she quickly squelched it. "They'd think I'm crazy the way I'm dressed tonight...Besides, I need to keep that as my last resort."

SIXTY-EIGHT

Upon entering Panatta's, she was immediately met by a formally-dressed host.

"Hello sir, I'm meeting with my lawyer, and I think he is already here..."

"Ah, yes," the man responded with an elegant accent. "Those gentlemen are just having drinks. But would *signora* care for a dinner menu?"

As if...

"No thank you. But you said 'gentlemen'; so the others are already here?"

"You will be the fourth, *signora*. Follow me please."

As she trailed the host up to the second level, dreading her looming encounter with Lynch, her stomach was in full-churn mode.

On the upstairs level, there were customers scattered about, but the place was far from capacity. It was easy to spot the large table with three male occupants in suits, including Lou Lynch—in the flesh. He was sitting next to a lawyerish-looking man and they were both across the table from John Natenberg. This was really going to happen.

The men stopped their conversation as all eyes turned her way.

Slow breaths...

Though she wished she could just fall through a trap door, she allowed the host to seat her next to John Natenberg.

"Great you could join us, Mrs. Santoro," he remarked, rising partially from his chair.

There was a minimal nod from Lynch—who also looked like he'd much rather be elsewhere and wanted everyone to know it—and a quick introduction by Natenberg of "Andrew King, of Ashe, Kramer & King".

Though she was happy not to have received any greater attention at the outset, she attributed it to the apparent intensity of their negotiations—as if she had just walked in on a high-stakes poker game.

A server intruded. "Would the lady care for something to drink?"

She hesitated as if whatever she ordered would be her first test for the night.

It's not a freaking party...

"Uh, could I just have a plain ginger-ale?"

Upon the server's departure, Natenberg stood up. "If you gentlemen don't mind, I need a few private words with Mrs. Santoro." He signaled her with his eyes and briskly started toward the other side of the room, causing her to stand right up again.

On their way, they passed the server returning with her soft-drink.

This could almost be funny if it didn't suck so much.

Natenberg stopped walking when they reached a relatively empty area with enough privacy.

"Mrs. Santoro, first of all, you do understand that there's nothing wrong with the four of us talking here tonight. In fact, we're treating it as a settlement discussion which the law encourages."

"Sure sir. I'm just following..."

"And, even though Mr. Lynch is just a witness in your case against Aceworth, he's got his own attorney with him..."

"Yes sir."

"And, above all, we've agreed that everything said is confidential. So that should put you at ease."

Put me at ease?

She nodded meekly, but sensed he wasn't done.

"I'm working on an acceptable settlement for you, Mrs. Santoro, but one reason I wanted you here personally is to be a witness as to what is said."

Even though it's all 'confidential'?

"I'm not resisting, sir," she whispered back. "But what exactly do you mean by me being 'a witness'?"

Natenberg, though seemingly in full-combat mode, managed a perfunctory smile. "I'm saying that, if it ever comes up later—which is very unlikely—I want you to back me up that I did not, that's capital N-O-T, threaten to pursue perjury charges against Mr. Lynch. That's very important."

She nodded, trying not to reveal her unease over how convoluted it was getting.

"You see," continued Natenberg, "King does real estate deals, not litigation. So I expect to have—shall we say—some leeway in negotiating our subject matter. But, just in case there's ever an issue, you will remember that I never ever crossed over that line. Understood?"

293

"Uh, sure sir."

But please don't cross over...

"So, then," he grunted, "let's go see if we can get you a good settlement."

Walking back with him, she wondered what would happen if Natenberg actually did threaten Lynch with perjury charges, and if he was just assuming she'd be willing to lie about it. It made her recall how she felt when Lynch included her in his meeting with the county commissioner.

Upon their return to the table, she peeked at Lynch. With a frown on his face, he still looked like he wanted to get up and leave.

She slunk down in her chair, wishing she could slink completely out of sight.

"If I may," said Andy King with a tactful smile, apparently trying to keep it as light as possible despite his client's negativity, "given that we've all agreed that this meeting is confidential, would you mind educating us, John, as to why you think we could somehow have any influence with Aceworth?"

"That's a fair question, Andy," Natenberg started out engagingly, "and I'm glad you asked, because I wouldn't want any misunderstandings."

"Well go ahead then, John, we're listening."

Including me.

"As for Aceworth," Natenberg remarked, "we believe that their settlement position would be, shall we say, much more reasonable if it weren't for your client's sworn statement."

"Well, if that's your pitch," replied King, "why don't you just show this new evidence directly to Aceworth's lawyers? I'm sure you'd know how to do that effectively."

"Makes sense to me," Lynch chimed in, as if he had equal expertise.

"I'm getting to that, gentlemen," said Natenberg, not seeming to be bothered by their double-teaming. "The lawyers for Aceworth could still figure they'd use Mr. Lynch for some other purpose, given that he says he was talking to Mr. Santoro near the end, and given that they obviously view him as friendly to their side."

"Isn't that quite speculative?" asked King.

"Not the way we see it. They don't have much else that's any threat to us. Their case now revolves around your client, so he would essentially be ground zero on the witness stand."

"So you say, John, but..."

"So, rather than have such an unpleasant battle in open court," Natenberg added, "my client is willing to forego the accidental death coverage, which would otherwise double the policy, just to get this case over with and get on with her life."

"All well and good with us," said King, "but that's completely up to Aceworth."

"And you say that, knowing that Aceworth isn't here tonight," replied Natenberg. "Nevertheless, the four of us who *are* together now must first reach a settlement of our own to the extent we can, as I'll soon explain to you."

295

While both King and Lynch looked puzzled at the last words, Natenberg fashioned a look of pity toward Lynch, then turned toward King. "Andy, I'm sure you can understand that, if everything doesn't settle, and I mean *everything*, it will be very—shall we say—*grueling* for your client when he has to be cross-examined in open court."

Dawn stole a side-glance at Lynch, hoping he might be looking toward his attorney. Surprisingly, he seemed to be in a momentary trance, more passive than she'd ever seen him before.

Is that his worried look, or is he just bored?

"Heck," Natenberg added, "I'll probably subpoena him to testify myself, if for no other reason than to show the bad faith of Aceworth."

With that, King became noticeably agitated, and Lynch's blank stare morphed into a snarl. But neither responded verbally.

"As I see it, gentlemen," continued Natenberg, "we will want you two to convince Aceworth's lawyers that Mr. Lynch would be absolutely no help to their defense."

"John, excuse me," King again tried to interrupt, "but do you really think..."

"Give me another second, Andy, because I'm not quite done and this is critical."

"Go ahead if you must."

"He can just say he was mistaken. Attribute it to him being focused on his business. They'll get the message."

Putting his hands on the edge of the table, King gave a look as if he was ready to stand up and leave along with

Lynch. "If that's really what you're after, John, we'll be happy to give it careful consideration and get back to you."

"No, Andy. As I indicated before, that's only part of what I'm after."

King and Lynch gave confused looks toward each other, then back at Natenberg as if he had lost them again.

Natenberg then caught Dawn's eye with a look that seemed to say, "Now, watch this."

"Andy, I'm now going beyond Aceworth because this meeting is also about settling matters between our respective clients that have nothing to do with life insurance."

King immediately scowled at Natenberg, while raising his hand in front of Lynch preemptively. "Okay, John, we've been extraordinarily patient with you up until now, but we didn't come here to listen to confidential fantasies. This is the first I've ever heard that your client *supposedly* has a claim against mine, damn it."

"Sorry there," said King to Dawn, with a respectful nod.

As if...

"In my view," said Natenberg, unperturbed, "the giving of a false sworn statement to Aceworth's lawyers would help support Mrs. Santoro's wrongful termination case because it shows a state of mind toward her."

Oh my God.

"Wrongful termination!" Lynch bellowed as he rose partway from his chair and pounded the table.

King, though showing increased anger himself, hand-gestured for his client to stay seated and keep it down.

Although Lynch initially seemed compliant, and reseated himself, he whispered loudly enough at King for all to hear: "That's not even fantasy; it's certified bullshit."

"I know, Lou," whispered King just as audibly.

"All I did was help her," Lynch snarled at Natenberg.

"Excuse me, but is that really *all* you did, sir?" John calmly replied with a cold stare.

Holy...

"Lou, don't lower yourself," said King. "Let me handle..."

But Lynch wasn't done, his face reddening. "I gave this *unqualified* woman a job that she desperately needed," he said through his teeth, while pounding the table again. "But it turned out that she didn't really like the work. Isn't that right, Dawn?"

It was Natenberg's hand this time that shot up in front of Dawn's face. "I'll handle this," he barked.

"Hell," Lynch smugly continued, "she even quit my office of her own free will when she first thought she was going to get all her life insurance money. Then, after her trouble with the insurance started, she came back to me begging to be reinstated."

Oh God, this sucks.

"Ask her yourself, counselor," Lynch scoffed, "since you won't let her answer me directly."

Despite the onslaught, Natenberg—to Dawn's amazement—maintained a confident smirk, as if he were merely toying with both of them.

Lynch shook his head in disgust, then turned toward Dawn and caught her eye with a look as if he were trying to appeal to her personal honesty.

Ugh...So now, You're the one who wants truth.

She looked back again at Natenberg, determined not to let Lynch play her.

"Come on, Dawn," persisted Lynch, the salesman, "I know you've got more integrity than that. Don't let him put such false ideas into your head."

Damn it, this is exactly why I did not want to be here.

She held up her hand to screen her face from Lynch and King, while grimacing toward Natenberg.

He gripped her arm, then resumed eying Lynch and King pugnaciously, as if they were no match for him.

Lynch's face started to flush. His hands grasped the table as if that was all that was stopping him from rising up and storming out.

"Easy, Lou," King finally said, "I haven't heard anything yet worth getting aggravated over."

"Oh, I'm not aggravated, Andy, just annoyed at having this much of my time completely wasted."

With the tension barely subdued, Natenberg looked at King and Lynch. "Gentlemen, I completely agree that aggravation isn't necessary. What I seek for my client should be relatively painless for you to provide and would help this widow avoid bankruptcy court."

Lynch exhaled forcefully as if to convey that he was unimpressed, but he also appeared ready to talk. "Well, counselor, I too would like an end to this nonsense. I was very close to Mr. Santoro myself, as Dawn knows, and her legal struggle is just generating some bad memories when Abel should be resting in peace as far as I'm concerned."

Lynch then leaned toward King and whispered something—too softly this time to be heard.

King, after a moment of apparent thought, looked at Natenberg. "John, my client would like to have a few minutes alone to speak with Mrs. Santoro. Why don't we make that happen?"

Say "No"!

"Hmm, that *might* be okay," replied Natenberg, as if the idea had never occurred to him. "But let Dawn and I first have a few words in private." With that, he motioned to Dawn to step away.

"Of course, sabotage me first," Lynch quipped.

"It's routine, Lou," said King, "and, unless I miss my guess, she might not be willing otherwise."

When John Natenberg and Dawn were far enough away, he had her stand with her back to the others.

"Any questions, Mrs. Santoro?" he calmly asked, as if she were merely being asked to play a friendly card game for the first time. "You are ready for this, right?"

"Sir," she forced herself to talk softly, even if through clenched teeth, "this was not supposed to be part of it...If I had known this was coming, I wouldn't have been willing to even come here tonight. Besides, Aceworth would still have to raise their offer. So, me having to talk to Mr. Lynch would probably be for nothing anyway..."

"Mrs. Santoro..."

"Sir, I'd really like to leave now..."

"Mrs. Santoro," commanded Natenberg, his heavy eyebrows bearing down so forcefully that she momentarily forgot about Lynch, "this is actually a *good* sign that I was hoping for. And all you have to do is *listen* to him."

"But, Mr. Natenberg..."

"You can even tell him that I told you to say nothing without first consulting again with me. Surely, you can do that much for the sake of your future and that of your child."

Though feeling set up, as well as pressured, she looked down momentarily to reassess.

Screw it, I'm here.

SIXTY-NINE

Upon their return, King sprung from his seat and motioned Natenberg toward the upstairs bar.

Lynch remained seated, eyes riveted upon her. He almost appeared sincere, aside from his usual arrogance.

With the table between the two of them, she remained standing.

After a look of mild annoyance, he forced a smile and motioned for her to sit.

She continued to stand.

"Please, Dawn."

Not wanting a prolonged standoff, she complied, but kept her arms folded.

"First of all," he announced, "I don't see why we're even here. Excuse my French, but don't you see that this is all bullshit?"

Knowing that such talk was not what Natenberg envisioned, she rolled her eyes, then waited stone-faced for whatever would be 'second'.

His eyes pressed her, but she outlasted him.

He changed his expression to that of concern. "Dawn, through no fault of your own, there are some important things about your case that you just aren't aware of."

She did not take his cue.

"I'm serious, Dawn. After Abel died, Aceworth sent out an investigator to question me. He thought that I might know something about Abel's mental state. I protected your

302

interests, but I think he could sense that I knew more than I was letting on..."

She listened, but intended to show no reaction.

"Then, later on, Aceworth's lawyer picked it right up again and was very persistent. That was when I was encouraging you to settle...Remember?"

As if...

She stared back blankly.

"It was only after you ignored my warnings," said Lynch, pointing his finger at her, "that I gave Aceworth's lawyer my sworn statement just to try to appease them. But I still hoped that it wouldn't hurt your case or do you any harm. I'm not a lawyer, Dawn."

She slowly shook her head just enough to let him know that she wasn't buying it.

"Dawn, think about it," implored Lynch. "Did you want my sworn statement to say that I *did* provide the legal opinion to Abel, so that he absolutely knew the risk to the life insurance when he ran in front of that truck?"

Though she wanted to instantly dismiss his question, it bothered her. And she suspected that he sensed it.

Say nothing...

"You might be upset with me, Dawn, but I never asked to be involved in all this."

So you're completely innocent?

He pointed his finger at her again. "Now, I face legal attacks for trying to protect you, and all because of your stubbornness."

Though still reluctant to respond, there was one question she had to ask: "Mr. Lynch, if all that's true, then why did you say in your statement that I personally knew that Abel was thinking of killing himself and that I even approved the idea?"

"Dawn..."

"Never," she railed at him, "would I have approved that!"

But to her surprise, her words seemed to have no effect upon him.

"Dawn," he calmly replied, "whether you like it or not, Abel told me that you knew everything, so how would I know otherwise?"

Frustrated by her inability to refute his tale—no matter how incredible—she looked away, sensing that this ordeal was going nowhere, no matter what Natenberg had been hoping for.

Seconds passed.

In the heavy silence, Lynch reached across the table and grasped her unsuspecting hand.

What the...

Rather than try to yank it free, she deadened herself to him.

"Dawn, I'm guessing that our private session may be about over. So, whether you accept what I say or not, I would still prefer to end all this friction. The bill you got for the attorney's fees only happened because you switched lawyers, but I have influence with Andy's firm."

Obviously.

"And, as far as that home loan," he continued, "you didn't expect that it could just go unpaid indefinitely, did you? Lending companies are subject to regulators..."

But what?

She waited.

"Still," said Lynch, easing his tone further, "there's less oversight on second mortgages, so I could take care of that for you as well."

She looked at him, waiting for the catch.

He smiled smugly and released his grasp. "All you have to do to get these freebies is settle your claim with Aceworth, so that everything is buttoned up just like your lawyer said."

Seeing no right way to answer, she looked away again.

"Dawn," he queried, "Can't you at least say something?"

She looked toward him. "Mr. Lynch, I appreciate your offers, but I still need more money from Aceworth to be able to raise my daughter. That's why Abel bought their life insurance policy."

"Aceworth!" growled Lynch. "You should just take whatever they offer and run.

"And run?"

"Like it's free money, because it is, Dawn. Abel took a risk and didn't get away with it. End of story."

"So you say, Mr. Lynch. But they've never proven that to me."

With his eyes wide, he again appeared at the limits of his self-control. "Dawn, you've got to be realistic here, even if it's just for your own sake. Don't you see that you and I are in the same boat with Aceworth? If you force me to testify, the full story will be that much worse for you."

That assumes that anyone would believe you.

"Mr. Lynch, I'm sorry, but, in addition to needing more money, I owe it to Abel to fight Aceworth."

He stared at her until he seemed convinced that she meant it. "My conscience is clear," he said, then stood up and started toward the bar until King noticed him.

Lynch waved them back to the table and, upon their arrival, he looked Natenberg in the eyes. "We talked, counselor—mostly I talked. I made some generous offers, just like I've been generous toward her all along. But now it's up to you to deal with the insurance company's lawyers, not us."

Natenberg looked at Lynch for long seconds, but said nothing.

Lynch took two twenty-dollar bills out of his wallet and tossed them onto the table, then nodded toward King. "Come on, Andy, let's go."

He turned and immediately started walking off, followed by King, who looked back with a quick smile and wave, while stepping fast to catch up with his client.

SEVENTY

With Lynch and King gone, Natenberg looked intently at Dawn. "So, *were* his offers generous?"

"Taking care of my legal bill and getting the house loan forgiven or canceled—whatever they call it."

Natenberg nodded smugly. "Pretty much what I was hoping for."

"I really am blown away, sir, at how you made that happen."

He studied her a moment, then motioned with his head toward the exit.

They walked, a nervous silence between them.

As they reached the parking lot, he stopped. "So, now that you have all that, Mrs. Santoro, I have something else to tell you."

"Okay..."

"I already *did* pressure Aceworth's attorney."

"What sir?"

"I told Tilden all about Lynch's lack of credibility, even including his antics with you, so that a jury would not give his testimony any weight. I also got him to admit that their truck driver could be vulnerable on cross-examination for the reasons I previously explained to you."

"Oh, my. So what did they say, sir?"

"After some back and forth, they upped their offer and agreed to keep it secret until I could find out what Lynch would contribute. I figured that Lynch might be more generous in a vacuum, figuring nothing might come of it anyway."

"Wow...Forgive me for being dense, sir, but then why did you start out tonight telling King and Lynch that it was up to *them* to negotiate with Aceworth's lawyer?"

"Oh, I knew they wouldn't want to mess with that. It was just another way of pressuring them."

"That's amazing, sir."

"The point is, Mrs. Santoro, that the strategy worked."

"For sure, sir."

"But, never mind strategy, don't you want to hear Aceworth's new offer?"

She grimaced.

"Why the look?"

"Because I'm afraid of not appearing grateful if I don't think it's enough—after you worked so hard and did so much."

"Seriously, Mrs. Santoro?"

She nodded apologetically.

"Are you that sure your goals are realistic? At this moment in time, the stars are aligned for you."

"Sir, I'm not trying to be unreasonable, but Aceworth's lawyers have still never proven anything to me. And now their case is even weaker, just like you just told them."

With his eyebrows furrowed to the max, Natenberg seemed on the verge of screaming at her right in the parking lot.

She gritted her teeth.

Somehow, he forced a smile. "Mrs. Santoro, you're still technically my client, whether you want to be reasonable or not. Therefore, I'm ethically obligated to convey Aceworth's settlement offer to you."

"Yes sir," she shakily replied.

"All I ask is that you don't just reject it right away. Give it a week. Get a second opinion if you want. Will you do that much?"

"Absolutely, sir. Please don't misunderstand me. I will give it serious thought, because I'll be the one who has to live with whatever I decide."

He studied her with apparent doubt.

She met his eyes.

"So then," he finally spoke, "I'm pleased to report that I got Aceworth to come up to ninety-five thousand—more than double where they were. And, with Lynch taking care of your first firm's fees, you'll get to keep quite a bit of it...But that's it; I can't do any more for you. Understood?"

"Wow again, sir. That's incredible."

"Excuse me, but does that mean it's good enough for you?"

He had to ask that.

"Sir, this whole meeting tonight, and the one-on-one with Lynch...I don't trust myself to decide right now. I do want to think about it, like you suggested."

"Fair enough, Mrs. Santoro."

"It's just that..."

309

"What, Mrs. Santoro?"

"Now that I see how good a lawyer you are, and with Aceworth now thinking that you're going to stay in my case, it's hard for me to understand why they're not offering even more..."

"Perhaps they would go higher one day, Mrs. Santoro," he said dismissively, "like on the courthouse steps right before trial. But, for now, I did what I could with them."

"I know you did, sir, and I didn't mean to sound the least bit ungrateful..."

"And, if this settlement fails, I'm still getting out of your case."

And with a clearer conscience, I'm sure.

"Certainly, sir. You've explained that fully."

"Then, good evening, Mrs. Santoro," he said with a quick hand-shake, "it's been a really long day."

He turned to walk toward his car.

She got into her own car and started the engine, while watching John Natenberg get into his Mercedes.

She sat and thought about his parting words, and how he had labored well into the evening, in a high-powered meeting, to try to help her. It reminded her of the hospital surgeon who had worked tirelessly trying to find a way to save Abel on that fateful day, but who eventually had to accept failure and move on.

But I too have ethical obligations. One of my clients can't even talk yet and the other isn't alive anymore to defend himself.

SEVENTY-ONE

Days later, while browsing through another newspaper's employment section, she pondered the disappointing phone conversation she had with her latest attorney prospect—this one named Yvonne.

The idea of retaining a female lawyer, or even consulting with one, had intrigued her. James said she had trial experience and "might" even be tough enough to take on Aceworth's lawyer—as if that was by no means a given for her gender.

To Dawn's disappointment, however, Yvonne's initial interest seemed to melt as soon as she learned that she'd be the third lawyer on the case. "Let me get back to you," she said. "Maybe I'll give John Natenberg a call."

Oh, great.

When Dawn asked how long before she would make a decision, Yvonne had simply said: "You are totally free to keep looking."

In the midst of her current struggles, Dawn seemed to feel the presence of Abel. Yet, strangely, it was not the selfless man she married. It was a demanding and impatient force that stood ready to judge her if she failed.

"What do you expect from me, Abel," she whispered. "Do you want me to take the easy way out and become a mistress—assuming he'd still have me?"

She tossed the employment section aside, then got up and started pacing. "I don't remember ever asking for this freaking mess," she muttered. "And, by the way, was there a particular conversation between you and good old Lou that I should really know about?"

But she caught herself before her frustration turned to anger. She sat back down and forced herself to use the controlled breathing exercise she had picked up in child-birth classes, which seemed to work as well as anything in calming her down.

She also thought back to the time she sat in her car trying to write out a full matrix of alternative paths, but found it too overwhelming. It helped once again just to realize that her life wasn't destined to be simple or safe.

She took another long, slow breath. "Abel, just don't forget that it's only me fighting them. Okay?"

She reached over to the discarded employment section, picked it up, and crumbled it into a ball for her wastebasket. "Enough torture for now, there's always tomorrow's paper. Today, I'm going to take Cora some place I can afford. Some place where there are everyday people...Oh my God, Chuck E. Cheese."

SEVENTY-TWO

That night, as she stared into the darkness of her bedroom, something different kept her edgy and awake. It wasn't just her money woes or even the pressure she still felt to protect Abel's memory.

Thinking of what Julie would probably say, Dawn allowed that the culprit might be her own body, stubbornly clamoring for its needs to be satisfied, as if nothing else mattered. Too much time had passed since she lost her life partner—the man who measured his own happiness by hers and who held her like she wanted to be held, especially at night.

There was also the bare loneliness of her battle, a relentless ordeal she had never volunteered to undertake, but which would be ready to challenge her the next morning and the next, no matter whether she had any other pressures or distractions.

After more long minutes passed, and with no relief in sight, she reluctantly opted for the promise of a sleeping pill, telling herself that she was already wobbly enough these days without also being sleep-deprived.

But, while back in bed, waiting for the single dosage to take effect, a vision of the entire bottle—just as it sat there in her medicine cabinet—flashed into her mind.

I wonder how many pills were left...

"Stop right there," she muttered into the darkness.

It would be so easy and painless...

"This is bullshit," she blurted out, loud enough to carry out of her bedroom.

313

Within seconds, Cora was making noises of her own, obliterating the audacious solicitations from the medicine cabinet.

Dawn rose from bed and quietly entered Cora's room, where she found her child just awake enough to look back at her.

She picked Cora up and held her tightly, gently stroking the child's puffy-soft hair. "Cora, sweetie-kid," she whispered, "Mommy thanks you so much for your love."

Cora offered a drowsy half-smile in return, before her eyes gradually closed.

Dawn gazed at her daughter, and gazed some more.

When she finally put Cora back down, and turned to leave the child's room, lightheadedness challenged her. The one pill she took was imposing its will upon her, as advertised.

She maneuvered back to her beckoning bed.

Lying there, in diminishing consciousness, she focused upon her last vision of Cora, the one person who would not judge her if she failed—at least, not anytime soon.

SEVENTY-THREE

Dressed in a dark blue pantsuit that she had hoped to wear at trial, she found herself back in what *seemed* to be Panatta's restaurant, but this time standing with her back to a wall.

Atmospheric jazz played through the sound system.

A gathering of men, apparently for some type of private event, occupied tables and booths as far as she could see in the dimmed lighting.

To her left, an authoritative-looking man sat alone at an elevated table. It was the Commissioner she met in Lynch's office. He was preoccupied for the moment, as were the others, but there seemed to be expectation in the air.

She stepped forward to peer further into the room and saw Louis Lynch sitting at a table with Andy King, just as at their meeting.

At the next table, Aceworth's lawyer, Ken Tilden, sat with investigator Frank Bayardo. The two seemed relaxed, like bar buddies telling stories or jokes.

Near them, she recognized Ari, the money lender from the pawn shop, who was sipping wine. He was alone, at least for the moment.

Other men, unknown or not recalled, were also interspersed among the tables.

Behind all of them, and across the room, she could just barely recognize two large men standing in front of the exit door. They appeared to be the bouncers from the Flashery.

Without any preliminaries, Commissioner Briggs banged a gavel on his table and the soft music stopped.

Dawn felt unease, but then heard a familiar female voice calling to her from behind. "C'mon, Dawn. You can do it."

Looking over her shoulder, she saw Rosemary, smiling and waving to her from the short hallway leading to the restrooms.

"Do what?" Dawn called back.

"Make yourself some good money," Rosemary shouted. "Most of these guys have bucks to burn."

"How?"

"Just start moving and the music will go with you," Rosemary chimed back. "You'll see."

Oh my God. As if...

She looked around for James, seeking any help he might give her, but could not see him anywhere.

"Dawn, what are you waiting for?" Rosemary called out again.

"I know what," Dawn said on an impulse, "I'll explain to these men that Abel never told me he was thinking of suicide...and also that I was tricked at my deposition."

She turned back to the male audience and walked toward their tables while trying to speak, but no sound emitted. Moving closer still, she tried shouting at the men while emphatically shaking her head "No". But she still failed to even register with them.

Commissioner Briggs pounded his gavel again. "Now, little lady," he bellowed, "I don't recall authorizing you to give us any speeches."

"But sir, if I could only..."

"Don't be foolish. These men aren't here to *listen* to you."

Though the Commissioner was apparently the only male she could communicate with, she was aghast at how an elected official could be so callous about her rights. "Well, I'm going to have a jury anyway," was all she could think of saying.

"Like hell you will, unless we think you deserve one," snapped the Commissioner. "And besides, we already know that you helped your husband plan his suicide."

"But that's not true, sir," she implored. "And it's my right to have a jury decide my case."

The Commissioner shook his head as if she were merely a nuisance. Then, with another bang of his gavel, he waved his other hand to motion her back to the wall.

Seeing no immediate recourse, she lowered her head and slunk back to her prior spot. When she then turned around, it was just in time to see the Commissioner nod toward the other end of the room. A spotlight instantly shined upon her.

Despite the sudden glare, she could see one man at a front-row table take something out of his wallet and hold it up for her to see.

The spotlight shot over to him, revealing that it was a hundred-dollar bill.

The man laid it on his table and sat back in his chair with both hands behind his head, leering at her.

The spotlight then shifted to another man, and then another, until there were large bills and lustful eyes in all directions.

"Now, little lady," the Commissioner spouted out, " I hope you can finally see why you're here. But, pretty soon, these men are going to get impatient."

"C'mon, Dawn," Rosemary again prodded her, "I know you can do this."

She turned toward Rosemary. "But, if I do what I think they want, they'll never take me seriously. My jury trial will never get approved."

Rosemary shook her head, apparently becoming as frustrated with her as the Commissioner.

Oh my...Am I being dense? These men could go see professionals...probably younger ones too.

"Okay, Rosemary, I'll try."

"I could announce you if you want," Rosemary eagerly suggested.

"Uh, thanks," Dawn said with a forced smile, "but I need to first boost my confidence a little. Let me see if I can ease into this."

She turned back toward the men, her hips slowly undulating.

The spotlight returned to her and the music energized, with earthy blues replacing jazz.

Unsure what she should do next, she peaked back at Rosemary, only to see her nodding and clapping.

318

"Keep going, Dawn," yelled Rosemary. "Yay Dawn!"

She turned back toward the men and added rhythmic shoulder movements and her sexiest smile to accompany her swaying hips.

Wolf whistles and crude howls started coming from all directions.

The music, however, suddenly became even louder and raunchier, as if jealously vying for control of the room.

She gave into the bestial beat, bobbing her head and letting her whole body undulate more brazenly.

More men laid out bills, while the primal sounds persisted.

"Yeah baby, now take it off!"

"Show us what you got!"

"Take it *all* off!"

We'll have to see about that...

She moved her hands suggestively all over her body, while her hips gyrated and swayed.

Still more howls and whistles followed, with cash now set out on every table she could see.

"Dawn," said Rosemary, her voice barely audible, "if this doesn't give you confidence..."

"Maybe," she yelled back. "Do you have any idea how much money is out there right now?"

"I'd say a helluva good start for you."

"For sure, Rosemary, but I need..."

"How completely shameless of you," an all-too-familiar voice intruded.

319

She turned around to see Lou Lynch standing in front of her.

"What do you think Abel would say about this?"

"I'm just trying to survive, Mr. Lynch," she pleaded, while she kept moving her body for the rest of the audience.

"And you'd rather be up here like this than with me?"

"I'd much rather be in a court, sir, for my trial."

"Won't you ever learn?" chided Lynch. "Even if you got your trial and then somehow managed to prevail, they'd just appeal it."

"Then I guess I'd just have to keep fighting, until I finally won out."

Lynch shook his head, turned and blended back into the audience.

With the spotlight solely on Dawn again, she tried to recreate her courage, but the music now had more ideas of its own, blasting discordant sounds as if chastising her for the interruption.

Feeling pressured, she looked over the heads of the men and locked her eyes upon the furthest chandelier she could see. Then, while continuing her sensuous body sway, she unfastened the top button of her coat.

The music blared louder still—*duh-duh, di-dah, duh-duh, di-dah*—bullying her as if it thought she needed it.

What the...?

Annoyed, she purposely slowed her movements, trying to de-synch from the oppressive sounds, while unfastening her other coat button, then removing the garment altogether.

But rowdy saxophones, backed by relentless percussion, demanded that she speed up her disrobing, while a strobe light started flashing in anticipation.

Exasperated to the point of anger, she stood completely still, with her hands at her sides, her white blouse still buttoned all the way up to her neck.

The music and lights, however, blindly continued as if on overdrive, while the men stomped, clapped and howled mindlessly.

More seconds passed, but the bizarre ritual still raged on without her.

"Screw this," she said as she strode toward the closest table, while all the men remained mesmerized as if she were still performing back near the wall.

She reached out for one of the bills, but, just as a hundred was close to her grasp, she heard a knocking sound, which somehow pierced through the ruckus.

She looked up at the two bouncers, but they appeared as oblivious as all the other men, with no visible activity in their vicinity.

She turned back to the cash and edged her hand forward again, but the knocking resumed and this time it woke her up.

SEVENTY-FOUR

Groggy from her sleeping pill and nightmare, she looked dumbfounded at the clock, wondering who could possibly be on her front porch at 8:15 a.m.

She put on her robe and hurried to the door, concerned that more knocking or the door bell ringing would wake up Cora.

"Any home buyers can just call Julie," she muttered.

Through the window, she saw a slender middle-aged man, carrying a briefcase and dressed in a navy-blue blazer with a white shirt and striped tie. He seemed harmless enough.

"Good morning, Mrs. Santoro," the man said respectfully. "My name is Jerry Rundle."

"Good morning," she cautiously replied. "Are you here about the house?"

"Oh, no, ma'am, I'm a VAMS private investigator," he replied, handing her his card.

"Oh, them..."

"I'm actually a co-owner, Mrs. Santoro. I'm sorry if it's a bit early, but I wanted to try and catch you before you went out today."

"That's okay, sir, I'm up."

"Mrs. Santoro, I have a delivery for you that could be important in light of your current situation."

"My situation?"

"I'll be happy to explain...Might I come inside, please, to go over this with you?"

"That's fine," she said, motioning him in. "As long as we talk quietly. My daughter's sleeping."

"Surely," he replied in a half-whisper. "And I do suggest that we sit down somewhere for this."

"Okay. But I just hope it's not some new problem," she said as she motioned him toward the dining room table.

"I doubt that, Mrs. Santoro. It's two sealed envelopes for you from your husband."

"From Abel?" she remarked incredulously, now wondering if it was a mistake to let Rundle in.

"I'm aware that he's deceased, Mrs. Santoro, and my sincere condolences for your loss."

She took a long look at him, then slowly nodded.

"Before your husband died," said Rundle with utmost deference, "he came to us with a delivery request that was only to be carried out if we determined that a certain condition was met. Apparently, your husband did not expect to be available for you."

"Whoa! Are you kidding me?"

"I am not, Mrs. Santoro."

"Oh my God."

"Mrs. Santoro, first, I need to tell you that we assigned your husband's unusual request to one of our operatives who we knew to be very capable and conscientious. But sometimes the ball can be dropped even in the best organizations."

"Dropped, in what way? Or does that even matter now that you're here?"

"We hope it won't adversely affect you at all, but we..."

"Mr. Rundle," she said anxiously, "how would I even know until I see what it is?"

"Very true, ma'am, and you'll receive it in a matter of seconds. But we do apologize in advance in the unlikely event that you think we should have made this delivery earlier. It was a combination of an unusual request and the man assigned to it having to leave town for an extended period."

"That's what I was told—a family emergency."

"Yes. But, as a result of your recent inquiry, it eventually got to my attention."

"Okay..."

"And also keep in mind that, under your husband's instructions, we weren't supposed to deliver this prematurely either. So, hopefully, you'll see that it all works out."

"Yes, sir, I hope so, too. But I have no idea yet what Abel's instructions were."

"Sorry, Mrs. Santoro...I'm trying to be methodical, so that you'll understand everything."

"Understood, sir. I'm listening."

"Mrs. Santoro," said Rundle, his voice and expression indicating something highly sensitive, "your husband asked us to periodically monitor your status and to only make this delivery if we concluded that you got into what he called a 'desperate situation'."

"Desperate?"

"Yes, meaning financial or legal."

"Oh my."

"And your husband understood that, to try to carry this out, we would primarily be relying on public information about you, which we routinely use in our trade. He didn't hire us to constantly tail you or do a stakeout, which would have been extremely expensive even on a short term basis."

"Well, I guess I'm glad of that."

"Ma'am, we've concluded that it's time to make this delivery based on two factors. First, the county recorder's office shows that a foreclosure's been started on your house..."

She nodded.

"...And according to district court records, you're also about to lose your second lawyer on your lawsuit against Aceworth Life Insurance Company."

"All true, sir, and with no third lawyer yet."

"So, Mrs. Santoro, I'm sorry to have to put it this way, but with all this going on and you being a widow with a young child, do you agree with us that your husband's requirement has been met as to you being desperate?"

"Oh, absolutely," she blurted out, momentarily forgetting to keep her voice down. "In fact," she said more softly after catching herself, "it's worse than you know. I don't have a decent job and my first law firm might sue me for legal fees even before my insurance case is decided. So, unless I agree to what I think is an unfair settlement, I could soon be even more desperate."

"Okay then, Mrs. Santoro, I'm sorry to hear all that, but I'm glad we didn't wait any longer. And I hope that whatever is in the envelopes will be of benefit to you like your husband hoped."

"Oh, wouldn't that be awesome."

As Rundle opened his briefcase, however, she couldn't help but be skeptical. How could Abel have written anything before his death that could possibly help her now, no matter what he might have thought or intended?

Rundle meanwhile laid two envelopes on the table face down: one white and rectangular, the other gold and in the shape of a greeting card envelope. He then placed a single typed sheet of paper, with his business logo at the top, directly in front of her and handed her a pen.

"Mrs. Santoro, my partner is a son-of-a-gun on paperwork. So, if I could just get your signature on this receipt, which basically says you agree that your husband's prerequisite for delivery has been met and that both envelopes are still sealed."

As soon as she signed, he slowly stood up. "I'll excuse myself now, Mrs. Santoro, and you can have your privacy."

She offered a distracted nod, but then stopped staring at the envelopes to consider how extraordinary this delivery was, no matter the timing or contents. Her eyes moistened.

"Mr. Rundle, if nothing else, it means the world to me that you fulfilled my husband's wish."

"Of course, Mrs. Santoro, and..."

But before he could finish his sentence, she was out of her chair and quickly stepping toward him. "I'm sorry, Mr. Rundle, but you're going to get a hug."

"Oh...," he blushed, then shyly spread his arms to receive her gesture.

"Thank you so much, Jerry," she said as she gently squeezed him.

"It's my job, uh, Dawn," he replied while waiting to be released, "but you're certainly welcome. And again, I hope that you and your sleeping child will somehow be helped."

SEVENTY-FIVE

With her front door secured again, she returned to the dining room table and eased back into the same chair she had just been sitting in when Rundle was present. With the house eerily quiet, and her dead husband's unknown writings before her, she felt almost as if she were at some sort of altar that was immune to the passage of time. She took a deep breath and let her hands fall to her sides.

When she finally felt ready, she picked up the gold envelope and read the inscription: TO MY DARLING DAWN AND CORA, LOVES OF MY LIFE."

She stared at it. "Oh my God—I can only open this once."

She slowly put back the gold envelope and focused upon the white one. She turned it over to see that it was taped as well as sealed. On it were the words, "Only to Be Opened by Dawn Santoro". It then said, in brackets, "OPEN THIS FIRST".

"Holy bejeezus," she muttered. "I could've easily blown that. Wished you would have warned me, Jerry."

Although satisfied with not having messed up the sequence, the white envelope's command seemed ominous to her. She stared at it cautiously, then held it up to the light, hoping that she might get an early clue on its contents. But she could not make out anything legible.

She took another deep breath and resolutely blew it all out as if in submission to whatever fate was now in store for her. "Whatever you're going to say to me, Abel," she whispered, "please don't make things any worse for me."

328

She took another deep breath and carefully unsealed the envelope, enabling her to extract two pages of white bond stationery, which she then laid out in front of her.

She trembled upon seeing Abel's handwriting:

To My Loving Wife:

This letter is to tell you what you need to know, but I could not let it be my final words to you and Cora. That's what the gold one is for. You can open that one whenever you think the time is right.

So far, so good...

My love, in case you did not find out by the time you read this, I had terminal brain cancer. (At the bottom of this letter are my two doctors.) But I bought life insurance from Aceworth Insurance Company, remember? The policy should still be with all the important papers.

Now comes the tricky part. The pain was getting worse and the doctors said I would wind up in a hospital full-time till the end. I did not want that, and I would not have been a good husband to put you through all that.

So I told my boss Mr. Lynch about everything and showed him a copy of the policy. I asked him if he thought I might have another choice, instead of just waiting for the end to come. (You can guess my idea.)

329

Oh My!

Even though I was letting Mr. Lynch down as an important worker for him, he was very kind and asked his lawyers about my idea. They told him that, if a doctor diagnosed someone as terminal (like me), then the life insurance beneficiary (that's you) would still get the normal payout even if the insurance company could prove that the death was not really an accident. This was a great relief and I thanked him.

Holy Freaking Shit!

Mr. Lynch also told me that he would make sure you got the insurance money whenever and however I died. But I started to worry that he might be too busy with his business matters, and I had no back-up plan. Now that you are reading this letter, something must have happened with him, so this was worth the cost. All you have to do now is take the insurance policy to a lawyer and explain the situation.

One more thing, my love. If you think my idea was wrong, then I beg your forgiveness. But never ever doubt that I did what I thought was best and that I loved you and Cora with all my strength right up to the end. (More on that in the gold envelope.)

Always With Love,
Abel

She put the letter down and covered her face.

"This is way too freaking crazy," she groaned. "Thank you, Mr. VAMS, or whatever you call yourself. My life was way too boring before this."

She got up, started pacing and thinking out loud. "So where does this now put me in the world of the living?"

She paced some more. "It definitely proves once and for all what a complete liar Lynch is...But it also means that the truck driver was right after all...And wouldn't Aceworth Insurance Company love to get their hands on this."

She walked back to the table and put Abel's letter back into the white envelope. "There it will stay," she vowed. "I know you meant well...but now I've got to come up with an idea of my own, Abel, or my case and my future could be terminal."

She again resumed pacing, her mind scrambling for a direction. But, like trying to do the matrix in the parking lot, it was too messy for her frazzled mind.

She stopped and looked upward, willing to invoke any available source. "Abel, if you had a Plan 'C', please tell me what it is?"

She slowed her breathing and thought some more.

"Damn it, I need a confidential meeting of my own," she whispered, "with someone I can completely trust...And no lawyers this time, thank you very much...Jewels, I need you again. Now, more than ever."

SEVENTY-SIX

Weeks later, while sitting at Abel's grave site, Dawn was able to show the hint of a smile.

"Hey, lover," she said softly, "I got your letters...For sure, I was desperate then, but I'm not anymore."

She kissed two fingers and touched them to the gravestone. "But first, sweetheart, I want you to know that I understand why you did it. Oh, my God, what you must have been going through..."

She carefully thought about her next words. "I also don't blame you for trusting Mr. Lynch...I almost did," she said with emerging tears. "But he never could have replaced you, no matter how rich he is."

She took a long breath. "I'm afraid that things didn't quite work out as you planned, darling, because he actually misled you on the legal stuff...But, don't feel bad, because he pretty much misled everybody."

She wiped her misty eyes. "The important thing is that, thanks to you telling me what *really* happened between you and him, and some help I got from others, I've been able to make it all work out."

She nodded her head and smiled. "We got Mr. Lynch to withdraw a lien he had on the house and we got the first lawyers that he set me up with to cancel their bill..."

"And it gets better," she chirped, with her smile broadening. "My second lawyer, John, got the insurance company to pay me almost a hundred thousand dollars. I know that seems low, but it was a lot better than zero, which is what could have happened thanks to Lynch..."

"But, here's the really neat part, Abel," her wet-eyed smile now a prideful grin: "With part of that insurance money, your little wife from Tucson became a full-fledged investor in Las Vegas real estate. Can you believe it?"

"Yup, my friend Julie—you remember her, the real estate agent—well, she and I came up with the basic idea and her broker went in on it too. We have what her broker says are 'options' that should make us lots of profits."

"So, my dear husband," announced Dawn, "you don't have to worry about me and Cora. Who knows, I might even be able to start my little studio one day."

After a moment of silence, she let her smile dissipate into a mild grimace, as she rubbed her hands together and cleared her throat. "Uh, just one more thing...and I hope you don't mind, honey...but Julie's going to be moving in with me to help cut both of our expenses—at least until we can cash in on our options."

She shook her head at the thought of Julie's increased presence in her life. "It's true that she can be a little wild sometimes, but she promised her best behavior around the house...And besides," Dawn snickered, "I'm not sure I'd be able to handle it if things stayed overly calm and peaceful for too long of a stretch."

She stood up, smiling again. "So anyway, my love, I hope you're at least a little proud of me. I sure am of you. And Cora will be too, every time I tell her what a great daddy she had."

EPILOGUE:

On a slow weekday afternoon, Louis Lynch sat back in his reclining executive chair, conversing on the phone with a friend:

"Hey Pete, when you get a chance, would you mind tracking down the name of the guy who did the paneling and cabinetry on your office remodel? I lost my guy awhile back and I've been through two others since then who couldn't cut the mustard."

"Great, thanks. Well, in other news, somebody beat us to a few of the properties we were tying up near that new mall project."

"No, they're using secret trusts. What the hell, that's how we usually do it."

"No, just a few, so we'll still do well. But here's the worst part: My partner thinks that I pulled a fast one on him."

"No shit. I flat-out denied it—which is the truth—but he's not satisfied."

"You got that right. I actually think it might be someone he doesn't remember tipping off. Maybe he had a few too many at some reception, or who the hell knows with him...But he's dead set on blaming me."

"Yeah, Amen to that...But anyway, I have to personally compensate him for his lost profits on the pieces we didn't get, even though I also lost the profits on them as well."

"It is a screw-job, but I've got no choice," said Lynch as he massaged his forehead with his free hand. "He knows he's irreplaceable."

"Yeah, that's life...Hey, we're still on for poker Saturday night, right?"

www.ingramcontent.com/pod-product-compliance
Lightning Source LLC
Chambersburg PA
CBHW030413180626
46812CB00005B/1995